Praise for J.L. Langley's *My Fair Captain*

5 Lips! "The mystery element to *My Fair Captain* is just as enjoyable and gripping as the relationship between Nate and Aiden which rounds out a perfect tale. I'll be watching for more of the Townsend brothers in the future!"

~ *Tara Renee, Two Lips Reviews*

Joyfully Recommended! "J.L. Langley did a masterful job in *My Fair Captain* creating characters and a world that you will want to revisit often. If you enjoy spicy and playful m/m romances I recommend that you pick up *My Fair Captain* today, but be warned you might stay up all night reading this book!"

~ *Sabella, Joyfully Reviewed*

5 Angels and a Recommended Read! "Ms. Langley has created a phenomenal story that encompasses many social issues and problems that we see in our own society."

~ *Teresa, Fallen Angel Reviews*

My Fair Captain

J.L. Langley

A Samhain Publishing, Ltd. publication.

Samhain Publishing, Ltd.
577 Mulberry Street, Suite 1520
Macon, GA 31201
www.samhainpublishing.com

My Fair Captain
Copyright © 2008 by J.L. Langley
Print ISBN: 1-59998-761-9
Digital ISBN: 1-59998-507-1

Editing by Sasha Knight
Cover by Anne Cain

First Samhain Publishing, Ltd. electronic publication: June 2007
First Samhain Publishing, Ltd. print publication: April 2008

Dedication

In memory of Charlie Mitchell. Friend and neighbor. He will be greatly missed.

Extra special thanks to: Dick D, my V.E.P.B. You really helped me see this whole story clearer. I'd have probably started killing off characters for stress relief if it weren't for you. I enjoyed our plotting sessions immensely.

And to the ladies of Jaw Breakers. I'd have ripped my hair out on this one if it wasn't for all of ya'll. This story was the king of all DIP disorder catalysts. Thank you for suffering along with me.

Prologue

January 26, 4811: Planet Englor: A glade outside of Hawthorne Proper in the country of Moreal.

A dried, crumpled leaf blew across the toe of his shiny black boot as he lifted his right foot. Nathaniel should have stayed home...honor be damned. It was all a misunderstanding, an accident. Now, he was going to pay dearly for it. He was going to die.

"Six."

Nate swallowed hard and seized a deep breath as he took his sixth step. The crisp morning breeze ruffled his hair, blowing an overlong lock of dark brown into his eyes. He blinked and shook his head to dislodge it, then wished he hadn't. His head still ached from the heavy imbibing he'd indulged in the night before. If by some miracle he got out of this alive, he'd never drink again.

"Seven." Baron White's voice sounded exceedingly harsh over the rustle of leaves and a neighing horse. Then again, maybe it was the circumstances that made it sound that way. Or perhaps it was the serenity of the glade in contrast.

With his mind dazed and his body on autopilot, Nate continued forward. He peered over the horizon, past the bare trees, where the sun was beginning to light the sky with its morning blush. When was the last time he'd been up early enough to see the sunrise? He couldn't remember, but knowing this might be the last time... His carefree existence as the oldest son of the Duke of Hawthorne suddenly seemed worthless.

Someone at the edge of the clearing coughed as the Baron's voice rang out.

"Eight."

Nathaniel advanced a pace. Why had he ever thought he could reason with the viscount? Daniel Bradford, Viscount Hargrove and heir of the Marquis of Oxley, had always been a hothead. Despite the fact their fathers were the dearest of friends and Nate had known Daniel practically since birth, there had never been any love lost between them. As children they'd been rivals. As adults, they merely ignored each other. Until last night. Last night, they'd become bitter enemies.

"Nine."

Closing his eyes, he planted one foot in front of the other. The ancient Terran gun felt heavy in his hand. He didn't want to do this. The accusation that had brought him here was false, but his alibi was just as damning. Everything in him screamed to run off the field and flee. He'd be called a coward, but at least he'd live another twenty years. And more importantly, he wouldn't have to disillusion his father.

"Ten. Fire!"

Nathaniel turned knowing exactly what he had to do. He could not kill Hargrove. If by some miracle Nate lived, his father would surely disown him. He might be a wastrel, but he adored his father and disappointing him was the worst fate Nate could suffer, more horrible than even death. He aimed over Daniel's left shoulder.

The sound of gunfire erupted and a searing pain blossomed in his side. Flinching away from the agony, his finger jerked the trigger.

Daniel's blue eyes widened, his mouth dropped open and he stared at his chest, where a red stain spread across the tan brocade waistcoat. He looked back at Nathaniel, his face pasty white, and crumpled to the ground like a rag doll.

A loud feminine scream tore through the air. Victoria, Hargrove's fiancée, ran onto the field and flung herself over the viscount.

Oh, Galaxy, what have I done? Nate stood perfectly still, watching for any movement from his opponent.

Someone rushed toward Nate. "Star dust, Nate."

Jared.

Nathaniel was vaguely aware of the hustle and bustle around him as he let the gun slip from his numb hand. It hit the dead grass with a soft thud. Staring at Hargrove's lifeless body partially covered by Victoria's blue riding habit, he willed the man to get up. But he knew that wasn't to be.

A flock of people crowded around the viscount, finally blocking Nate's view, but the sobbing and sounds of disorder continued.

Fingers prodded his side, making the dull twinge flare into sharp pain. He hissed out a breath and glanced down at Jared's dark head. Why was his younger brother here?

Jared perched on his knees, examining Nate's side. "It's only a flesh wound." Rising, he moved in front of Nate. "We have to get out of here." His brother clasped his shoulders and shook him. "Nate, are you listening to me?"

Nathaniel tore his gaze away from his sibling's worried brown eyes and looked past his shoulder. Hargrove couldn't be dead. He couldn't. Nate hadn't meant to kill the viscount, he was the one who was supposed to die.

The physician stood over Daniel shaking his head. Victoria sobbed harder, raking her hand through Daniel's blond hair, begging him to respond. Even Baron White had waddled his portly body over to stand by the downed man.

"Nate." Jared shook harder.

Nate touched his injury, wincing at the pain. What was he to do now? He yanked his hand away from the sticky mess and brought it up between him and Jared. Dark red coated his fingertips and dripped down his hand.

"Dammit, Nathaniel." Jared slapped him, jerking Nate's head to the side and nearly knocking him off balance. "Get it together. We have to go."

The sting snapped Nate from his daze. Jared was right. Dueling happened quite a bit, but it *was* illegal. No one would say a word unless the authorities happened along, then they would all be incarcerated. Which was no less than he deserved.

"Did you ride Nabil? Or did you come in one of the lifts?" Jared asked, tugging him toward the horses. Right past the tree line, horse-drawn coaches and the Low In-Flight Transports hovered above the ground just off the road.

"I rode Nabil." Nate freed himself from Jared's grip as they cleared the trees, looking for his black gelding. "What are you doing here, Jared?" Nate knew for a fact his brother had not been in the glade when he'd started pacing off. He'd purposely come to the duel alone, not even bringing a second.

Nabil stood several yards away from the lift bearing his family crest. As Nate and Jared approached, the gelding pranced toward them, sensing his unease and the need for urgency.

Jared tilted his boyish face in defiance as he walked to the lift. "Open door. Steps down." The door slid into the doorframe and steps descended from the side of the vehicle. "I came to watch your back, brother mine. I woke and you were gone. You should've told me you planned to go through with this. I barely made it here in time." Jared climbed into the carriage. "Steps up." The stairs disappeared into the side of the black metal conveyance as Jared braced his hands on the doorframe and turned his attention back to Nate.

For the first time, Nate noticed his brother's disheveled appearance. Jared's wrinkled black knee britches had been worn the night before. He was without waistcoat and cravat and his pale blue shirt had one sleeve rolled above his forearm. His shoulder-length dark brown hair hung loose as though he hadn't even run a comb through it. The handsome face, a slightly younger version of Nate's, was shadowed with stubble. By the looks of it, Jared had rolled out of bed, with no assistance from his valet, and into the lift to follow Nate.

Feeling anesthetized from head to toe, Nate hefted himself into the saddle. "I wasn't going to go through with the duel. I came to talk Daniel out of it, but he wouldn't listen." Turning Nabil toward the trees, he tried to see through the dried brush. His stomach dropped to his feet, feeling the full impact of what he'd done—however inadvertently. He'd killed a man.

"I'm sorry." Jared's voice was so quiet, Nate barely heard him.

"So am I," he whispered back. Turning Nabil, he gave his only sibling a sad smile. "Let's go home, Little Brother."

Jared nodded and backed out of sight. The lift's door shut, then the lift whipped off the grass onto the road. It floated at a fast clip in the direction of Hawthorne.

Looking back at the clearing one last time, Nate closed his eyes. His life would never be the same again. Heeling Nabil, he nudged his horse into a gallop toward home and his father's censure.

Chapter One

November 5, 4829: Planet Regelence: Townsend Castle in Classige, Pruluce (the ruling country of Regelence).

An ear-piercing screech echoed through the castle followed by the slap of bare feet on marble floor. The sound of skin hitting the polished stone in the entryway suddenly muted into a soft thud. Aiden looked up from his sketchscreen.

Muffin, his oldest brother's ward, barreled through the door of the parlor, naked and dripping wet. Her shoulder-length red hair was plastered to her freckled face and around her neck and shoulders. She ran as fast as her short thin legs would carry her, trailing water on the blue carpet and looking over her shoulder. Barely sparing Aiden a glance, she dove under the chaise he reclined on.

He bit his bottom lip to keep from laughing. *It must be bath time.* Saving his latest painting, he put the stylus in its holder on the side of the screen and set it aside. Leaning over the edge of the chaise, he lifted the gold damask ruffle. He brushed back a dark lock of hair that fell over his brow and focused on a pair of blinking wide blue eyes.

Muffin brought her tiny finger to her pursed lips as rivulets of water ran over her rosy cheeks. "Shhh... I owe ju, Aid'n."

Dropping the fabric, Aiden sat back up, still fighting off his mirth. The four-year-old hadn't figured out that Jeffers, the castle computer, knew everything that happened under its roof. Doubtlessly, Nurse Christy would ask Jeffers to pinpoint the child.

Aiden decided to take pity on the waterlogged sprite. Sure she needed her bath, but it was good to rebel now and again. It kept things interesting. "Jeffers?"

"Yes, Lord Aiden?" the disembodied baritone asked.

"You have not seen Lady Muffin."

"My Lord, you know I'm not allowed to lie to castle guardians and chaperones on your behalf, including Lady Muffin's nurse."

Aiden sighed. He did know, darn it. Inside the castle and on its immediate lawn were the only places he and his siblings were allowed without a chaperone. Which was why they had to resort to trickery to get any time by themselves. *Speaking of alone time...*

He glanced at the clock on the mantel above the white marble fireplace. *9:12 a.m.* Three minutes until Payton shut down Jeffers, assuming Payton could circumvent Jeffers' cameras, the other castle servants and a security system to get to the access panel in the basement. The last time Payton flipped Jeffers' switch, their parents responded by implementing more defense measures. "Fine, let me rephrase that. You do not *see* Lady Muffin, she is hiding somewhere in the house."

"That is true, Lord Aiden. My cameras cannot see under the chaise, although my heat sensors tell me she is there. I will tell Nurse Christy thus."

Aiden snorted. Jeffers would probably word his response to Christy exactly like that. Not that it would matter, Christy could easily follow the water trail to her missing charge. But it would give the little rascal a chance to assert her independence and cause chaos in which he could escape. As long as Christy wasn't in the parlor at the time Aiden had to make his getaway.

A loud clacking of heels clipped down the hall outside the parlor. Aiden held his breath until the footsteps moved on past. He glanced at the clock again, *9:14 a.m.,* then out the open parlor door. "Jeffers, close the parlor door. I'd like privacy, please. Also, close all cameras, heat sensors and microphones in this room until further notice."

The blue-curtained French door closed with a snick. "Yes, milord."

Hopping off his seat, Aiden looked under the chaise. He debated several seconds on whether to tell the little girl about the scheme he and his brothers had concocted. He didn't want to chance the imp going outside and getting hurt, but even she should be able to take advantage of the rare freedom. Knowing her, she'd likely use her stolen minutes of independence to sneak into the kitchen and get some sweets. "Muffin, Payton is turning off *The Spy* today. Promise me you won't go outside?"

Her damp head bobbed, a bright smile lighting her cheeks. "Promise."

"And no telling Rexley."

Again she nodded. "'Kay."

"Whew." Muffin told Rexley everything, and what his oldest brother knew, their parents knew. Rexley was heir to the throne and probably pictured in the dictionary under responsible. If he got word of Tarren cajoling Payton into shutting Jeffers off, Rexley would be honor-bound to go straight to their father and sire.

Aiden dropped the concealing material and gathered his fourteen by eighteen inch sketchscreen he'd brought with him for his afternoon of freedom under his arm. He'd considered bringing a traditional sketchbook and some charcoal, but with

14

the sketchscreen he could do more things. Even though he loved to use the time-honored methods, with the screen he could make the work larger, add color, even have it printed into a finished piece. He could alter his renderings anyway an artist would wish to do so and it had nearly unlimited storage, where as with the conventional means he eventually ran out of paper.

He glanced at the fireplace. The mantel clock read *9:15 a.m.* "Jeffers?"

There was no answer.

"Jeffers? Are you there?"

Still the computer didn't respond.

Yes. Payton had done it. In all of Aiden's nineteen years, he'd never known Jeffers not to respond after the first call. Even after asking for privacy, speaking the computer's name would bring him back into the room.

The French door opened and shut.

No. He was so close. Aiden spun around, expecting to find Christy. He breathed a sigh of relief when he saw Colton leaning against the door.

His brother clasped one large hand to his muscular chest and ran the other through his short black hair. Predictably, he was dressed in his buff-colored pants, a white poets blouse and his favorite brown riding boots. "Whew. That was close. Muffin flew the coop and her nurse and Cony are looking for her."

Muffin's head popped out from under the gold damask. "Cony?"

Colton started, then the corner of his mouth turned up. "Yup, Cony finished his meeting early and Christy intercepted him on the way to his study."

"Dust." Aiden's shoulders slumped. If their sire was out and about in the halls, they'd never make it past him. Their parent was a very astute man. He probably already realized Jeffers was out of commission. Which meant... "We have to hurry, Colton."

Colton nodded. "Exactly what I was thinking." Turning toward the door, he lifted the edge of the curtain and peeked out.

Walking up behind him, Aiden tried to see over his brother's towering form, without luck. Colton was the tallest of his brothers and he'd inherited Father's muscular physique. Aiden, even though a few months older than Colton, was the shortest of his siblings, but at least he'd inherited Father's broad shoulders too. "Well? Is Cony out the—?"

Colton jumped away from the door, his sherry-colored eyes wide. "Come on. Now Father is there too. We'll have to go out the window." He shooed Aiden to the front of the room.

"Father?" Muffin asked.

Hurrying to the window, Colton knocked the heavy velvet drapes aside and got tangled in the gold gauzy panels underneath. "Yes, Muffin. Father is, at this moment, on his way into the breakfast room."

Great. The breakfast room was across from them. Aiden set his sketchscreen down to hold the curtains out of the way before Colton tore them down and they got in trouble for that too. "Where are you going?"

Unlatching the wood frames of the window, Colton pushed the panes open. "Riding. Where else?" Colton was an avid horseman. He'd spend his entire day on horseback, if he were allowed.

"I meant, where are you going riding?"

"I'm going—"

The door opened.

Aiden let go of the curtains and dropped to his stomach, hoping the loveseat in front of the window would conceal him.

Only a second later, Colton dove to the ground next to him.

The door shut and the sound of panting followed.

Dust. So close, yet so far. Now they were surely caught. The sofa had mahogany legs and an eagle claw foot, with an eight-inch gap between the bottom of the beige material and the floor. Anyone who bothered to look would see them. If it were Cony and Father, he and Colton were dead in the water.

Aiden tried to see under the loveseat, but the chaise blocked the view of the door. Catching Colton's gaze, Aiden tipped his head, indicating his brother should peek and see who was in the room with them. Colton was on the other side and could peer around the edge.

Shaking his head, Colton mouthed the word, "You."

The big coward. *If you want something done...* Aiden belly crawled to the edge of the sofa, but before he could glance around it Muffin squealed, "Payton," and scrambled from under the chaise.

Payton? Aiden glanced around the side of the loveseat.

His second oldest brother hurried farther into the room, catching Muffin as she leapt at him.

Payton's gaze landed on the open window and his brow scrunched. Looking down, he spotted Aiden. "Wha—"

Colton stood. "Payton, what are you doing here?"

Payton rolled his eyes, then glared at Colton. "Running for my life. What are you doing here? I sacrifice myself so you can get out, and you're still here?" Frowning, he arranged Muffin in his arms and rushed to the window. "Muffin, you're naked."

She giggled and nodded.

"And you're wet." Payton wiped his hand on his pants and moved the curtain aside. "Why is she wet?"

"Bath time." Aiden, Muffin and Colton answered together. Only when Muffin said it, it sounded more like, "Baff time."

Groaning, Payton peeked out the window. "I forgot about that. Bad planning all the way around. I'm going to throttle Tarren." He set Muffin down, did another quick surveillance outside and climbed out of the room. Reaching back inside, he snagged Muffin. Once he got the little girl settled onto his hip again, he motioned to Aiden and Colton. "Come on. You have mere seconds before our father and sire come in here. They're going room to room."

Aiden grabbed his sketchscreen while Colton disappeared through the billowing gold fabric and midnight blue brocade. His brother was kind enough to reach back and offer to hold his screen while he climbed out.

After taking his screen back from Colton, the three of them and Muffin snuck around the perimeter of the castle. Colton took the lead, leaving Payton and Muffin to bring up the rear. If they could make it around back, the hedges and rosebushes in the formal garden would conceal them as they made their way to the stables.

"Psst." Payton tapped Aiden's shoulder. "Give me your cravat."

"What?" Aiden turned to his older sibling. Payton had on a pale blue waistcoat over a snowy white shirt *and* neckcloth. "Why?"

Payton rolled his eyes and blew a dark hank of hair off his forehead, like the answer should have been obvious. "So I can fashion some sort of cover for Muffin. I can't walk around with her naked."

Aiden didn't see why not, she was a baby. It may not be acceptable for her to go unclothed, but it would look much worse for Aiden to go around disheveled. Not that he particularly cared, but Father would have his hide if he caused a scandal. Aiden nearly scoffed at the thought. How many times had he heard and discarded the rules of propriety? Just going out un-chaperoned would result in a scandal if he were caught. "Fine. Colton, hold this." Handing off his screen to his brother, Aiden untied his cravat and tossed it to Payton.

"Thank you. Now take her so I can take off my own." Payton passed the naked sprite to Aiden and proceeded to unknot his cravat.

Grabbing Aiden's cheeks with her chubby little hands, Muffin planted a big sloppy kiss right on his lips. "I wuv aah-ven-chures."

"Would you three hurry?" Colton hissed over his shoulder, already several yards ahead of them.

They jogged to catch up, with Muffin clinging to Aiden's neck and Payton stripping as he followed. When they made it to the side of the garden, directly across from the stables and transport barn, they stopped for a breath.

Aiden set Muffin on her feet and Payton wrapped the neckcloths around her, fashioning a sort of toga/bikini. It was an interesting ensemble, but Muffin didn't seem to mind.

She preened for them. "Pretty?"

Aiden chuckled. "Yes, Muffin, you're pretty."

Groaning, Colton handed Aiden his sketchscreen. "Rexley will throttle all of us if he sees her dressed like that."

Picking Muffin back up, Payton snorted. "Well, it's certainly better than her going in the buff."

Colton shrugged. "I suppose that's true." Looking back toward the castle, he cocked his head to the side. "Now we have to sneak to the stables. I need to get Apollo if I'm going to ride to the creek."

"Why are you wasting your free time riding by the creek? You can do that with a chaperone."

Grinning, Colton raised a brow. "Yes, but if I run into Lord Wentworth on his day off with a chaperone, I can't—"

Payton started shaking his head before Colton ever finished his sentence. "No. You are *not* to go near Viscount Wentworth without a chaperone. Sebastian Hastings may be the head of the Royal Guards but he's a widower and single, not to mention a known rake. You'll be compromised. Then what? Father and Cony will blame me, because I shut off *The Spy*."

Aiden nodded his agreement. Payton would be in as much trouble as Colton. But Colton would be forced into a nuptial ceremony with Lord Wentworth. Knowing Colton, that was probably his goal. Unlike Aiden and Payton, Colton actually enjoyed being out in society and seeking a consort.

Shrugging, Aiden nudged Colton. "Come on. I want to get one of the lifts and go to the docks before someone catches us. I've been dying to sketch the hydro-space freighters and the water ships."

03

The docks were busy and loud, booming with life, unlike anything Aiden had ever seen. He'd been with his sire and his father to the Regelence Space Docks. He'd even been on the customs pier of the Space Docks, but it was nothing like this.

On the customs pier it was rare to see cargo moved off a ship. Usually an inspector boarded, examined the contents and left, clearing the freighter for travel in the Regelence solar system.

Here, on the docks at the Bay of Pruluce, sailors busily distributed their freight to different ships for delivery. Large, shiny-metal space freighters hovered over the wooden docks where their cargo was lowered. Once on the ground, the goods were transferred, some to hover trucks and trailers for land distribution, and others to the water ships for allocation to other countries on Regelence. Some of the ships, the Cargo Hydro-Space Crafts, could even be used for water travel or space travel. They had an open deck on top used for sailing and a massive enclosed hull for space travel. No matter the ship, it was all very fascinating watching the people hurrying about them.

The country of Pruluce was a contrast, a mixture of old and new. The port piers, people and buildings looked much like they would have in Earth's eighteen hundreds, but most of the vehicles were top-of-the-line new technology. For an artist it was a veritable dream come true with its variety of textures, colors and shapes.

Captivating as the port was, the stench of fish and rot permeated the air, making Aiden glad he'd picked a spot overlooking the docks. If the odor was this strong from thirty feet away, it was probably suffocating near the water. On the hill, the grass was soft beneath his stomach—his preferred working position—and he could still enjoy the experience. It was rare for a young lord to get the opportunity to see the core of Regelence's interplanetary commerce. Until Aiden was twenty-five years of age it was likely to be the only time he'd witness it. Therefore, he was determined to capture it. The more settings an artist could portray the better, and he was nothing if not committed to his art.

Shifting his attention away from the scene below and back to his sketch, he frowned. He'd already used half the memory on his screen rendering several of the Cargo Hydro-Space Crafts, and now he was trying to perfect the water compulsion system under the water ships. The technology made the ships much faster and more efficient than the regular boats used for pleasure, but not nearly as easy to depict. *Draw what you see, Aiden, not what you think you see.* The thing was, he wasn't sure what he saw, the water was constantly in motion, going up into the hovering vessels, then back down into the ocean.

He'd mastered portraits, landscapes, still lifes and even architecture, but some of the technology gave him fits. He closed his eyes and tried to picture it in his head, really *see* it. He *could* picture it. Now, if he could only render it.

"Oi there. Wotcher doin' 'ere, boy?"

Startled, Aiden opened his eyes.

Three men clambered up the small incline toward him. They were a fierce looking threesome. One was tall with short blond hair and broad shoulders, another was short and pudgy and yet another was somewhere in between. Their loose black tunics and formfitting uniform pants proclaimed them sailors.

Aiden's stomach churned with apprehension. He couldn't imagine what they wanted with him. Maybe it was his overactive artist's imagination, but the word "pirate" grabbed hold of his brain and wouldn't let go. Of course, it was ridiculous, pirates wouldn't be in port with all the legitimate sailors. Would they? Aiden dropped his stylus and scrambled to a sitting position.

The men came to halt, staring down at him. The tallest man might even be considered handsome if not for the surly expression. The middle one was downright scary looking, with his bald, bumpy head, beady eyes and hawklike nose.

The shortest one—with greasy brown hair and a scraggly beard—glowered at Aiden. "I asked wot ye were doin' 'ere, boy?"

"I—" Aiden hurried to his feet. His gut feeling told him these were not nice men. The scowling looks on these three's faces hinted at trouble. He may not care much for societies dictates, but he certainly didn't want to be murdered or kidnapped because he'd disregarded them. But he wasn't about to let them know he was alone. If they thought he had a chaperone with him... Clearing his throat, he jerked his head toward the lift he'd appropriated for his trip. "My chaperone brought me here so I could draw the ships, not that it's any of your business."

Spying the sketchscreen, the blond man's brow furrowed in a fierce frown. He bent and snatched the screen from the ground and used the buttons on the side to flip pages.

"Hey, give that back." Aiden grabbed for his screen but the swine jerked it from his reach.

"Go check the carriage. I'm bettin' the wee lordlin' is alone." The blond's gaze traced over Aiden's frame and a nasty smile curved his lips. "My, yer a pretty wee fin'. I fink we'll take ye wiv us."

Aiden's stomach dropped to his feet. He could either stay and fight or make a break for it. He'd never been bad at self-defense and weapons training, but they'd never been his strong point either. He was more of a strategist, a fight-with-your-mind type. The deciding factor was the weight difference. The three sailors were much bigger. Which hopefully meant he was faster than them. Aiden was no idiot, the odds were clearly in their favor. He bolted, running past the heavy man. If he could get to the lift first he could get away. He'd have lost the drawings he'd risked propriety to get, but he'd be safe.

His eyes, locked on to the open door of the black metal vehicle, narrowed to tunnel vision. Nothing mattered but getting inside. It had been programmed to respond to his family's voices and their servants—no one else could use it. It alone was his haven out here on his own. He dove in without using the steps.

Before he could pull his feet inside and order the door closed, someone grabbed his ankles.

A maniacal laugh echoed through the lift as Aiden was dragged from it.

He kicked at his assailant while trying to catch ahold of something...anything. When nothing came within grabbing distance, he dug his nails into the polished wood floor and continued to lash out with his feet. There was a grunt when his foot connected. Then an arm wrapped around his calves, forcing his legs tight together so he could no longer kick. *Bloody black hole.*

"Come now, pretty, don't ye want ter play wiv us? Ye 'ave no care for society's rules or ye would not 'ave come 'ere by yorself. Didn't anybody tell ye the bleedin' docks are no place for yung innocents?"

It was the tall blond thug who had him. Aiden recognized the voice. *Wonderful.* The other ruffians had more weight, but this man looked to be stronger and probably had more endurance than the others.

A hand groped Aiden's arse, making him freeze for an instant. *Good Galaxy*, no one had ever dared to take such liberties. Aiden scrambled harder, to no avail. His fingers squeaked across the floor as he was pulled toward the opening of the coach. Throwing his arms wide he tried to wedge himself inside the doorway. The pressure on his underarms was unbearable, but he held on as long and he could. When his arms gave way, he clasped his hands around each side of the doorjamb.

"Ye've been caught, give it up and come along nice and quiet-like before ye 'urt yorself," the tall sailor said.

Was it his imagination or did the thug sound tired? Sweat dripped into Aiden's eyes and very ungentlemanly grunts left his lips. His teeth clenched together so tightly his jaw hurt but he would not go down without a fight.

"Henri, Russell, get over 'ere and 'elp me," Aiden's captor rumbled.

Another set of arms wrapped around his belly and Aiden was yanked free of the coach.

"Arugh." His fingers were on fire. Aiden shook his hands trying to relieve the pain. That had really smarted. Luckily his fingernails were still attached. Looking over his shoulder, he glared at the bald hooligan. "Let me go!" He made a fist and swung backward, clipping the man on the ear.

Bellowing in agony, the man clutched the side of his head and released Aiden's middle.

Aiden braced for impact with the ground, catching himself on his hands. The jolt sent a stinging twinge through his wrists, but it didn't slow him down. Once his hands were planted on the grass he used the surprise to his advantage and jerked his knees into his chest.

The other thug didn't let go, but he did lose his balance, falling to the grass with Aiden.

Aiden rolled onto his back and bolted into a sitting position. As hard as he could, he brought his hands together and cuffed the blond's ears.

Still the man didn't release his hold. He bellowed, "Henri."

Aiden twisted and thrashed like a man possessed, knocking his hair into his eyes. He had to get free...now.

Suddenly, the man loosened his grip, allowing Aiden to scuttle away. His heart pounded and his lungs pleaded for more air, but he didn't stop moving. The safety of the coach was only a yard away.

"Would you like to explain what you think you are doing with my son or shall I just run you through?" a deep, steady voice inquired.

Cony? Aiden froze, turning back around. His sire was here? He brushed the black curls from his eyes and peered at his savior.

His sire stood with the tip of his sword under the bearded man's chin, his long legs spread in a fighting stance. Cony studied Aiden before relief registered on his face, then he glared back at the three men. "Aiden, go gather your things." Cony dipped his head toward the art screen.

Aiden hurried past the men, who were scurrying like crabs out of Cony's reach. Grabbing his sketchscreen, Aiden ran back to his sire's side.

Cony clipped the blond upside the head with the flat of his blade, then pointed the tip toward the other two. Stomping his foot at them, he yelled, "Get!"

The men swiftly obeyed, running down the hill and toward the docks.

Watching them leave, Cony shook his head. "If it wouldn't stain your reputation with investigations and trials, I'd have dispatched them." He lowered his sword and turned his attention to Aiden. "What in the bloody hell were you thinking?"

"I—"

"Get in the carriage, Aiden." Cony grabbed Aiden by the back of his neck and led him to the lift. There was a second lift next to the one Aiden had borrowed. Which was probably why Aiden hadn't been aware of Raleigh's arrival, the carriages were remarkably silent.

After sending one carriage home, Cony motioned for Aiden to precede him into the other. Aiden climbed inside. Only then did fear set in. He could have been in some serious trouble if Cony hadn't come along.

Cony entered the carriage and ordered it back to the castle as he put his sword in its scabbard. Tossing it on the seat across from them, he sat, crossing his long legs in front of him and leaning back against the burgundy leather seat. He stayed motionless for several minutes.

Aiden bit his bottom lip and watched his sire. The confines of the family coach were comforting in its familiarity. Now, if he could only stop the jittery feeling in his stomach.

Cony's jaw clenched and he closed his eyes, letting out a sigh. Running his hands over his face, he sat forward, resting his elbows on his knees. Turning his head, he faced Aiden. He took a deep breath and let it out. "You could have been kidnapped, raped or, Galaxy forbid, murdered, Aiden." Cony stared at him for several seconds then ruffled his hair and pulled him into a hug. "What am I going to do with you? With all of you...you and your brothers are going to be the death of me, I swear it."

Leaning into his parent's touch, Aiden gave thanks that he was alive. Finally, his heart slowed back to normal and the jittery feeling lessened. He hadn't thought of the consequences. He only wanted to get away. No one would take him to the docks, so he took himself.

Pulling out of his sire's embrace, he shrugged, trying to act normal and not let Cony know how much the near mishap had bothered him. "You should probably lock Colton and Tarren up and throw away the key. Rexley is too responsible to be a problem and Payton needs a challenge. He's too smart by half. Me? Send me to art school? Allow me to seek an apprenticeship?"

Cony stared at him, blinking twice, before bursting into laughter. Groaning, he pinched the bridge of his straight, narrow nose and leaned back in his seat, closing his eyes.

Aiden tried not to let the abrupt silence bother him. Either Cony would punish him or he wouldn't. The important thing was that he was still around to be punished.

They rode the rest of the way home in silence, Aiden toggling through the great sketches he'd gotten and Raleigh staring out the window. The coach stopped when they reached the front of the castle.

Tucking his screen under his arm, Aiden stood.

Cony caught his arm and turned him before he could exit the lift. "I understand, Aiden. I really do. I was young once too."

Aiden nodded, not knowing what to say. He didn't doubt the sincerity in his sire's statement. But it didn't change the fact that Aiden was determined to be an artist and he needed different subjects if he were going to gain more experience.

Raleigh chuckled and cuffed his shoulder. "Stop fretting, Son, I'm not going to beat you. But rest assured we will discuss this with your father."

A lecture. Aiden groaned but managed not to roll his eyes. He was thankful that he'd made it through the ordeal. He almost welcomed the sermon.

"In fact, I left him stewing in the study." Cony pushed past him and stepped out of the carriage.

Great. Aiden dismissed the carriage and followed.

Before they reached the front door it was thrown open. Which wasn't unusual, Jeffers was probably operational again. But it wasn't Jeffers who greeted them, it was Thomas, their human butler.

His face was red, gray hair bedraggled, and his burgundy uniform disheveled, which was highly irregular. Thomas was normally more uptight than Jeffers. Obviously, he'd taken up the slack when Jeffers was offline. He took a deep breath and stood aside. "Jeffers is rebooting. I've been asked to inform you that his majesty is waiting for you both in the study." Thomas held out his hand. "May I have your sketchscreen and have it taken to your chambers for you, milord?"

Nodding, Aiden handed his screen to Thomas. "Thank you, Thomas."

Thomas bowed.

Aiden's stomach plummeted as he followed his sire down the hall.

Father was waiting for them behind the desk. He sat with his hands folded on top of the huge wood desk, his brow furrowed. First, he gazed at Cony then at Aiden. The tension melted from his shoulders. "Have a seat, Aiden." He glanced at Cony. "Well?"

Aiden took a seat on the loveseat sitting perpendicular to the big desk.

"He was at the docks as Muffin said." Perching himself on the corner of the desk, Cony angled to see both his consort and son.

Father groaned and put his head into his hands. "Aiden."

Cony frowned, shaking his head. "Oh, but that's not the worst of it, Steven." He looked at Aiden. "Tell him what happened, Son."

Father's head shot up, his eyes wide, glancing at Cony then Aiden.

Aiden prepared himself for the inevitable and told his father about the three men. After he relayed the story he sat back and waited for the outburst to come. It never did.

Leaning back in his chair and closing his eyes, Father stayed quiet for several minutes. His chest rose and fell with deep movements and he rubbed the heels of his hands into his eyes. Finally, he dropped his hands and opened his eyes. "You could have been killed. What if your sire hadn't gotten there in time?" He leaned forward, resting his elbows on the desk. "Aiden, this has got to stop."

Here comes the punishment. "Yes, sir. We shouldn't have turned Jeffers off again."

Father heaved a sigh and exchanged a glance with Cony before returning his attention to Aiden. "I'm not talking about the sneaking out and meddling with Jeffers. That is a whole other situation. Which, rest assured, you will all be punished for. I'm talking about your obliviousness when you get into your art. You didn't even see the men until they were right on you, did you?"

"No, sir." Aiden shook his head.

"Aiden, you need to get your head out of the clouds. Have you even looked at available men this season? Just today I received a request for your hand."

Aiden's stomach flip-flopped. They'd been through this before and his parents promised never to give consent without having Aiden's permission first, but it still unsettled him to hear of a proposal. "From who this time?"

"Whom," Cony corrected.

"From whom this time?" Aiden automatically rectified his mistake.

Having witnessed countless grammar lessons, Father never batted a lash. "Lord Braxton."

Aiden groaned. Braxton would expect him to be a societal and political paragon and further Braxton's own political agenda—he'd practically said as much the other night. Aiden tried to get it across to Lord Braxton that he wasn't interested, telling the man point-blank how important his artwork was, but apparently the man couldn't take a hint. "You refused him, I hope."

"I told him I'd consider it after speaking to you."

"I don't want a consort."

"Why ever not?" Cony asked. "Braxton is a good catch. He's wealthy, connected, strong..."

"And handsome," Father added.

Cony frowned, reaching across the desk to flick his spouse's ear.

"Ow." Father slapped at Cony's hand. "What? He is."

"He's very influential in parliament and he comes from a long line of not only Regelence navy officers, but IN officers as well," Cony continued.

Aiden suppressed a grimace. If he could find someone as well suited to him as his parents were to one another, he might consider it. But Braxton wasn't that man, even if he was handsome, with his tall, lean frame and his prematurely silver hair. "I want to be an artist. And Braxton is too..." Aiden waved his hand. "Overbearing."

Cony nodded his agreement. "Yes, the man does seem a bit dictatorial." He gazed at Steven. "That can be troublesome."

Father scoffed. "I'm not domineering, Raleigh." He looked back at Aiden. "You need to take a consort some time."

"Why? I want to paint and draw. I want a career in art, not helping some lord manage his estate, decide what investments to make and further his political career." Aiden dropped his gaze to his lap and wrung his hands, feeling dejected. How could he make them understand?

Cony pushed off the desk and knelt in front of him, taking his hands. "Don't you want a family of your own?"

Aiden shrugged. He had a family, a family he loved. Most of the time he even enjoyed being around them. Why did everyone think a man needed a consort and children to make him complete? Who really cared what family had what fingers in what pies? He didn't want to be some trophy because of who his family was.

Standing, Father walked around the desk and leaned on it a mere foot from Aiden. "We want you to be happy, Son. And we want you to be safe, to know you're taken care of. It seems every time in the past year you've gone off to draw somewhere, you've gotten yourself into a situation. The last two weeks alone you've nearly been trampled by a heard of cattle, almost fallen off a cliff and stung by bees."

It was only a handful of cows and they'd completely missed him—except for the one who stepped on his foot—how was he supposed to know Tarren's dogs were going to chase a cat through the field behind them? And he'd been in no danger of falling off that cliff—even if he had skidded over it chasing his stylus—he'd merely been stuck on the outcropping until Jeffers notified someone. He'd gotten some great compositions of the creek from up there. And the bees, well in the future he'd be careful and make certain there weren't any hives in the next tree he decided to climb. It had all been worth it though, he'd captured several nice pieces for his portfolio.

"You must take a consort. It is the way of things. You will need a family of your own. Eventually, your brothers will all have their own families and your sire and I won't be here forever," Father said.

Aiden rolled his eyes. His parents were a long way from the grave, they were only in their early forties. And by the time his brothers had children and spouses, Aiden would be well on his way to being a master artist. "Why can't I stay here until I'm ready to be on my own?"

Pinching the bridge of his nose, Father closed his eyes. "You're the son of a king, not a common man. We find a suitable spouse, we have families, we lead the country, we don't do middle-class labor."

"But that's just it, Father. I am the son of a king. I should be able to do as I please. I don't care about a career in politics or the military or any of that."

The room fell deathly silent for several minutes while Aiden pleaded with his eyes. Finally, Cony stood. Nodding like he'd come to a decision, he turned to Father. "Being a consort isn't for everyone, Steven."

"Raleigh, do you want him to grow old alone?" Father stepped forward, brushing back Aiden's hair with one hand and reaching for Cony's hand with the other. "I only want him to be happy. You didn't want to be my consort, but would you go back now?"

Grabbing Father's hand, Cony shook his head. "You know I wouldn't, but you allowed me to be myself and work. It was never about aligning yourself with my family or furthering your political career. That can't be said for a lot of other lords."

Work? Cony didn't work. Well, that wasn't exactly true, he did work. Cony helped Father with national and planetary government and diplomacy.

Father nodded. "You're right. You're both right." Lifting Aiden's chin, Steven made Aiden meet his gaze. "I'll make you a deal, Aiden."

"A deal, Father?" Aiden cut his eyes to Cony.

Cony gave a slight shrug, but he smiled. Dropping Father's hand, he took a seat next to Aiden.

Father looked at Cony. His lip twitched, then his face hardened and he bent to stare Aiden in the eye. "You keep out of trouble—and I mean no incidents at all—and I'll hire you an art teacher." He shook his head when Aiden opened his mouth to speak. "My main problem—your safety—has not changed. I love you, Son, and don't want anything to happen to you. If you can keep out of trouble for three whole months, I'll hire a teacher to come here and teach you. And on your twenty-fifth birthday, I'll settle an estate and an allowance on you. But I don't want you to close your mind to the possibility of taking a consort. You may find someone who suits you very well. I'm still not convinced that isn't the best thing for you."

Cony patted his leg. "Your father is right, you need to keep an open mind." He looked up at his spouse. "You do know that you will have to hire a master, yes? The boy is good. Very good. I seriously doubt a regular art teacher, like he had in the schoolroom, will be able to teach him anything."

Father snorted. "I know that. I had planned on hiring Contenetti. I doubt I'd have much problem convincing the man to use the east tower as a studio and taking an apprentice."

Aiden smiled so big, it was almost painful. Contenetti was the most famous artist in Regelence, possibly even in the entire Regelence system.

"Do we have a deal?"

Aiden nodded. "Yes."

Father narrowed his eyes, trying to look stern, but he wasn't entirely successful. "If you endanger yourself again, you will not be so much as allowed to leave your room without a chaperone. And furthermore, I'll find you a consort myself. Are we understood?"

"Yes, sir."

The lights flickered, drawing all their attention. The lights never flickered unless Jeffers was involved.

His parents shared a smile, then Cony frowned. "Now, about Jeffers—"

Oddly enough, Jeffers picked that exact moment to speak. "Your Majesty? Your Highness?"

"Welcome back, Jeffers," Father responded.

"Thank you, sir, but I've a spot of bad news. There has been a theft."

Chapter Two

The Lady Anna: Intergalactic Navy space frigate, under the command of Captain Nathaniel Leland Hawkins.

Nate stopped at his cabin, braced his hands on either side of the entry and rested his forehead against the smooth steel of the hatch. Sometimes being in charge was a real bitch. Today in general qualified as one of those times.

"Captain, first mate Kindros has been taken hostage by the prisoner. The prisoner has already shot two security guards."

Fuck.

Not two seconds after the ship's precise feminine voice finished delivering the bad news, someone came running around the corner breathing heavily. "Captain, the prisoner got a fragger and is holding Lieutenant Kindros captive."

The hatch lifted, squeaking across Nate's forehead, before he stepped back.

"Are you coming inside?" Trouble, his son, stood in the hatchway, a big smile on his lips, until he caught sight of Nate's face. Trouble's aquamarine eyes widened and he looked past Nate to the crewman who'd hailed him.

Sighing, Nate turned around, spying Thompson, one of the Lady Anna's junior officers, wringing his hands. "How did the prisoner get a weapon?"

"Umm—" Thompson bit his bottom lip, his gaze darting around, looking at anything but Nate.

Nate held up a hand. "Never mind. Are the security guards still alive?"

Thompson nodded.

"Are they expected to recover?"

Again Thompson's head bobbed.

Well, that was at least something. Nate pinched the bridge of his nose with his thumb and forefinger and stared at the dark purple carpet. He never should have left the damned interrogation room.

"You got a headache, Hawk?" Trouble asked.

Yeah, several headaches, a stolen shipment of weapons, a traitor, some new carbon scoring on the hull of my fucking ship, and now... "Yes." Nate dropped his hand. "Anna, what is Lieutenant Kindros' location and status?"

The ship's steady voice answered promptly. "First mate Kindros is in corridor Q. She is alive and well, Captain."

"And the prisoner?" Nate turned toward Trouble. "Get my pistol and com-con."

Trouble rushed off, his blond curls bouncing as he ran back into the cabin.

"The prisoner is also in corridor Q. He is holding the lieutenant against his chest with a fragger gun to her temple, sir," Anna answered.

Turning back to the nervous junior officer, Nate pointed. "Make sure everyone stays out of the corridors and call the rest of the security team back to the gangway to protect the bridge. I'll handle this."

"Y-y-yes, sir." Thompson saluted and hurried off down the hall.

Nate shook his head. "How did such a timid man make it to his rank?"

"He isn't timid. He's only that way around you."

Frowning, Nate glanced down at his son. He held out his hand for the gun, gunbelt and command-connection earpiece that would allow Anna to speak to him privately. "Why would he be that way only when he's around me?"

"You scare the crap out of everyone." Trouble grinned, showing off his straight white teeth.

Yeah, everyone except the pest in front of him, apparently. Nate put the com-con in his ear, the belt around his waist and glared at Trouble. "Stay put, Trouble."

"Aye, aye, Cap'n." The kid saluted, clicking his bare heels together, and pushed the button on the bulkhead next to the hatch making it swoosh shut.

Insolent pup. Nate started down the corridor toward his first mate and the prisoner she allowed to escape. "Anna, where are Lieutenant Kindros and the prisoner now?"

Anna's voice sounded only in his earpiece. "Traveling down corridor P, headed toward corridor M, Captain."

"Has security reported back?"

"Yes, Captain."

Nate hurried through the passage, his boots muffled by the carpeting. When he reached where it intersected with corridor M he stopped. He could hear his first mate threatening her captor.

Nate pressed his back against the cool metal bulkhead, holding his gun in front of his face at the ready. "Hey, Jansen, if you will let Lieutenant Kindros go, I'll take it easy on you." *Well, as easy as I can considering you're a fuckin' traitor and that you've pissed me off.*

A bolt zipped past Nate's head and struck the bulkhead opposite him, making a small black carbon burn where it hit. *I guess that's a no.* Nate crouched lower.

"Fuck you, Cap'n." Jansen punctuated the decline with another blast of his fragger.

Kindros' feminine gasp echoed around the corner, followed by the sounds of a scuffle. There was a dull thud and then an angry masculine grunt. "I told you to be still, bitch."

Nate growled, imagining the butt of the fragger cracking against his first mate's skull. "Brittani?"

"Still here, Hawk," she replied faintly.

Another thud, then a yelp from Kindros.

Shit. He didn't want to have to kill the idiot, not that he was opposed to killing the pain in the ass, but Nate wanted answers first. "Anna, I need a SITREP."

Lady Anna's detached voice came through his earpiece immediately with the situation report he requested. "Prisoner Jansen is advancing on your location, Captain. His weapon is still aimed at the first mate's head. My sensors tell me he is highly agitated. Lieutenant Kindros is dazed but still conscious."

Nate touched the earpiece linking him to the ship's computer, glad he'd thought to use it. "His weapon is set to a penetrating bolt?"

"Yes, sir."

Of course it was. "Is his finger on the trigger?"

"Yes, sir."

Figured. "How close to the corner of my corridor is he?"

"About three feet four inches, sir. He's angling away from the bulkhead closest to you."

Fuck. Nate wished he had a way to see what was going on. He checked his fragger, making sure it was set to stun, just in case Kindros got caught in the crossfire. The problem was, with Jansen's finger on the trigger, shooting him with any kind of bolt would get Kindros killed. The whole body inevitably spasmed when hit with a bolt, whether it was set to penetrate or stun.

"Sir, Jeremy is advancing rapidly toward the south end of corridor M," Anna reported.

Nate's jaw clenched. "Fuck." Jansen and Kindros were at the north end of corridor M. The boy was headed right into the thick of things, as usual. Nate was certain he'd ordered all personnel to stay out of the area until he had this cleared up. Hell, he told Trouble to stay put when he'd left the cabin. "I want a three-second warning before Jeremy arrives at corridor M."

"Yes, sir."

Nate got to his feet, inched closer to the corner and readied his fragger. This may not be a bad thing. In fact, Trouble might just escape punishment if this worked.

"Jeremy approaching in three...two...one."

"Hawk?" Trouble shouted.

Nate stepped around the corner in time to see Jansen aim his weapon on Trouble. Nate fired, striking his son, cabin boy and all-around pest center mass.

Trouble's body stiffened and fell to the deck.

Nate fired again, hitting Jansen before the man figured out what was going on.

Jansen's weapon discharged then he dropped it. The bolt directed exactly where Trouble had been standing before the shot disappeared down the corridor. Jansen crumpled to the deck.

Kindros, getting the residual effect of the pulse bolt through connection with Jansen's body, slithered to the ground in front of Jansen.

Nate engaged the safety on his weapon and shoved it into the holster on his belt. He rushed to Jansen, grabbed the fragger beside the downed man and flipped the safety button. "Anna, please notify the security team that the prisoner has been recaptured and is awaiting an escort to the brig."

"Yes, sir. They are on their way, Captain."

Kindros came to first, having gotten a lesser jolt than Jansen or Trouble. She sat, running fingers through her long dark hair, smearing blood across her forehead. She blinked drowsy brown eyes at him. "Hey, Hawk."

Nate offered her a hand. "Brittani."

She reached up and, noticing the blood, wiped it on her black pantsuit. Then she put her slim palm in his and allowed him to pull her to her feet. She held his hand, when Nate would have turned away, and squeezed. "Thanks." Letting go, she straightened her uniform, dusting off the gold bars on the shoulders signifying her rank. Once again she touched her forehead and drew her hand back, studying the red smudge.

"You're welcome." He knew she was a little more shook up than she let on. He hadn't worked with her for going on ten years not to know how she reacted to stress. She was rattled, sure, anyone would be having had a weapon pointed at their temple, but she'd rather die than show it. The woman had more pride than most people he knew. "Are you okay?"

"Sure." Kindros groaned and followed him toward his unconscious son. "I feel like a total idiot, allowing that schmuck to get the drop on me and get out of the interrogation room though."

Nate nodded. "What happened?"

Brittani grimaced. "He asked for some water. I ordered Johnson to get some, feeling a bit sorry for him after you scared the piss out of him."

Nate arched a brow. Really, people's reaction to him was downright ridiculous—not that he would do anything to dissuade them. It worked to his advantage—but it was outrageous nonetheless. Okay, he'd earned some of his reputation, but he didn't go around killing people for the fun of it. "And?"

"And when Johnson came in with the water, the prisoner surprised us. He shoved me, grabbed Johnson's weapon and then me. I thought he was still shaken up over having been captured and taken on board *your* ship. I slipped up."

It wasn't like Kindros to let down her guard.

She groaned and threw her hands up. "For crying out loud, Hawk, the man was so petrified at coming face-to-face with you he peed himself. I didn't think he had the balls to try something like that."

"See that it doesn't happen again." Nate stopped and looked down at his son. Then something occurred to him. He sniffed and tugged Kindros around, surveying her backside. A wet spot stained the right side of her black uniform. "Did you realize you have urine on your pants?"

Her face scrunched. "Eww... You bastard. This is your fault."

Nate chuckled. "I'm a bastard, but I'm not completely heartless, therefore you may change uniforms before you carry on." He felt much more amused than he had when this whole ordeal started.

The fifteen-year-old lay on his side, his mouth hanging open. He seemed fragile and very pale against the plum-colored carpet, his blond curls appearing almost white in contrast. Muffled groans from behind Nate caught his attention.

The security team members were hauling Jansen to his feet. The man was still mostly out of it. The bigger of the two crewmen bent down, lifted the prisoner over his shoulder and walked back down the corridor. The other crewman dipped his head at Nate and then followed.

"Asshole," Kindros hissed.

"It wasn't his fault *you* let him get away."

She winced. "Ouch, rub it in."

"That's my job. And, Lieutenant Kindros, for the record, letting a prisoner loose is a court-martial offense. I'm letting you off easy. Since you were the one held hostage, consider this a severe dressing-down. Don't let it happen again."

"Yes, sir. Thank you."

He bobbed his head in recognition to Kindros. "Make sure you get your head checked out."

"Yes, sir." She sauntered off.

A smacking sound brought Nate's attention back to Trouble. The boy squinted and made a chewing motion then rolled over onto his other side, pillowing his hands together under his cheek. "Can we dress down Lieutenant Taylor too? I have been trying to catch him in the showers since he came aboard."

Nate nudged the back of Trouble's thigh with his foot. "You're in some serious trouble. And since you mentioned it, I've been meaning to talk to you about—"

Trouble grabbed his leg and moaned. "Oh, the pain. I think my leg is broken. I'm going to die. I probably even have a severe concussion and—"

Nate scowled at his son thrashing around the deck. Now that the danger was over his stomach felt queasy. The pest could have been killed.

Trouble stopped moving long enough to crack open his eyes. Catching sight of Nate, he moaned louder and began thrashing about again. "Oh, I'm dying…"

Nate scooped the little phony into his arms and started toward their cabin. "Pain or not you will be punished for disobeying an order."

Suddenly, the cherub face tensed, all pretense of pain leaving. "I almost forgot. The admiral is on the televid. He needs to speak to you right away!"

೮೩

His headache was coming back with a vengeance. Nate let go of the bridge of his nose, running his fingers over his mustache and beard, trailing his hand down his neck. He looked back at the monitor on his desk. "Okay, let me get this straight. You knew they had weapons before you sent me in there and you didn't tell me?"

Admiral Jenkins waved his chubby hand back and forth, shaking his head. "No, no, no. I knew we were missing weapons. I didn't know where they got off to until I got the report from your ship saying you'd found them." He stretched and yawned, staring at Nate when he was done. The man was purposely hedging.

Nate shoved himself out of his chair and walked around to the other side of his desk. If he sat still any longer he was going to fall asleep. If it was any of the other IN Admirals he wouldn't have dared break protocol, but this was Carl, who had been his friend for damned near twenty years, since Nate joined the Navy.

After swiveling the televid to face him, Nate paced back and forth. "Carl, I've had a bad day. You sent me to a supposedly unarmed dinky backwater planet to deliver supplies for the resistance and my ship got shot at. After my crew captured the aggressors, we discovered they had a stash of IN class three weapons. The leader of the group of rebels took my first mate hostage, shot two of my crew and put carbon burns on my bulkheads before I re-apprehended him. We've had no luck getting information out of the group on where they obtained the guns, and now you're telling me you knew the weapons were stolen, but not who stole them." Nate stopped in front of the screen, raising an eyebrow at his commanding officer. "I'm bringing the detainees into headquarters. What else do you want from me? The last I heard, torturing prisoners for info was against IN policy."

The admiral grinned, his blue eyes crinkling at the corners, making him look younger than his sixty-two years. It was a grin Nate knew well, and it made his headache kick up a notch. That smile from his friend didn't bode well. The old man had something planned, something Nate wasn't going to like. "So you were paying attention, Nate."

Nate snorted. "Of course I was paying attention. What are you scheming, Carl?"

Carl chuckled.

Fuck.

"How do you feel about a little undercover work?"

Nate barely kept his mouth from dropping open. Spying? Carl wanted Nate to spy? Nate couldn't intermingle with a crowd if his life depended on it. Forget the fact that he had a reputation as the IN's infamous Captain Hawk. He was six-foot-five and two hundred and forty pounds—he did not blend into the background well.

"Oh, cool. Can I come?" Trouble's platinum curls preceded his grinning face around the hatch frame.

Closing his eyes, Nate counted to ten. How many times had he told the pest not to eavesdrop? Hadn't he just given the kid a severe dressing-down for disobeying?

"Hi there, Trouble," the Admiral said cheerfully.

Nate opened his eyes and shot his son a glare. "Out." He pointed his finger toward the hatch.

Flicking him a quick glance, Trouble waved at the televid. "Hi, back, Admiral Carl. How are Betty and your son?"

"Trouble..." Nate gritted his teeth.

"Bye, Admiral. Gotta go." Jeremy took off, disappearing from sight.

Smart kid. "Carl, I'm a naval destroyer captain, not a spy. Why in the universe would you want me to do undercover work?"

"You better have a seat, Nate."

Great, just fucking great. It looked like the news was getting better and better. Nate went to his chair and turned the monitor back around.

Leaning back in his own chair, Carl crossed his hands over his stomach. "I want you to use your title."

"You want me to go undercover as an IN officer?"

The older man shook his graying head. "No, I want you to go as an Earl...the Earl of Deverell, heir to the Duke of Hawthorne."

Nate's gut clenched like he'd taken a fist to the abdomen. He swore he could hear his blood pounding through his veins and his mouth felt like he'd eaten that bitter granular candy Trouble had a penchant for, but his composure never faltered on the outside. "I'm no longer the heir to Hawthorne. I'm sure the honor has long since passed to my younger brother."

"That is beside the point, Nate. No one will know that you haven't been in contact with your family for nearly twenty years. I need you because you've lived in a regency society before. You know how to act as a lord, a gentleman."

"Are you commanding me to go or are you asking me?" He thought about it for a moment. "No. I won't go back to Englor. Find someone else."

"No, no, not Englor, but a planet akin to it. It's a planet called Regelence. They've similar customs. Their society is, like Englor's, based on Earth's Regency period. Like Englor, it's also under the jurisdiction of the Aries Fleet."

Nate closed his eyes and leaned his head back on the headrest. He didn't want to do this. It would bring back way too many memories. Memories he'd just as soon stayed gone. Well, if not gone, buried away in his past where they couldn't bother him. "Why?" He opened his eyes, meeting Carl's gaze.

"Because that is where the guns you found on the vessel that attacked your ship were stolen from. We need to find out who is involved. It's a weird coincidence I know, but it will be easier for you to fit in. Otherwise, we'll have to train someone to their customs and that will take time. Time we don't have. We cannot allow our weapons to be used against us if we are to maintain peace between the planetary systems, Nate."

Damn the man. He had to bring the cause into it. Carl knew damned well how Nate felt about his job and what the IN did to keep peace.

"I need someone I can trust, Hawk."

"All right. I'm in."

Carl's smile was radiant. "Good. You will need to report to the base on Regelence Space Dock. You will be outfitted with a wardrobe there. Take Trouble with you. You will need someone who can get in with the servants."

"Yes!" Trouble's triumphant shout came from the other room.

Nate barely managed not to laugh. *The little shit.*

The Admiral did laugh. "Train him to act as your valet. You will be staying at the planetary royal palace in Pruluce, the capitol country of Regelence."

Nate's eyebrows shot nearly to his hairline. Carl wasn't kidding when he said they needed someone who knew how to act titled. "The royal palace?"

Carl's lips twitched. "Yes, you'll be the guest of King Steven and his consort. Raleigh is employed by the IN. But since he is too close to the case he cannot officially be involved. I doubt you will be recognized, but if you are it will not be a big deal. And while we are on the subject, Steven and Raleigh are the only ones who will know the true reason you're there. Off the record, I know both of these men personally. They are good men and they aren't involved. You can trust them fully. However, officially you report to me. You'll be briefed fully when you—"

Nate blinked, totally losing track of what the admiral was saying. *Did he say—surely not.* "Wait. Did you say *he*? The king's consort is a man?" Societies like the one they were discussing, like the one Nate grew up in, did not tolerate same-sex relationships.

The admiral laughed. "Did I forget to mention that Regelence is a very patriarchal society? So much so, in fact, that the aristocracy makes certain their offspring, especially their heirs, are male and genetically altered to have a preference for the same sex."

♋

The Lazy Dog Tavern, downtown Classige, Pruluce on planet Regelence.

Ralph Benson leaned against the wall, holding his breath. When he'd followed the other valet here, he'd had no idea the man was on the take. He'd come with the other castle servants to share a pint after the royal family turned in for the night. He never suspected this info would fall into his hands.

Taking a drink of his ale, he nodded at a passing waitress, still listening intently to the valet as he spoke.

"I think I have our man set-up to get the cloning technology once he marries into the family. After he gets his new spouse addicted we'll work on influencing the father." The valet stopped talking briefly, listening to whomever he was talking to on the televid, Ralph supposed. "No, the royal bitch does not know. She only knows that she will get the money when she gives him the schematics." Again the valet paused. "Azrael has no idea I am here but I think he might suspect us. And remember, we always have her child to use if we have to—"

Ralph pushed away from the wall. He'd heard enough. He didn't understand most of what he'd overheard but he knew enough to discern their Queen was involved, which was what he was here for. He had to get word to Colonel Hollister somehow.

Chapter Three

Townsend Property: the outskirts of Classige, Pruluce, the capital country of Regelence.

Gazing out the window at the passing landscape, Nate felt like he'd been transported back in time to his youth. The whole thing seemed surreal, the clothes, the coach, everything. It brought forth conflicting emotions. He found himself sitting more rigid than normal. Whether it was his repressed "lord" surfacing or the assignment he couldn't say. The thing was, he'd never been what one would consider a pretentious lord, even when he was one, but this was a role, an acting job. The sooner he figured out who was in on the stolen weapons the better.

A growl combined with a rustle of fabric brought his attention back inside the lift. He suppressed the urge to smile, knowing Trouble would only take it as encouragement. The kid had been fidgeting and bitching since they'd changed clothes on the space dock three hours earlier.

Nate knew damned well the pest was trying to gain his sympathy and it wasn't working. If he had to wear a waistcoat and cravat, so did Trouble. The kid should be thankful Regelence had a nice temperate climate. There had been days on Englor when it was downright unbearable to be anywhere but lounging at home in the air conditioning.

Squirming and nearly worming himself off the leather cushions, Trouble made agitated little grunts and groans.

"Stop fidgeting."

Trouble snorted and fell to his side on the seat. Grabbing the fabric over his thighs, he tugged and wiggled, assumingly trying to ease his britches downward a bit. Soon enough one hand came up, yanking at the neckcloth, followed by melodramatic choking sounds. With much production, the kid finally slithered to the polished wood floor and glared up at Nate.

Nate raised a brow.

"Kill me now." The pest's arms flopped to his sides on the floor. His face screwed up and he closed his eyes on a wail.

Nate's lip twitched. The kid really did have a flare for dramatics—he was quite the drama queen. "What happened to 'I'm super spy Double-o-Trouble'?"

The pale brows drew together and one aquamarine eye cracked open. "That was before I was forced to wear smothering clothes. This rains meteors, Hawk." Trouble pushed himself off the floor and back onto the seat with a sigh. "These pants are so tight my balls are practically in my throat. Or rather they would be if this noose I have around my neck wasn't restricting the space in there." He pulled at the starched white cloth tucked into his collar again. "I don't see why I have to wear this getup. I'm supposed to be a servant."

"You're a valet. How can you be expected to dress me, if you can't even dress yourself?"

"I didn't dress you. *You* dressed me." He motioned to the cravat that Nate had tied into an intricate knot. "Why can't I be the earl and you be my valet?"

"Because an earl does not flop around on the floor and complain about his unmentionable anatomy being in his throat."

Trouble's eyes widened. "Damn, Hawk, you sound like you have a stick up your ass."

Nate turned back toward the window, studying the vibrant green grassy slopes and trees, keeping Trouble from seeing his grin. "Lords don't mention foreign objects up people's arses either."

"Speaking of things up people's asses—"

"Trouble..." he warned. He had no idea what the pest was about to say, but it certainly wasn't the kind of talk the imp should use. It wasn't at all proper and he needed to be getting into character. Of course, it was Nate's own fault because the kid had been raised around sailors for half his life.

"Whaaat? I'm just saying... This is a gay society, right? So, does this mean I can find a boyfriend?"

Nate groaned. "No, you may not. This is a job. You are supposed to be gathering information." The thought of his son in possible danger wasn't a pleasant one. It brought to mind the pest's last escapade that nearly got him killed.

A smile crept across the boyish face. "What if I have to get cozy with the enemy to get information?"

"Now why do I have the feeling you will find yourself in just that sort of situation?"

The pest shrugged and squirmed a little, pulling at his waistcoat.

"Remember, you are the prestigious servant of an earl. We are not on holiday."

The red light over the hatch blinked, indicating an incoming transmission. Nate peeked out the window again and noticed they were approaching a large, ornate iron gate. Looking at Trouble, he pressed a finger to his lips and touched the intercom button.

"Good afternoon, Lord Deverell," a baritone male voice greeted as the gates swung open allowing them entry. "I'm Jeffers, the head butler. Welcome to Townsend Castle. Thomas, my assistant, will meet you at the front entrance."

"Thank you, Jeffers. Will you please send additional servants to help my valet with my belongings?"

Trouble rolled his eyes.

"Yes, milord."

"Thank you." Nate frowned at his son. It was time to get serious. The sooner they figured out who stole those damned weapons and how, the sooner they could get back to the Lady Anna and stop living a farce. The intercom clicked off.

Apparently, the pest had decided to behave and take on the role he was to play. He still wore a grimace and was stretching his neck strangely, compensating for the cravat, but he sat straighter and had composed himself.

"Remember, when we stop, you will go through the side servants' entrance and stay either downstairs or in my room. Likely your own room will be a very small one connected to mine. *Try* to act proper, no cursing, watch your posture, and for Galaxy's sake, stay out of trouble."

"Yeah, yeah, yeah, I got i—"

"Ahem." Nate gave him an arched look.

"I mean, yes, milord." Trouble sighed. "I remember the lesson on proper behavior and in case I need further instruction, I have an electronic reference book on my reader in my suitcase."

Nodding, Nate retrieved the beaver hat from the seat next to him. "Good, go get things settled in our room while I handle things with our hosts."

The lift came to a stop, the door raised and the steps descended from the vehicle. Nate put on his hat before exiting the carriage. A quartet of servants stood at the bottom of the front stairs, judging from the uniforms, a head servant and three footmen.

A tall, slender, gray-haired man stepped forward and bowed. "Greetings, Lord Deverell. I'm Thomas, the assistant butler. Welcome to Townsend Castle."

"Thomas." Nate tipped his head slightly. "My valet will need help with my things."

"Yes, milord." He snapped his finger and the three younger men rushed toward the lift and began removing luggage from the storage below the passenger compartment. "If you will follow me, milord, I'll take you to the study for your meeting, unless you'd prefer to freshen up?"

"No, thank you, Thomas. I'd prefer to meet with their majesties now."

"Very well, milord."

Trouble got out of the coach and talked to the footmen.

Giving one last hope that Trouble stayed out of trouble, Nate ascended the wide cement steps leading to the gothic style castle. It was a beautiful structure with ivy clinging to the gray stone walls. It reminded him vaguely of Hutchins Hall, the estate nearest his boyhood home, Hawthorne. Only, Townsend Castle was considerably larger than Hutchins Hall.

The large wooden door opened, revealing a vast marble entryway. It spoke of refinement and wealth, yet it was quite masculine. The foyer was brightly lit by a crystal chandelier that sparkled off the gleaming jade-colored marble. It was like walking into a museum, pristine and showy. It had been a while since he'd been anywhere so classy.

"Might I take your hat and gloves, sir?"

Nate pulled off his gloves, handing them and his hat to Thomas.

Acutely aware of how his boots clicked on the natural stone and echoed in the stillness of the vestibule, he followed Thomas.

The door shut with a heavy thud behind Thomas and the voice that had greeted Nate in the coach spoke. "Thomas, please show Lord Deverell to the study. You are needed in the conservatory posthaste."

Grimacing, the butler turned to Nate, bowing again. "If you will come with me, milord." He raised his arm, indicating a door ahead of them and to the left before the hallway became a huge open space. It was massive with two grand staircases along the side walls.

Somewhere in the castle a door slammed and a huge ruckus ensued. It sounded like...barking? The yapping grew louder and frantic clicks reverberated off the marble.

Thomas' shoulders drooped and he groaned before he quickly remembered himself. He glanced back at Nate and smiled, hurrying his steps. "Right this way, milord." Thomas reached the door and it swung open.

Around the corner a herd of about ten dogs, large and small, scrambled down the hall toward the entry. Their toenails clicked and scraped, trying to obtain traction on the marble.

"Ho there. Jeffers, the door!" A handsome man with an abundance of short, dark curls barreled around the corner following the dogs, nearly trampling Thomas.

Only Nate's quick reflexes kept the butler upright. He caught the older man's shoulder, steadying him, and watched the young man sprint after the pack of wild beasts.

The teenager was dressed for riding, in buff-colored pantaloons and shiny black boots. His blue coattails flew behind him as he slipped and slid over the polished stone. "Sorry, Thomas," he yelled over his shoulder and continued out the door after the dogs.

Placing a hand against the wall, Thomas took a deep breath. "Thank you, milord." Under his breath he mumbled what sounded like, "Lord Terror."

Before Nate could ask what that was about, a squealing, naked, wet, little girl ran past, followed by an older woman.

"Lady Mischief," Thomas muttered.

Nate blinked. Good Galaxy, he'd landed in a fucking nuthouse. "Pardon?"

Thomas' eyes widened comically. "Oh dear. Nothing, Lord Deverell, nothing. I was talking to myself. Bad habit, that." He extended his arm toward the room again.

Entering the dark masculine room brought back memories of Nate's father's study at Hawthorne. It had wall-to-wall mahogany bookshelves and large leather furniture. Nate inhaled deeply. Sweet tobacco, bay rum and leather filled his senses, just like the study in Hawthorne Manor. He'd always loved that room.

"Please make yourself comfortable. Is there anything I can—"

Stomping ensued, followed by, "Muffffinnnn!" A tall man, who looked to be slightly older than the one chasing the horde of canines, stuck his head in the door. His golden eyes widened at the sight of Nate. "Oh, excuse me, I didn't realize we were expecting company." His dark head popped back around the door and his hurried footfalls trailed off.

A grin tugged at Nate's lips as he took a seat on a small burgundy sofa vertical to the desk.

Thomas grimaced and glanced at the door. He was obviously in a hurry, but reluctant to be rude and leave Nate without seeing to his comfort. "Milord—"

Nate waved him away. "I'm quite all right. Go."

"Thank you, milord." The older man bowed and left the room.

If the household was always so unruly, it was no wonder the thieves had not been detected. According to the information he had, Jeffers, the castle computer, had been out of commission at the time of the theft. Nate had not been given any details about the computer's downtime, other than to say Raleigh Townsend would brief him when Nate arrived at the castle.

The window to Nate's left shattered.

Shit. Nate hit the ground, landing flat on his stomach. A white polo ball rolled across the wood floor and onto the rug, coming to a stop inches in front of Nate's face. *What the...* He picked up the ball, got to his feet and crossed to the broken window.

"Hello there." A young man with wide shoulders and a friendly smile waved from atop a sorrel horse. "Sorry about that. I didn't hit you, did I?"

Nate shook his head. "No, you didn't hit me." He held up the ball. "Would you like this back?"

"Yes, please. Are you the earl?" the horseman asked.

"Yes, and who might you be?" Nate tossed the ball out.

"I'm Prince Colton. Pleasure to meet you, milord." He tipped his head and heeled his mount off toward the ball.

Colton? The second to youngest prince. Judging from the looks of him and the similarity to the other two gentlemen Nate had seen since his arrival, he realized they were probably siblings. Good Galaxy, the royal family was a handful. He was starting to get a suspicion as to why Jeffers was shut down.

Stepping away from the window, a rustling sound made Nate stop mid-stride. Leaves rained down and a grunt came from above. "Bloody black hole and imploding stars," a soft masculine voice hissed.

Way up in the tree closest to the window, a boy balanced precariously on a thin tree limb. He reached toward a flat computer screen of some sort that had snagged on an adjacent branch. At his unbalanced angle a fall seemed imminent. Likely a shout to be careful would bring the teen plummeting to the ground, so Nate raced to a set of French doors on his left. Hurrying outside, he got to the base of the tree just as the branch the kid balanced on snapped.

"Whoa." The boy wobbled and fell against the limb holding the computer, knocking the device loose. "Dust!"

The flat screen clipped only one bough before falling free. Nate caught it before it hit the ground.

The young man gasped, his gaze meeting Nate's.

Nate started. The boy—no, that wasn't right, he was young, yes, but not a lad—was absolutely gorgeous. Nate stared into the big gray eyes, mesmerized. The man was simply beautiful. He had a small frame that had, at first, deluded Nate into thinking him a child. A mass of ebony curls surrounded a handsome face, and a full bottom lip was caught between even white teeth.

"Uh, thanks. I, uh— Whoa." The man's booted feet slid off the tree, leaving him dangling from his hands ten feet in the air.

Nate set the computer screen down and held his arms out. "I've got you. Drop."

"Uh..."

"Drop."

"Okay. Please don't miss." The man let go with a reluctant whimper.

The negligible weight landed in Nate's outstretched arms. He bent his knee slightly to keep from jarring the young man. Nate glanced at the handsome face and his gut clenched. Up close the man's eyes were the color of molten steel. He had flawless ivory skin and full lips. The heat of his body pressed against Nate's chest made his cock stir. The man was slim and not very tall, but he had broad shoulders that spoke of nice muscles under the well-tailored clothes. What he wouldn't give to see this slim body completely bare of clothing and those pretty lips wrapped around his hard cock. Closing his eyes, Nate concentrated on getting his pulse back to normal. He was here on a mission, not to get involved. Besides, this was most likely his hosts' offspring.

He opened his eyes in time to see a pink tongue dart out and wet the beguiling lips. Nate's cock—fully erect now—strained against the placket of his pantaloons.

The man's gaze roamed over Nate's face as long, elegant fingers came up to trace his beard. "Who are you?" he asked in a seductive whisper.

Nate hadn't even realized he'd leaned forward until the smaller man jerked, nearly spilling himself out of Nate's arms. Setting the man on his feet, Nate watched him straighten his waistcoat. When he brushed off his trousers, he seemed to realize he had a problem.

Good, the young lord wasn't unaffected, just surprised. Not, of course, that it mattered. Nate wasn't interested. *Yeah, right.* He bowed. "Nathaniel Hawkins, Earl of Deverell."

The younger man's gray eyes shot wide and he hastily tried to hide his obvious erection. He squirmed before spotting his computer. Picking up the screen, he held it in front of his groin and met Nate's gaze. His enticing mouth formed an "O", followed by an inhalation of air, then the man blinked and shook his head as if to clear it. "Thank you for rescuing me, milord. I, uh, got my screen caught on the way up."

Nate was about to ask the man's name and why he was in the tree in the first place when an older version of the young man appeared in the window. "What in stars happened to the window? Aiden?"

The younger man, Aiden, frowned. He darted his gaze to Nate and gave a barely perceptible shake of his head. "I didn't do it, Cony. I was trying to get a different perspective on the garden." Aiden glanced back at Nate, his eyes pleading, and bowed. "Thank you again, milord."

Before Nate could respond the vision bounded off toward the back of the castle. How odd. Apparently the imp didn't want Nate to mention his fall from the tree. Or did he not want Nate to mention who broke the window?

"Lord Deverell?"

Nate dragged his attention from Aiden's retreating backside and turned toward the window. "Lord Raleigh?"

Raleigh smiled. "Yes, please come inside. You wouldn't happen to know what became of the window, would you?"

CZ

Nate swirled his scotch in its snifter and uncrossed his legs, settling back into the comfortable leather of the sofa. This place was definitely different from his normal, orderly life.

He'd spent nearly two hours talking with King Steven and King-Consort Raleigh—they'd long since stopped using each other's titles and started calling one another by their first names. Nate found he liked them both quite a bit.

Both men were a little older than Nate and not what he'd expected. Steven was quite laid-back. He gave the impression of laziness, but his form spoke of anything but. He wasn't overly tall, but the man was powerfully built, wide through the chest, lean through the hips. He wasn't a man who laid around all day.

Raleigh wasn't tense exactly, but he wasn't as easygoing as Steven. He brought to mind a big cat, always alert and ready to pounce. Like a large feline, Raleigh was tall and athletic looking. Nate had no doubt the man would be as fast as he was strong. It made Nate wonder what exactly the man did for the IN.

Nate took a sip of his drink while he tried to get a grasp on his most recent discovery, that the Townsend offspring were responsible for the computer being off. He'd come to suspect it before Raleigh revealed the truth. "Let me get this straight. The princes shut Jeffers off in order to have an adventure?" Nate frowned. It seemed to him the princes did as they pleased already.

Steven nodded from his seat, an armchair across from Nate. A lock of black hair fell into his eyes. "Raleigh's children are brats."

Brushing the hair off his spouse's face, Raleigh got up from his perch on the wide arm of the chair. "Why is it whenever they do something good and noteworthy they are yours, but let them foul something up and they are mine and mine alone?" He crossed to the desk, sitting on the edge.

"Need I remind you that you are the one who wanted six children?" Steven's lip twitched and his sherry-colored eyes twinkled. The man clearly took delight in teasing his spouse. "Besides, they do have your DNA, how could they not be hellions? And since I'm quite positive it is your genes, not mine, that make them that way..." He shrugged and caught Nate's gaze, the mirth evident in his grin and raised brow.

Raleigh snorted. Raleigh was one of the classiest and commanding men he'd ever met—the snort seemed so out of character. It made him appear even more like Aiden.

The thought of Aiden immediately brought to mind the way the man looked in his arms a couple of hours ago, and Nate's cock began to rouse. He crossed his ankle over his knee again. "Ahem. I thought the two of you only had five children? Was I misinformed?"

Steven chuckled. "We only have five because I managed to talk some sense into him at last."

Picking up a pen from the desk, Raleigh flung it at the king, then turned his attention on Nate. His gray eyes twinkled. "No, you were not misinformed. There are only five and Muffin."

"Muffin?" Nate blinked. He assumed they were talking of the little girl he'd seen earlier, but he had no clue who she was...to them.

Laughing louder, Steven hurled the pen back, clipping his consort in the chest with it.

Raleigh ignored the pen altogether. "Muffin is our eldest's charge. I suppose in a sense she is our ward, but Rexley found her when she was a newborn. He was shopping with his chaperone and he heard her crying. She'd been abandoned in an alley behind a shop and reminded Rexley of a muffin, all round and plump. It was before he ate lunch." Raleigh chuckled.

Nate frowned. From what he had learned, Regelence's citizens subscribed to the artificial creation and incubation method of procreation. It was clear from what was said that the princes were created from such a process, because they obviously had both Steven and Raleigh's DNA. There was an egg involved, of course, but in most cases during the creation process the egg donor's genetics were removed until it was inconsequential unless the child being spawned belonged to that woman. "Why would someone abandon a baby that they'd had made. Could they not have designed her the way they wanted?"

Steven shook his head. "I presume she was conceived naturally. But, regardless, our laws do not permit designer babies other than a few minor things. In a case of male mates, the couple is allowed to specify if they want a male or female child. But other than that, and being predisposed to sexually prefer men, in the landed gentry our laws prohibit designer offspring."

Interesting. Nate took a sip of his scotch. Most planets that utilized the artificial procreation and incubation procedure used the all-or-nothing philosophy. They eradicated all undesirable traits and diseases and did not allow natural conception. "You allow natural gestation?"

"Oh yes. Actually, the ratio of natural-born children to synthetically created children is about eighty to one outside of the aristocracy. The procedure is very expensive. We are a patriarchal society, therefore, among the titled it is nearly one hundred percent. Occasionally, a lord will be born without having been altered to prefer men and..." Raleigh shrugged. "It's very rare though."

Nate liked how they did things here. It made sense to him. If everyone were perfect and lived into their hundreds, then the population would be outlandish. Not only that...how boring would it be if everyone were ideal specimens? And same-sex partners were not only accepted, among the landed gentry they were the norm. Too bad his own home planet didn't have similar values. If it had, he'd have never been forced into that duel... A duel that made him lose his family. Nate shook himself out of his ponderings, it was irrelevant. He was here to investigate a crime. "You said the children shut off Jeffers?"

Sighing, Raleigh picked up a drink coaster from the big mahogany desk, toying with it. "Yes. And I know what you are thinking, Nate, but they're innocent. They do not even know of my involvement with the IN, much less about the weapons stash we harbor for them."

He believed Raleigh, but something didn't add up. Nate needed to understand to eliminate the princes from suspicion. "I have no reason to doubt you. You say they aren't involved, fine. But why would they need to shut off the computer?"

"They wanted freedom away from the castle," Steven said.

"What do you mean? They appear to have plenty of freedom." *Shit.* That didn't come out right, but he wasn't going to take it back—it was the truth.

Steven chuckled. "Yes they do, more than most young lords I would say. We rarely deny them a request as long as it's reasonable and they take an acceptable chaperone with them. But that is the crux of the situation. They didn't want to be bothered with a chaperone."

"Why must they be chaperoned? They are all adults, are they not?"

Steven looked at Nate like he'd lost his mind.

Tossing the coaster aside, Raleigh pushed himself off the desk. He crossed to Steven and began kneading his shoulders. "On Nate's planet, it is a young lady's virtue that is guarded not the young lords."

Steven nodded and dropped his head slightly forward. "I see."

It impressed Nate that Raleigh had bothered to research Nate's origins.

Raleigh caught Nate's gaze. "Here it's the young gentlemen of the ton who are highly sought after. Until a lord reaches his twenty-fifth year, or is contracted into a consort ceremony, he must remain chaste. It is essentially like our fore-society, the nineteenth century, in Earth's England. Nevertheless, we are a male-dominated society, hence it is our young lords not our young ladies." The consort's dark head cocked. "Englor is exactly like our fore society, is it not?"

"It is." Nate took a drink of his scotch. "But I don't understand the rationale. In our society it's to insure a man's heir is his own, but here... Why would you need the young lords to be virginal?"

"We don't necessarily, that's just how we've always done things," Steven said.

Raleigh nodded his agreement. "Military and politics have always been of major importance here, due to how we gained our freedom from our neighboring systems. And consequently, we are now the ruling planet in the Regelence system.

"Unfortunately, the IN only deals with intergalactic affairs. We had to ensure we had the brightest and strongest warriors to fight for our continued freedom inside our own system. Are you familiar with ancient Terran history and the Sacred Band of Thebes?"

Nate had learned all sorts of things in officer training, but he remembered that part of history well because of his own sexual orientation. "Legendary warriors of ancient Greece. The group was formed of lovers who fought together side by side."

"Yes. The theory was lovers would fight better together than non-lovers because they would be less willing to disgrace themselves in battle. It's a bond even greater than that of family or tribe. Essentially our society was based on the same principal. Young men were kept pure and paired up at adolescence and enlisted together. The practice also served to align certain families. It worked very well and over the centuries we evolved into the male-dominated society we have today. Even though not all men are drafted now, nor are the majority subject to arranged matches, all lords are to remain pure until marriage."

"I'm surprised. No one has a problem with this?"

Raleigh shrugged. "Like I said, it goes back to tradition. Even though we now have the advanced technology to create offspring with both male partners DNA, it still goes back to what families once wished to align themselves with, political power. As a teen I hated it too, but it is custom and in all honesty, it has worked so far. We have one of the best militaries in the galaxy. And we have a much lower crime rate than most planets. Steven, myself, the kids, Parliament, we don't even need security in our social circles. Don't get me wrong, we have guards and we have castle security, but we walk freely amongst our people. Not all planets can boast of such. And I'm not saying it's all due to that rule, but if you start changing things around... There is something to be said for allowing mature men to run the planet."

It still seemed unfair to Nate, but at least he understood it better. "Women are free game, but stay away from men under twenty-five?"

"Oh. You prefer women?" Steven asked.

"I do not." Which was part of the problem, he was liable to find himself with a spouse if he wasn't careful. That was just what he needed.

Cocking a brow, Steven grinned. "Do you have a consort?"

Nate shook his head. "No, I've been on the Lady Anna so long I haven't had the time to look. It's only me and my son." Watching Steven's eyes light up in a glee made Nate want to kick himself for admitting his sexuality. That look was one Nate knew well and one he'd never thought to see again.

"Do you dance?" Raleigh inquired without removing his hands from his consort's shoulders.

Damn. Nate dipped his head.

The king's smile brightened even more. The man was clearly scheming. "Then you will join us tonight. We are attending Duke-Consort Keithman's ball this evening."

Opening his mouth to protest and tell the royal couple he needed to question staff, in particular Jeffers, Nate found himself silenced by Steven standing. Nate jumped to his feet, showing his respect.

"Excellent. You will need to keep up the pretense of being only our guest anyway. We don't want the staff wise to the fact you are investigating them. We will see you this evening, Nathaniel. Please take the time before the ball to rest. You will have all of the next day to investigate." Steven walked to the door. "Jeffers, you may come back in and release the security measures on the room. And please open the door." The door opened and Steven left, a spring in his step.

The man looked like the marriage-minded mamas Nate remembered from his youth. And did Steven just chuckle? Nate glanced at Raleigh, still behind the chair his mate had vacated.

Raleigh grimaced. "Meet me here tomorrow morning after breakfast and we will go over all the information I have obtained. Remember to keep your ears peeled at the ball. At this point, I can only assume the perpetrator is someone who works inside the castle or on the grounds, but..." He headed toward the door. He stopped before exiting and looked back at Nate. "No worries about compromising any of the boys inside the castle or on castle grounds. Jeffers is a reliable chaperone." With that he fled the room.

Nate stretched. A movement from the corner of his eye caught his attention. He turned to the window in time to see a mess of ebony curls and big gray eyes disappear from sight. *Aiden.*

Chapter Four

He nearly had it. A little sharper angle on the jaw and a bit higher cheek line. Using his stylus, he added some shading. *There.* Aiden sat back, eyeing the drawing critically. He'd managed to capture the man exactly, right down to the predatory gleam in his eyes. The squarish jaw, neatly trimmed almost black beard and mustache, and straight thin nose, all were rendered to perfection. Even the wavy dark hair on his head appeared soft, beckoning one to try and run their fingers through it. All that was left was to add color. A burnt umber, and ebony with some touches of red and gold, for the man's hair. Smooth shades of chestnut for his eyes. His skin wasn't fair like most gentlemen. It was a dark gold, maybe even a light bronze. The man was an artist's dream.

Aiden stared at his medium-sized sketchscreen. *Good Galaxy*, the mysterious stranger was handsome. He looked dangerous. Who was he? Really? He was an earl, the Earl of Deverell, Nathaniel Hawkins. Aiden had learned that much. They had been called to greet the earl formally and then told to get ready for the ball. Something was going on. Aiden just didn't know what. He had a sneaking suspicion it had to do with whatever went missing during his trip to the docks. Unfortunately, he was clueless as to what the stolen item was. He'd asked Cony about it twice and Cony had effectively changed the subject each time by saying it was something to do with business. Jeffers professed the same. What were Father and Cony up to?

Aiden pushed the save button on his screen. He should be getting ready for the ball instead of sitting at his dressing table obsessing over a drawing of a man he didn't know.

Nathaniel Hawkins elicited all sorts of emotions Aiden would rather not think about. Being in the lord's arms this afternoon had sent his body into a whirlwind of feelings. It'd felt like when he and Payton had gotten into Father's brandy when they were thirteen—lightheaded and...happy? His prick had even enjoyed the earl's nearness, just as it did now. Aiden rubbed the hardness through his pantaloons. That felt very good. He rubbed a little harder. Walking around with it engorged the way it was would be scandalous, therefore he *had* to get rid of it. Closing his eyes, he imagined wavy, dark hair, wide shoulders and long, muscular legs. *Nathaniel.* He got two buttons undone before the door to his dressing room opened.

"Aiden?"

Aiden jumped, removing his hand and pulling the screen off the marble tabletop and into his lap. Couldn't anyone knock around this castle? *Star dust.* He'd nearly been caught touching himself. How indecent. Nathaniel's eyes seemed to twinkle at him from the screen. Aiden frowned. When had he started thinking of the man by his given name? How very familiar, as if the man were an intimate. Aiden groaned. Deverell was definitely not good for his state of mind.

"Aiden? Why aren't you dressed?" Payton put his hands on his hips, looking around. "Where's Benson? He's supposed to be getting you ready."

Benson had laid out Aiden's evening clothes for him, but after that Aiden had dismissed him. He didn't want his valet fussing about while he completed the drawing. Aiden shrugged and focused on his sketch, which did nothing to alleviate his prick's interest. "I told him I'd dress myself."

"Why are you blushing?" Payton snatched the screen from Aiden's lap.

Aiden gasped and sputtered, reaching for the computer. "Hey!"

Payton seemed more interested in the drawing than his younger brother, much to Aiden's relief. He turned his back to Aiden, keeping his prize out of reach. *Thank Galaxy.* The fear of discovery did wonders for Aiden's erection. It wilted quickly.

"Payton..."

Crossing to the emerald green chaise near the door leading to Aiden's bedroom, Payton sat, still studying the sketchscreen. "What do you think is going on? Don't you find it strange that neither Cony nor Father have mentioned this man before?"

"I do. I think it has to do with whatever was stolen when you shut Jeffers down last."

"I agree." Payton frowned and looked up. "I still haven't discovered what was taken. Have you?"

Aiden shook his head. "No. Have you asked Rexley yet?"

"He didn't know either, or so he says."

Aiden arched a brow. "You think he's lying?"

"With Rexley, there's no telling. I know Father tells him more than he does the rest of us. Because he's the heir, I suppose." Looking at the drawing again, Payton cocked his dark head one way then the other. "He's handsome, in a fierce, rough kind of way, isn't he?"

Dust, yes. "I suppose. I tried to spy on him, Cony and Father today. Colton broke the study window, so the room—"

Payton's head shot up, his amber eyes wide. "Did you learn anything?"

71

Not hardly. Jeffers may not have been allowed to record what went on in the study, but he had guarded the room from eavesdroppers, nonetheless. "Not anything of importance. I couldn't get close enough without Jeffers threatening to sound the alarm. By the time Father left and allowed Jeffers back in the room there was nothing to see, or hear. Well, other than Cony asking the earl to meet him back there tomorrow after breakfast so they could discuss what Cony knew again. Cony thinks that whatever was stolen was taken by one of the servants."

"Interesting." Payton stared off into space, worrying his bottom lip. Something he nearly always did when he tried to figure something out.

Aiden looked at the clock on his dressing table. He had about twenty minutes to get ready for the ball. He should get ready, but he didn't want to. Going to parties imploded stars. All the power-hungry lords trying to match him with their sons was bothersome. When was everyone going to get it through their thick skulls that Aiden wasn't going to take a consort?

Aiden sighed, gathering the navy blue knee britches and white hose Benson had laid out. "Jeffers, please download the information on my sketchscreen into my art file."

"Yes, Lord Aiden," the computer answered.

Unfastening his pantaloons, Aiden pulled his shirt out of the waistband. He had taken off his waistcoat and cravat earlier. "Payton, will you turn off my sketchscreen? I'm going to take my small one with me tonight."

"Huh?" Payton blinked and focused on him, coming out of his daze. "Sure." He turned off the computer and set it aside before coming to his feet. "You know you're not supposed to draw at social gatherings. Father will have your head if he finds out." He paced back and forth between the door leading to Aiden's bedroom and the one leading to the water closet.

"*If* he finds out." Aiden pulled his knee britches on. "I need to talk to Deverell."

"Why? I seriously doubt he'll tell you what was stolen and why he's here."

Snorting, Aiden sat to don his stockings. "That would certainly make things easier. But I fell out of the tree next to the study today."

Payton's eyes went wide. He ceased his pacing and perched on the chaise across from Aiden. "How?"

"I was trying to get a bird's-eye view of the formal garden, when my sketchscreen got hung on a branch. I fell and Deverell caught me."

"Uh-huh." His eyes narrowing on Aiden, Payton smiled. "Why are you blushing?"

"What?" Aiden busied himself pulling his shirt over his head and going to the dresser where Benson had laid the one for this evening. "I'm not blushing."

A hand caught his arm and turned him around. "Aide—"

Bloody black hole, he had to get ahold of himself. He couldn't go around blushing every time Nathan—Deverell—was mentioned. Especially with Payton. Payton was better than anyone at needling information from him.

The bedroom door slammed, drawing his and Payton's attention. *Whew.* Saved by yet another sibling who couldn't remember how to knock on a door.

"Oh my Galaxy. Did you see him?" Tarren rushed into the dressing room and flopped on the chaise. "Do you think he's a spy? Or maybe a mercenary or something? He looks shadowy, in a sexy sort of way."

Letting go of Aiden, Payton went to Tarren, waving his hands at their obnoxious youngest sibling. "Tarren, get up. You're going to wrinkle yourself."

"Bah." Tarren scoffed at Payton, but sat anyway, brushing his hands over his gray evening coat. "You're so fussy sometimes." Grinning, he let out a breath, blowing the black hair off his forehead. "Did the two of you see him? Isn't he fascinating? He's going to the ball with us. Do you think he'll ask me to dance? And what if he does? He's so, so, big and..." Tarren shuddered.

Aiden very nearly growled. He didn't want to think about Tarren that close to the earl. If anyone was going to dance with the... Whoa, what was he thinking? He did *not* want to dance with Deverell or any other gentlemen. He hated to dance.

Aiden quickly finished dressing, blocking out Tarren's chatter as best he could. He needed to talk Deverell into keeping quiet about his fall. That was his only interest in the lord. *Sure, Aiden.* His darned prick started filling again. Aiden tugged a little harder on his neckcloth than he'd intended, making himself cough.

After his choking ceased, the room got very quiet. He turned toward Tarren and Payton. "What?"

"You don't agree?" Tarren asked.

"Agree with what?"

"That Lord Deverell would make a dashing consort." Payton rolled his eyes, stating more clearly than words that the comment was not his.

Aiden glowered at Tarren.

Furrowing his brow, Tarren gazed at Aiden. "Well, there's no need to get snippy. I had no idea you had staked a claim, big brother."

"Wh-what?" Aiden sputtered.

Payton drew close, slapping Aiden's hands away, and proceeded to tie Aiden's cravat. "You're glaring, Aiden. Is there something you'd like to tell us?" Payton stepped back and turned Aiden toward the mirror, showing him his immaculately tied neckcloth. "Well?" Payton grinned, letting him know it wasn't the cravat he was asking about.

Darn meddling siblings. Aiden strode to his bedroom, his brothers' laughter trailing behind him. He snagged his small sketchscreen from his nightstand and stuffed it into the inner pocket of his evening coat...or tried to. He'd stormed off and left his waistcoat and evening coat in his dressing room.

He didn't want a consort. Just because he found the man attractive didn't mean he wanted to make a life with him. His life was his art, end of story.

CB

Aiden sat in the large lift directly across from Nath—Lord Deverell—doing his best not to look at the man and failing miserably. The way the light of the streetlamps and moon filtered through the window, casting the earl in shadow, made Aiden's fingers itch to pull the small sketchscreen from his pocket. The chiaroscuro effect made the man look even more enigmatic and deadly than before. The splendor of the man himself was almost enough to risk Father and Cony's wrath, and being forced to take a consort.

Deverell turned from the window, his gaze landing on Aiden before he could look away. One side of the older man's lips turned up in a smile and Aiden's heart nearly pounded through his chest. He'd seen many stunning men in his short life, he'd even drawn most of them, but the earl mesmerized him.

Aiden's stomach fluttered and his prick filled with blood. Shifting, he tried to conceal his problem and make it go away at once.

Nathaniel arched a dark brow.

For several seconds they stared at each other. The heat of the man's gaze did nothing to calm the thundering heartbeat in Aiden's ears or his throbbing prick.

"Dance cards. Try not to lose them," Father announced, holding up the pocket-sized thumb scanners.

Tearing his gaze from Nathaniel's, Aiden joined his brothers in the chorus of groans.

Not long after Father passed out the cursed cards, the lift pulled in front of the Duke of Keithman's downtown Classige mansion. With a last admonishment to behave from Father, they all exited the coach. Thankfully, the reminder of where they were going squelched his body's reaction to the earl.

After getting out of the coach, Aiden followed Payton absently, contemplating possible scenarios to get Nat—Deverell alone. He needed to speak with Deverell long enough to ask for his silence regarding the tree incident. And maybe he could think of a way to find out what the man was doing here and what was stolen from the castle.

Payton looked left and right, tossed his card to the ground, stepped on it—grounding it under his heel—and let out an exaggerated, "Oh dear."

Having been so caught up in thought, Aiden nearly forgot about the dance card. One of these days Father was going to get tired of replacing the stupid things. A person would think their parent would get the message after the first ten dozen times they'd "lost" their cards. Aiden ascertained that both his parents were too far ahead to notice, took a quick peek to each side and tossed the card over his shoulder. He stepped up next to Payton and peered down at Payton's smashed dance card. He shook his head. "That's too bad."

Payton turned, a hand to his chest, looking positively stricken. "Indeed. Oh well, let's go inside." Even Aiden was impressed with the serious expression Payton maintained. If the Townsend boys had inherited anything from their father, it was his flare for acting.

Side by side, he and Payton entered the mansion. Outside the ballroom, they stepped in line behind Tarren and Colton and waited their turn to be announced.

"Excuse me, Lord Aiden?"

Nathaniel. Aiden's breath caught. He'd forgotten the man was behind them. What could the earl possibly want with him? He turned, noticing three of his siblings, the ones in their immediate vicinity, did the same. "Yes, milord?" Did his voice crack? Aiden's attention zeroed in on the spot where the man's snowy white cravat met his charcoal waistcoat, under the black evening coat. Slowly his gaze drifted upward to chestnut eyes. *Amazing, he has gold flecks in his eyes.*

"Ahem." Deverell grinned. "I believe you dropped this." He held out his hand.

Looking down, Aiden nearly groaned when he saw the dance card resting in the older lord's large, white-gloved hand. *Ugh.* A glance up assured him Nathaniel knew well and good that Aiden had *not* dropped the blasted thing.

Nathaniel brought the scanner to his gloved thumb. A red light flashed as the card scanned through the fabric. After it beeped, indicating it had recorded the identity of the person requesting a dance, the older man brought it close to his lips. "The first waltz." Again, the card beeped, then Nathaniel handed it to Aiden. The entire time the wicked gleam in his eyes challenged Aiden to protest.

Aiden didn't say a word, he couldn't, he was too busy concentrating on making his body behave. He could not walk into the ballroom with an erection.

After a slight bow, Nathaniel stepped past Aiden to where Cony was motioning to him.

Tarren bumped Aiden's shoulder with his own. "I don't know whether to be jealous or concerned for you."

Aiden was too stunned to respond. What had just happened? He'd either found his excuse to talk to the man in private or he'd obtained the means to embarrass himself in public.

When it was their turn to be announced, Payton took the card from his hand and ran it under the dance line-up scanner to the left of the ballroom entrance. The light on the black box turned from red to green, indicating that it had registered the line-up on Aiden's dance card and his list of partners—that consisted of one—on the mansion's main computer.

Aiden could only watch with his mouth ajar as Payton sealed his fate. Even if he lost the card now, he had at least one dance of the evening promised to another.

Payton handed him the card back. "Be careful, Aiden, that man is dangerous."

"What?"

"You're obviously not the only one interested, little brother."

Cʒ

Bannon Thompson's dance card landed in the crystal punch bowl with a plop. Aiden bit his lip to keep from laughing as it sank in the sea of red liquid.

"Oh no." While the men standing around the refreshment table let out refrains of "too bad", Bannon slapped a hand to his lips. His green eyes twinkled with mirth and his dark auburn hair fell into his eyes as he shook his head. He hid his smile behind his hand, all the while achieving a perfect facsimile of distress.

Aiden had to leave. He was so close to laughing he would give up the game and then Bannon would likely throttle him. Brushing close to his friend, he whispered a, "good one", before slinking away. That had been truly innovative. He'd never thought to discard dance cards in such a way. Speaking of... His own card still needed to meet its demise or, at the very least, gain its freedom from his person, preferably in a secluded place.

It wasn't that he was above lying and saying his dances were full or that he had a terrible headache or a bum knee or some such, but his father would undoubtedly ask to see his card afterward to make sure he socialized enough. Thank goodness society deemed a young man properly chaperoned as long as their parents were there. He'd hate to have Christy or Thomas following him around, goading him to dance and flirt. Father and Cony were excellent chaperones. They went about their business, checking to make sure their offspring were still within eyesight on occasion but rarely did they pester their children to mingle more at a soiree. Their own social and political life was way too active for that. Parliament members used parties to further their agendas, and it seemed all of them wanted to discuss those agendas with the King and King-Consort.

Ah, a potted plant. Aiden made his way across the ballroom, getting waylaid several times to talk to acquaintances, but finally he made it to the ficus. He was in luck, the plant was potted in a dark violet hydrogel. It would help conceal the card.

He pulled his handkerchief from the breast pocket of his evening coat, then dug into his inside pocket and palmed his dance card. Pretending to mop the nonexistent perspiration from his brow, he dropped the pristine linen square. "Oops." Bending to retrieve it, he reached behind him and pushed the card, concealed in his other hand, down into the hydrogel. *Yuck.* The tips of his fingers sank into the wet, slimy substance. Standing quickly, he wiped his fingers nonchalantly before stuffing the handkerchief back into his pocket. *Nothing to see here. Just a man picking up his handkerchief.*

"Lord Aiden."

Aiden nearly jumped out of his skin. He turned to find Lord Chadwick Manchester, the Marquis of Braxton, standing next to him. If it weren't for the way the man was peering down his nose, with his head slightly elevated, he would be quite handsome. He had a wonderful head of prematurely silver hair, cut short on the sides and longer on the top. His evening dress was in shades of a subdued navy and cream, accentuating his lean frame. He wasn't as tall as Deverell but he was taller than Aiden's own five-foot-eight-inches. "Lord Braxton." Aiden tipped his head.

"I went by the palace the other day to speak to your father."

"Yes, he informed me." *And the answer is no.* Aiden smiled.

Braxton raised a brow. "Did he?"

Wasn't it impolite to speak of marriage to an innocent? Aiden decided it should be. Or maybe he should be thankful that Braxton cared enough to speak with him about it instead of going over his head. No wait, he'd done that first. Before ever mentioning a thing to Aiden, he'd gone to Father. That was another strike against this man. "Yes, milord, he did. And I'm sorry to say I must refuse such a generous offer. I'm afraid we really don't have much in common." *See me be diplomatic.*

Braxton scoffed and waved a dismissive hand. "Of course not. You're too young to know what you want. As your consort, it will be up to me to teach you my interests and your place in society."

Why, of all the arrogant... Aiden's jaw tightened and his fingers flexed. He wondered briefly how much trouble he would get in for planting the pompous arse a facer, then decided the man wasn't worth his attention, much less his anger. "And that, Lord Braxton, is why we don't suit. I do know what I want and I will not be molded into something else. Good evening, milord." Aiden turned to make a hasty retreat but was brought up short by a hand touching his sleeve.

"Forgive me, milord. I didn't mean to offend. I think rather highly of you and truly wish you would consider my offer further. I believe we'd go well together. It's rather pleasing to find that you do have a backbone." Braxton smiled, looking contrite.

Aiden wanted to hang on to being miffed, but Braxton seemed very sincere. "Apology accepted."

"Good, perhaps you'll dance with me this evening?"

Not on your life. "I'm sorry, milord. I seem to have misplaced my dance card and I'm not certain what dances are taken."

Braxton's smile faltered a bit, but he recovered quickly. "Then another night? I would like to get to know you better."

"I'm sorry, milord, I still don't see any point. I want to be an artist, not a consort."

"You are a beautiful man and should not sully your hands with such menial labor, but as my consort you could dabble in art to your heart's content. Please, give it some thought." The man bowed over Aiden's hand, pressing a kiss to the back of his glove, then turned and walked away.

Aiden stood there for several minutes, aghast. What in the Galaxy was that about?

Someone bumped his shoulder. Rupert Cavendish, Aiden's friend and fellow artist. "He really is handsome. I've always had a preference for light-colored hair."

Aiden frowned at his blond friend. "Just last week you were gushing about Lord Wesley's dark good looks."

"Okay, fine, never let it be said I'm finicky."

No Rupert wasn't picky, not when it came to men. He liked any and all. The man was a hopeless romantic.

"Did you lose your card yet? Bannon's needed a drink apparently. It's in the bottom of the punch bowl." Rupert chuckled.

"I saw. I had to leave to keep from laughing." Aiden grinned. "That definitely wins for originality. Payton's jumped from his hand and met the bottom of his shoe."

"And where did yours end up?"

"Plant food." Aiden pointed to the plant behind them. "Poor thing looks hungry, doesn't it?"

Rupert's lips twitched. He composed himself by looking across the ballroom. After a few minutes he waved and smiled. "Is that the earl who's a guest at the castle?"

Aiden looked where Rupert's attention was focused and found Deverell across the room staring straight at them.

Chapter Five

Standing off to the side of the ballroom partially hidden by a large potted plant, Nate turned his attention away from Aiden. As much as he hated to admit it, he hadn't liked seeing the gray-headed gentleman kiss Aiden's hand. Nor did he want to explore those feelings. And how weird was that to see a man kiss another man's hand? Nate nursed a tumbler of scotch and waited for the first waltz.

The loud hum of chatter and the beginning notes of the quadrille assaulted his ears. He'd finally escaped the throng of people vying for his attention. It had been a long time since he'd been sought out because of his title. He had no delusions that his status as the guest of the king and the king's consort didn't weigh heavily on his popularity as well. However, he didn't miss the hopeful expression on the faces of matchmaking fathers introducing their offspring to him. Steven wasn't the only one interested in him as a possible son-in-law. This society was going to take some getting used to.

Watching the swirl of dancers, Nate determined that there were a few women in attendance, and a few of Regelence's military officers—from both the Navy and Marines and even a handful of IN officers—but most of the assembly was comprised of older lords and their sons. He'd seen men dance together before but never in this type of setting. It would have been disgraceful for men to do something so intimate together on his home planet. He actually liked the idea—he enjoyed dancing and men, so why not mix the two together? Studying the couples gliding around the dance floor, it appeared that the older of the men always led, which was quite a relief because he had no idea how to follow and didn't relish the thought of tripping over Aiden's feet and ending up on his ass in the middle of a crowded ballroom.

Turning away from the dance floor, Nate studied the mural behind him. It was similar to some of the paintings he'd seen in Townsend castle. Greek warriors in the midst of battle. There was lots of blood and gore in front of beautiful scenery but that wasn't what fascinated Nate. The warriors were nude except for shields and helmets. Throughout history there were several bands of warriors who fought nude, but it was surprising to see them depicted where so many virginal young men were present. Although, it made sense in a way. On Englor, female nudes decorated the walls. They were the predominate subject matter in Englorian art. Regelence glorified male beauty and strength and it showed in their artwork. Nate glanced around the ballroom. The white marble columns around the wooden dance floor were carved into picturesque soldiers, all nude. Even the dome over the dancers depicted a war scene, with men surrounding the base and the sky appearing in the very top and center.

As he turned back toward the dance floor, Raleigh sidled up beside him, a smirk on his handsome face and a tumbler in his hand. "Go ahead and ask your questions. You won't offend me."

"Ask?" Nate watched the dancers whirl by.

"Yes. How our society works. It must be quite foreign to you." Raleigh took a sip of his drink.

"It appears to be age. Am I right?"

"Partly. It is age, but also title."

"I see." No, he didn't see at all. As far as the dancing went it appeared the older of the partners led, but how could they base things on age? That was hardly fair. Come to think of it, it wasn't right that on Englor, women couldn't decide for themselves either. He'd never actually considered it when he was the one at the top of the food chain, figuratively speaking, but what if he'd been raised here?

Raleigh turned toward him. "Ask."

What the hell, he'd give the man what he wanted. "If a man marries an older lord he is always, what...property?"

Raleigh laughed. It took him several moments to compose himself. When he was finally able to talk, it was with a huge smile. "No. It's all based on age and rank. A man is not considered of legal age until he is twenty-five years of age. Until then he must defer to his parents, guardian or his consort."

"So until the age of twenty-five they are essentially, what? Treated as children?"

"Not at all. They are educated. Some join Regelence's armed forces or the IN. It's much like the unmarried females on your planet, with the exception of the military of course. However, when a man reaches his majority, then he has rights, unlike the women on your planet. His consort's land becomes half his. He, in essence, becomes his consort's heir." Raleigh took another swig of his beverage and set the glass on the tray of a passing waiter.

Interesting. "What if both consorts have titles? It's the higher title? Your title is King-Consort?"

Raleigh nodded. "Yes and yes. Take my children for example. Rexley, when he takes a mate, will be Prince Rexley, and his spouse will be Prince-Consort. But the rest of the boys would take their spouse's title. As princes they are the higher title but they are empty titles—they don't come with land or power, other than the heir apparent, Rexley. If say...Tarren were to take a marquis to partner, then his title would be Marquis-Consort and only then would he get a seat in the House of Lords. Essentially, every title has two seats in parliament, one for the lord and one for his consort. If a lord is unmarried he has only one vote until he takes a consort, or if he is underage, his guardian and his guardian's consort control both votes. But only those lords whose titles include land."

Raleigh shook his head, staring out over the room.

Nate followed his gaze to Tarren, who was trying to obtain a glass of brandy.

Shoulders slumping, Tarren set the glass back on the waiter's tray and turned toward the punch bowl.

Nate laughed. "Very impressive."

"They keep me on my toes." Raleigh chuckled. "Sorry, where was I? Oh yes. I'm Steven's heir and Rexley is my heir to the throne as the first born. Any lesser title is given to the second born."

The whole thing was rather fascinating and much more fair than Nate had first thought. Much more civilized than his home planet, where the women had few rights. But... "Only those who have passed their majority can choose a spouse?"

"No. Anyone can choose, but unless they have a title, they must have means to support themselves. It actually works out very well."

"Yeah, it sounds like a good concept, but being a naïve virgin doesn't sound like much fun."

Raleigh laughed.

"When Steven asked for your hand, he was not of age?"

"Steven didn't ask for anything." Raleigh snorted. "The conniving bastard compromised me, but that is a whole different story. But to answer your question, no, he was only seventeen." Raleigh grinned, taking the heat from his words. He searched the crowd until his gaze rested on Steven dancing with their oldest son. "Let that be a lesson. Don't get caught with any unmarried gentlemen in private." He patted Nate's shoulder. "Have fun, enjoy yourself. Tomorrow we'll start going through Jeffers' data banks. I'm going to go give my two wallflower children the evil eye and make them go dance. You should do the same." With that Raleigh walked away.

Nate was pretty sure which two of the princes the king-consort was referring to. Nate had had no intention of dancing tonight himself, but after seeing one of the wallflowers toss his card over his shoulder, Nate couldn't help himself. He was fairly certain the prince hadn't overheard the conversation in the study today, because the butler would have notified them, but this gave him the perfect opportunity to make sure. Not that it would be any hardship to dance with Aiden.

Nate remembered those full lips parting in surprise when he'd scanned his thumb. It was obvious the young lord was used to getting his way and he'd intended on going the night without dancing. He knew the rules, but he seemed to have no qualms about breaking them. In that, he reminded Nate a little of himself. But Nate would be lying if he said that was his only interest in Aiden. The young man intrigued him, like no one had in a long time. Society seemed to hold no appeal for him. When the gentleman kissed Aiden's gloved hand, Aiden had appeared almost annoyed. It tempted Nate to see if he could seduce him. Unfortunately, there were several factors interfering with that. First, Nate was here to do a job, not have fun. Second, Raleigh would likely kill him if he so much as laid a finger on the prince. And third, the prince was an innocent.

He wouldn't have the first clue how to handle what Nate expected of his bed partners. More to the point, the man would probably faint dead away if he found out.

The song came to an end and he tried to ignore the excitement of getting to hold Aiden near. He tried to persuade himself he only wanted to be able to question the young lord in relative privacy, but his cock wasn't at all convinced.

Looking around the ballroom, he spotted Steven and Rexley on the dance floor. Payton hid behind a potted plant on the other side of the room, opposite the one Nate was hiding behind. Or at least he thought it was Payton, Nate couldn't get a good glimpse of the face, but the dark green evening coat and the fact that Raleigh was headed directly for him spoke volumes. Tarren held court near the punch bowl and a large ice sculpture of the Greek God of war, laughing as a group of lords vied for his attention. Colton flirted shamelessly with a very dangerous-looking fellow dressed all in black, but Aiden was nowhere in sight. *Damn.*

Nate scanned the crowd once more. He didn't see Aiden anywhere. The heavy black velvet curtain covering the open patio doors swung closed, drawing his attention. Could the prince be outside?

Setting his glass on the tray of a passing servant, Nate made his way across the ballroom, being careful to stay on the white and black checkered marble rather than the wood dance floor. He scowled at anyone who looked remotely interested in hailing him, so no one did. Being big and intimidating was nice. And even if he didn't look unapproachable enough, he had rank. Forgiveness went a long way when one was the heir to a dukedom or, in this case, the esteemed guest of the king. It took him several minutes to walk around the large room and through the crush of bodies, but he finally managed.

Upon moving the curtains aside he saw nothing out of the ordinary. The terrace was illuminated with candles neatly placed in sconces along the wall. Several couples strolled along the balcony talking while others ambled around the formal garden below.

Aiden sat on a bench against the wall of the house with a pocket-sized computer in hand. At a brisk pace, he wrote on the small screen with a stylus.

What the fuck was he doing with a computer at a ball? Nate watched him for several seconds completely unnoticed, which wasn't a huge feat. Aiden seemed oblivious to his surroundings. Couples walked past him laughing and chatting. A man bumped into Aiden's leg and stopped to apologize. Aiden never even looked up. Whatever he was doing on the computer held his undivided attention.

Creeping forward, Nate tried to catch a glimpse, hoping it would give him insight into the young man. Regrettably, the screen was at an angle and Nate couldn't make out a thing. Probably a game—they were rare in this part of the galaxy, but not unheard of. "Did you forget our dance?"

Aiden jumped, clutching the screen to his chest. "Lord Deverell." Pulling the computer away from his torso a tiny bit, he peeked down at it, then darted a glance back at Nate while hiding the device against himself again. He blanched and pushed a button on the top, turning the thing off, before hastily tucking away the stylus and depositing it in his inside coat pocket. "It slipped my mind."

Nate raised a brow. Had it? Aiden seemed earnest, but given the circumstances of their promised dance... What was he hiding? He hadn't wanted Nate to see what he'd been doing on the computer. Nate held out his hand. "Would you like to go dance? We haven't missed it."

"Listen, Lord Deverell, I've been wanting to talk to you."

"Yes?" Nate took a seat next to him. This should be interesting.

"About the tree incident." He stared right into Nate's eyes, meeting his gaze.

Ahh... "Yes?"

"I was wondering if we could keep that between the two of us?" Aiden fixed him with a pointed glare, almost daring Nate to refuse him.

Nate suppressed a grin. The man had grit, he'd give him that. There was a lot of substance behind the handsome face. "Why?"

"Why?" Aiden parroted.

No way was Nate going to make this easy. "Yes. Why?" He took hold of Aiden's chin, forcing him to keep his gaze. It was rather forward, but he couldn't seem to help himself. He longed to touch the man, even if only through gloves. His errant cock seemed to like the idea of touching Aiden too. It began to fill with blood, hardening, just as it did every time he thought of the prince since laying eyes on him that afternoon. Not for the first time he cursed this society, his own honor and especially Aiden's innocence.

Aiden's gaze drifted down to Nate's lips for several seconds before meeting his eyes once more. Blinking, he pulled back. "Well...because it's not at all proper for me to be in a tree."

Now he thought of that? How convenient. What was he thinking before? Nate already figured out that Aiden had little care for what society thought. If he did he wouldn't have tossed the dance card, nor would he be out here on his computer in the middle of a ball. The corner of Nate's mouth twitched. "Then why were you?"

Aiden bit his bottom lip and wrung his hands together in his lap, making his shoulders flex.

Damn, the man was something else.

"Because I was dra—because I needed some fresh air." Aiden frowned and dipped his head once.

He was lying, that much was obvious, but why? Whatever the reason, Nate had the absurd urge to pull the man forward and try to kiss the truth out of him. The sooner he got the prince back inside with a roomful of people, the better. "Aiden?"

"Yes?"

"Come on. You promised me a dance." Nate grabbed hold of one firm arm and tugged Aiden off the bench and toward the ballroom. Holding him close was going to do nothing for his peace of mind—but at least being in front of a crowd should abolish his erection and the yearning to kiss the man.

They entered the ballroom as the orchestra started the waltz. He turned Aiden to face him and swept the prince into the dance.

Aiden felt good—right—in his arms. Aiden had to look up a little to meet Nate's gaze. He was stiff at first, but it soon became apparent he was a very graceful dancer. It surprised Nate. As adverse as the prince seemed to be to dancing, Nate half expected him to be a bit awkward and on the clumsy side, but he wasn't.

The man was an enigma. He didn't like to dance, yet he did it beautifully. He was attracted to Nate, although he obviously didn't want to be. Then there was the computer.

Aiden was distracted at first, his gaze raking over Nate's face, like he was cataloguing features.

What was he looking at? Nate grinned. "Did you finally manage to ditch the dance card?"

Aiden's eyes widened, a blush spreading across his face, then he nodded. "Payton beat me tonight though. And my friend Bannon wins for the most original card extermination this time. He accidentally dropped his in the punch bowl."

Nate chuckled. "Is it a contest?"

"It's ongoing. We judge on promptness and originality of destruction. Usually, I'm the first one to lose my card. Payton is generally the most original."

Pulling the younger man a bit closer than entirely proper, Nate squeezed Aiden's waist where his hand rested and used his thumb to caress Aiden's palm. He could feel the heat of Aiden's body, smell him. The scent was nice, like bayberry, one of Nate's favorite scents. Aiden's ebony curls moved a little on every turn, tempting Nate to run his fingers through the locks. Instead he tried to concentrate on the conversation. "What do the winners get?"

"The satisfaction of knowing they won."

The man was charming and competitive...not a bad quality to have. His innocence was obvious and extremely appealing, making Nate long to corrupt him.

Mirroring Nate's steps, Aiden never faltered. He grinned, his eyes gleaming. The younger man's face grew flushed with excitement, then he chuckled, throwing his head back a bit. "Thank you for catching my dance card."

Nate laughed back, truly enjoying himself. "You're very welcome. You don't dance much, do you?"

Aiden shook his head, his gray eyes wide. "Not unless I'm made to, and then my mind is usually on something else."

"Oh? And what is your mind usually on?"

"My art." He bit his lip and gave Nate another one of those pointed stares. "I'm an artist."

"That explains the computers. They're sketchscreens?"

Aiden bobbed his head.

It made sense. Nate had noticed him watching things closely, as if in a daze. "What do you draw?"

"A little of everything. Still lifes, portraits, landscapes. Anything possible. I want to be good at all of it."

Something about the way he said it, the zest, made Nate realize how important it was to him. Nate would be willing to bet Aiden was already very adept at it. "I'd love to see some of your work."

Aiden relaxed again, a grin slowly spreading across his face. "You would?"

Nate nodded and twirled them around. "I would. I've always enjoyed art. I try and visit museums when I go to a new planet. I can't draw a lick, even with the help of a computer, but I like to look. My mother loved the arts, painting, music, acting, but especially paintings and printed media." It was one of the few things Nate held onto from his youth.

The smile Aiden gave him was absolutely radiant.

Nate smiled back and before he knew it, they were staring at one another, caught in the magic of the waltz as they danced around the ballroom. It was truly one of the strangest moments of Nate's life.

The song came to an end but they barely noticed.

Nate gazed into the upturned face right below his own. The man had such a beautiful mouth. Dipping forward, Nate licked his lips.

Aiden tilted his head, his eyes closing.

Nate closed his own eyes, inches away from Aiden's lips.

"Aiden!"

They jumped apart, the spell broken.

Fuck. Nate dashed a quick look around to see if they'd been noticed standing in the middle of the dance floor making eyes at each other.

The young blond man Nate had seen talking to Aiden earlier rushed toward them, stealing peeks behind him. Everyone else seemed to be leaving the room, oblivious to them.

When the young man stopped in front of them, he bowed.

Aiden motioned to him. "Lord Deverell, this is Lord Rupert. Rupert, Lord Deverell."

Rupert bobbed his head. "Pleasure to meet you, Lord Deverell." Turning his attention to Aiden, Rupert snagged Aiden's free arm and started pulling. "You have to come to dinner with me. My sire is trying to get Lord Cromley to escort me into the dining room."

Aiden glanced at Nate, wide-eyed. "But—"

Rupert looked at Nate, seeming to realize how rude he'd been. He gave a dip of his head. "Lord Deverell?"

Nate tipped his head. "Lord Rupert?"

"Might I borrow my friend?"

It was on the tip of his tongue to say no. He didn't want to give up Aiden's attention, which was rather disturbing. "Of course." He let go of Aiden's slender hand reluctantly.

Rupert beamed at him. "Thank you."

Watching Nate the whole way, Aiden was dragged off the dance floor by his friend.

Nate stood there for several seconds feeling like he'd been hit upside the head.

Chapter Six

They left the ball at one a.m.—which was relatively early as far as balls went—but Nate was glad. It may be important for him to look like a guest to the staff, but he wanted to get a head start on the investigation. Raleigh had given him the pass code to get into Jeffers' memory and Nate had every intention of using it. But first he went to his room to check on Trouble. With any luck the kid would have gotten some information from the servants.

When he entered his room, his son was sprawled out on his bed on top of the covers snoring. The pest wore a pair of flowered pajamas and the ridiculous white, fluffy bunny rabbit slippers he'd bought last year at one of the ports they'd visited.

Sitting on the edge of the bed, he nudged Trouble. "Trouble, wake up."

The pale, freckled nose wrinkled and he snuffled before opening his eyes. "Huh?" He blinked several times and sat up, his blond curls sticking out at different angles. He yawned, and a goofy, lazy grin slid into place. "Did you get lucky?"

Nate groaned. The kid had a one-track mind. "No, I did not get lucky. What are you doing in this getup?" Nate motioned to the flannel pjs. "I thought you were given sleep shirts."

Trouble snorted. "No way am I wearing a gown. Gowns are for girls."

Nate closed his eyes and pinched the bridge of his nose, a smile threatening. Trouble was wearing baby blue flannel adorned by little pink and yellow flowers, with floppy-eared bunnies on his feet, yet he was worried about looking feminine. "What are you doing in here? You are supposed to be sleeping in the room over there." Nate pointed to the small room adjoining his.

"I was waiting on you. Besides, that bed isn't very comfy and the room is tiny."

Ignoring the gripe he'd heard at least three times since Trouble saw the room this afternoon, Nate stood and went to the nightstand on the other side of the bed. There was a decanter of scotch and two tumblers. *Thank Galaxy.* He poured himself a drink. "Did you learn anything?"

"Nah, not really. Can I have one?"

"No. And what do you mean not really? If you didn't learn anything, why were you waiting up for me?"

Trouble eyed the glass of liquor and frowned. "You're no fun, you know that?"

"Yes." Nate made a "continue" motion with his hand.

Trouble sighed. "I was waiting to see what you'd learned."

"Not a lot." Crossing to the window, he peered out into the garden. The way the moonlight fell over the ivy-covered faux Greek ruins was picturesque. A sudden vision of Aiden lying out on the grass in the center of the fallen columns flashed across his mind. Damned, if that wasn't a pretty picture. His prick threatened to harden. Nate took a drink. He had to get the man out of his mind. Maybe learning more about him would douse Nate's interest. It sure couldn't peak it any more, he could hope anyway. "Have you heard anything at all about the princes?" Nate turned his head from the window.

"Oh, I've heard a lot about their studlinesses." The pest waggled his eyebrows.

Nate quickly downed the rest of his scotch. Something told him he was going to need it to get through the conversation without choking the shit out of Trouble.

"What do you want to know? There are five of them, all dark-headed, all gorgeous and available. But every last one of them is a virgin." Shaking his head, Trouble made tsking sounds.

"Trouble..." he warned.

"Whaaat?" He held up his hands and smiled. "I'm just saying... Come on, even you have to admit it's a shame. There is some prime male flesh there, all of age and all unconquered. It should be a crime."

It should, damn it. Crossing the room, Nate poured himself another drink.

"Okay, okay. The staff has nicknames for them. Rexley, the oldest, they call him Lord Responsible. He's a bit of a stick in the mud. Great ass though and he—"

"Jeremy."

Trouble groaned. "There is Payton, his nickname is Lord Plague. He's a little too brainy for his own good and the absolute plague of the staff because of it."

"How so?"

"Apparently, he's the one responsible for shutting the computer down. And he is always making messes doing experiments and stuff. He's a computer genius." Trouble hopped off the bed, went to the washstand and poured himself a glass of water. "You sure I can't have scotch instead? All right, all right. Stop glowering at me." Taking a drink, he set the glass back and padded to the bed, perching himself between the large end posts. "Tarren is the youngest—he's known as Lord Terror. Which is pretty self-explanatory. Personally speaking, he seems like a lot of fun. He likes to hunt and has a lot of dogs. And from the looks of him in those tight pants...hung like a— Oh and speaking of horses, Colton is the horseman. His nickname is Lord Calamity, again it's pretty obvious why, but boy does he have some great thighs. Muscular and—"

"What about Aiden?" If Nate sounded a little anxious, Jeremy didn't seem to notice.

"Lord Audacious. He sort of has his head in the clouds. He's an artist and a rather gifted one if the rumors are correct. Some of the maids and footmen were going on about a portrait he did of the king's consort. The whole staff has a bit of a crush on Raleigh. And who can blame them. The man is gorgeous. Lord Aiden looks a lot like him. Don't you think?"

Nate started to inform Trouble that Aiden was much more attractive, but grunted instead. Who knew what his son would do if he thought Nate had a thing for Aiden. It didn't bear thinking on. "What else? Do you know anything about Payton shutting Jeffers off?"

"Nah, just that Tarren had something on him and blackmailed him into doing it."

Interesting. "See if you can find out what he used to blackmail him with. Anything else?"

Trouble shook his head and yawned, lying back on the bed. "Nope, other than daily operation stuff. All the servants were here the day the guns disappeared, but no one saw anything unusual."

"Figures. All right, I'm going downstairs. Go to bed."

"Okay." Trouble scooted to the middle of the bed and started plumping pillows.

"Your bed."

Groaning and mumbling, Trouble got off the bed and headed toward the valet's room. "You should have to sleep in here, Hawk. You're the one who makes sure we're both dressed right, not me." He shut the door, still grumbling about how small and uncomfortable the bed was.

Nate made a mental note to see about getting the pest a softer bed.

It was quiet downstairs, all the servants having gone to bed, which suited Nate fine. He didn't want to be bothered. Slipping into the study, he went to the desk. "Jeffers?"

"Yes, Lord Deverell?"

"Please secure the room."

"Yes, sir. The room is secured. You will be notified if anyone approaches it."

Nate sat in the chair behind the desk, stretching. *What a night.* It had been forever since he'd gone to a ball. Oddly, he'd enjoyed it. He'd expected this entire ordeal to be nothing but a pain in the ass, but he was finding it rather refreshing. As much as he hated to admit it, given the circumstances of him leaving, he missed home. He missed his father and Jared, he even missed the attention that came from being the Duke of Hawthorne's heir. As strange as Regelence's customs were, it was too bad he hadn't been born *here*. His sex life would have suffered, but he'd still be an earl and he'd still have his family. If only Englor had been more open-minded and accepted all types of relationships, not just the norm. Sighing, he ran his hands over his face. It didn't matter. That wasn't his life. He was an IN captain and he was here on a mission.

Scooting back from the desk, he looked for a button to bring up the access panel to the house computer. There had to be one, because there was a hairline seam in the top of the desk. Ah, there on the inside of the opening. Nate pushed the button, and a screen came up. Where was the keypad? The computer was voice controlled, but he'd need a keypad and thumb scanner to access it. "Jeffers, where is the keypad?"

"Top left-hand drawer, milord."

He opened the drawer, punched in the numbers Raleigh had given him and pressed his thumb to the scanner. Thankfully, his print had been added to the system earlier.

Jeffers acknowledged him as soon as he set his thumb down. "Welcome, sir. What can I help you with?"

Nate shut the drawer and got comfortable. "Jeffers, please show me the video you have of the basement right before you were taken offline and right after you were brought back online."

A video of an empty corridor flashed onto the screen. It looked like an ordinary hallway with mahogany wainscoting, pale wallpaper above and sconces interspaced throughout. Except for the color of the wallpaper it could have been the hallway outside of Nate's room, but there were only two other doors, one to the left and one at the end.

"Jeffers, where is the room with the weapons in relation to this shot?"

"The camera is over its door, milord."

"Show me."

The screen changed. It looked to be the same hallway, only it was a shot of double steel doors and a single door to the right of it. On one of the double doors and on the single door were thumb scanners and keypads. Both entries needed security clearance.

"The double doors lead to the storage room?"

"Yes, milord."

"Where does the other door go?"

"My maintenance room."

Nate yawned again, then focused back on the single door. That was more than likely where Jeffers' off button was. "Let me see all the shots in this general vicinity before and after you were out of commission."

The next shot was of the inside of the storage room. Three flights of stairs led down into the huge storeroom where large wooden crates lined the walls. There was a large metal cargo door along the far wall. The screen continued to change views, showing the same room. There appeared to be only two points of entry, the doors leading into the hallway and the cargo door. The video suddenly went dead. When it came on again it started where it had left off. When Jeffers showed him the first shot again, Nate noticed the door on the left was partially opened. "Jeffers, where does the open door lead?"

"Into the main house."

"And where does the other doorway lead?"

"Into the servants' corridor."

"Can you show me the other side of the door, before the outage?"

"Yes, milord."

The computer showed another hallway, this one with dark green wallpaper above the wainscoting. There were three doors spaced evenly along one side and two doors on the other. Nate frowned. There was no activity in the hallway. Which didn't mean much, Jeffers was off for nearly two hours. The theft could have happened anytime during that time. "The camera is above the door leading to the basement?"

"Yes, milord."

"Are there any other views of this hallway?"

"No, milord."

"Damn. What is this hallway?"

"It is the corridor outside the princes' suites."

He wondered which one was Aiden's, then quickly dismissed the thought. "Show me this hallway immediately after you regained power."

The monitor blinked, indicating the picture had changed, but the screen was the same as the prior one. There was no activity in the hallway or any sign that anyone had gone to the access panel. Why wasn't Payton in any of the prior shots if he was responsible for Jeffers' hiatus? "Is there any video of the inside of Payton's room?"

"No, milord. I only have audio access to the bedchambers and no information is recorded like it is in the public areas."

Interesting. "Which rooms belong to what prince?" Nate didn't want to think too much about how he'd phrased that question. He only needed to know the location of Payton's room.

"The rooms on the right, starting at the closest, belong to Rexley, Tarren and Colton. On the left are Payton and Aiden's rooms."

So Payton and Aiden were next door to each other. "Do you have thermal access to this hallway?"

"No, milord, I only have full access to the public and secure areas. I have video and audio to the private corridors."

He knew it was Payton who flipped the switch. He really didn't need to know how, but he'd have felt better if he could see it. "Do you have full access to the servants' hallway?"

"Yes, milord."

"Show me the servants' hallway leading to the basement directly before and after the shutdown."

A narrow white passageway came on the screen. There were doors interspaced throughout it. It was empty. The screen blacked out and came on again. The hallway appeared the same except there was a door partially open. "Jeffers, where does that open door lead?"

"The valet chambers adjoining Lord Aiden's room."

Nate closed his eyes and leaned back in the chair. His gut instinct said the man was innocent of anything involving the IN investigation, but he kept turning up in the oddest places. Aiden made him desperately want to be the trusting man he'd been before he left home. He made Nate want a normal life, the life he'd left. But Nate wasn't that man anymore. He was a captain, in charge of a whole ship full of people...in charge of this investigation. Resorting back to his old life wasn't an option. That unquestioning, relaxed attitude led only to heartache, he knew that. So what if no one had ever stirred the feelings Aiden inspired.

Love at first sight? Nate groaned, sitting back up and opening his eyes. *Complete and utter bullshit.* It was a case of him not having gotten laid in forever. He had to get Aiden out of his mind. But the coincidences were just too many to ignore— Aiden spying on him, the vow of secrecy he'd tried to extract from Nate, and now this, his door being open. It was coincidental, he knew it was—it had to be—the king and his consort were good men, he couldn't see them raising a traitor. Somehow Aiden was tied into this case and Nate was going to find out why, whether his idiot body and mind liked it or not.

CŽ

He couldn't sleep. Aiden rolled over and plumped his pillow again, trying to get comfortable. It was no use, his prick was so hard it ached. Getting those laughing chestnut brown eyes out of his mind was a lost cause. Nathaniel's smile, the heat of his body when he was near, his powerful shoulders and intimidating height, the way he smelled, it all haunted Aiden, refusing to let him doze off.

He couldn't remember the last time he'd had as much fun. Dancing with Nathaniel had made him feel special, not just one of the royal brats. Deverell had truly been interested in his art. It was something they had in common. The attention had nothing to do with Aiden's title and everything to do with mutual attraction. Nathaniel saw Aiden as a person, and Aiden liked what he saw in Nate.

Aiden pressed his hips into the mattress, trying to get some relief. What would those big, strong hands feel like wrapped around his cock? Aiden groaned. Nathaniel wasn't the only one who saw what he liked. The man made Aiden want things he shouldn't. Realizing he was grinding his prick into the bed, he stopped. He flopped over onto his back, his cock throbbing. The heck with it, it wasn't going away.

Snaking his hand underneath the covers, he lifted his sleep shirt. If his valet caught him, he'd get another lecture on how he shouldn't touch himself and how he should save it for his future consort, but Aiden couldn't bring himself to care at the moment. Benson was asleep and the door adjoining their rooms was closed—he wasn't likely to come in Aiden's room at this time of night without being summoned. Wrapping a hand around his erection, he tightened his grip. *Ah.* He stroked up, then back down. What if Nate were his consort? Would they do this together?

Nathaniel's prick would be as big as the rest of him, Aiden just knew it. The earl's arms would feel good holding him. They'd kiss the whole time they touched each other, their fingers exploring, driving each other mad. Aiden's hand sped up. His testicles pulled closer to his body. There was a little tingly sensation at the base of his spine.

104

Using his thumb to rake over the tip, Aiden squeezed harder. He imagined Nathaniel's fist around him, Nathaniel talking to him in that low deep voice, encouraging him to take his pleasure. Then they would rub against each other like Aiden sometimes did against the mattress. All that bare skin— Nathaniel would be so warm and hard. Using his other hand, Aiden pinched a nipple, making it stiffen. Maybe Nathaniel would take the nipple into his mouth? Aiden trembled and moaned at the thought. Nathaniel would suck and bite. Then he'd lick and nibble his way down Aiden's chest, swirl his tongue around Aiden's navel. Continuing downward, his lips would brush across Aiden's prick—

"Unh." Aiden's eyes flew open, his body convulsing as his climax rushed out of him. Semen shot against the sheet. The heated spunk oozed down his shaft, over his hand, onto his stomach.

Aiden gasped, surprised. The image of Nathaniel's mouth on his prick should have scandalized him, but it didn't. He'd heard Rexley and Payton, having caught two of their footmen in the act, whispering about it once. Aiden shivered.

Climbing out of bed, careful not to let his shirt fall into the mess on his stomach, he went to the washroom to clean up. He brought a wet cloth back and cleaned the top sheet to avoid Benson's lecture when the bedding was changed. After returning the cloth to the hamper in the washroom, he got in the other side of the bed, avoiding the wet spot. He lay there for several minutes, waiting for the usual drowsiness that a release brought. It didn't happen. His mind kept conjuring images of Nathaniel and the things they could do together.

Maybe if he drew a little it would help clear his mind so he could sleep. He got up and padded to the chest at the foot of his bed where he kept his sketchscreens. He wanted his large one, the one he'd taken to the docks. He'd work on the water compulsion system under the boats...anything but Deverell. Thinking about the earl was what was keeping him awake—drawing the man wasn't likely to help any.

Where was his large screen? There were paints, a conventional sketch pad, some oil crayons, graphite pencils, charcoal, even a small folding easel, but none of his screens were there. The small one he'd taken to the ball was on the nightstand, the medium one was in the dressing room. Aiden frowned. He hadn't seen his large screen in several days. Thomas had taken it to Aiden's room the day he'd gone to the docks, so why wasn't it here? Maybe Thomas had gotten busy and left it elsewhere. "Jeffers, do you know where my large sketchscreen is?"

"No, milord."

Hmmm. Well, he knew where his medium screen was. Aiden shut the trunk lid and went to the dressing room. He found the sketchscreen right where Payton had left it, on the chaise. He went back to his room and climbed into bed with the screen. "Jeffers, did you download the information from my large screen?"

"Yes, milord, as you requested. All data on your screens are updated and synchronized into your files upon leaving and entering the castle."

"Upload the sketches from the large screen onto my medium screen, please." Aiden hit the on button then glanced at the small screen on his nightstand. He sighed. *What the heck.* Maybe if he finished the sketch of Nathaniel he'd started at the ball, he'd get the man off his mind. "Jeffers, also add the data off my small screen onto the medium one."

"Yes, milord."

Why did the man have to be so...so...so compelling? Captivating? *Bloody black hole*, the man was becoming an obsession. He'd like to think it was from strictly an artistic standpoint—and it was, partially. He'd initially forgotten their dance because he'd had the urge to draw the man laughing. The image of Nathaniel's smiling face, when he was talking to Cony, was permanently etched in his brain. The man didn't seem to be the type to smile a lot. Aiden's prick regained interest at the thought, making him groan.

"Lord Aiden, the data transfer is complete."

Aiden started. "Thanks, Jeffers." He toggled through his files and found the one he'd begun at the ball. The one Nathaniel almost saw. Aiden had nearly jumped out of his skin when the man had appeared before him. He'd been completely caught up in rendering the laugh lines around the man's eyes when he smiled.

Maybe Cony and Father had a point about him having a one-track mind when it came to his art. He'd almost missed the chance of a lifetime, the chance to dance with Nathaniel. Luckily, the man himself had shown up to remind Aiden of their dance. He'd never forget that dance, it had been miraculous. He hadn't wanted to leave the man's company. *Darn Rupert.* Aiden desperately wanted to learn more about the earl. He wanted to know why the man was here. How long would he be staying? Would he pose for a portrait? How did his lips taste?

Aiden shook himself away from that line of thinking. Finding the sketch he'd done of Nathaniel earlier, he removed the stylus from the side of the screen. The man was so mysterious looking, like a dashing hero out of the romance novels Tarren was addicted to. What would it have been like if he'd let Nathaniel kiss him when he'd caught him from the tree? He was certain that was exactly what the earl had intended. Then this evening... He should be glad Rupert interrupted when he did.

This was getting him nowhere. His prick was on its way to throbbing, already fully erect again after the session with his hand.

Turning off the screen, he put the stylus away. Maybe food would help get his mind off Deverell.

Aiden climbed from the mattress and dug underneath his bed for his slippers. He should probably put a dressing gown on over his sleep shirt, but everyone had long since retired for the evening. Besides, it wasn't like he'd run in to anyone in the kitchen—the staff was asleep and other than Payton or Cony, no one else would be caught dead there. If his other brothers or Father wanted something to eat at this time of night, they had Jeffers wake someone to bring it to them.

Thankfully, by the time he made it down the stairs, his wayward cock calmed down. He reached the bottom of the main steps and took two steps toward the dining room, intent on going through the servants' entrance to the kitchen, when he heard talking. Aiden paused and listened. Jeffers was talking to someone in the study. He thought about going back upstairs to put on more proper attire, but decided it wouldn't hurt to take a peek. Tiptoeing toward the study, he heard Nathaniel's voice. Immediately his stupid prick decided it wanted to perk up and listen to the smooth intonation too. Aiden looked down, hoping his problem wasn't noticeable in the billowy calf-length shirt.

It was.

"Milord, Lord Aiden is outside the study."

Aiden froze. *Dust.* Before his brain clicked back on and told him to run, Nathaniel appeared in the doorway.

"Hello, Aiden."

"Uh..." Aiden peered up at the object of his fixation. His pulse actually sped up and his stomach got a fluttery feeling. He was standing here in his nightclothes, completely indecent

108

with an erection straining against his shirt. "Hi. I was just..." He nodded. He had to get out of here before Nathaniel noticed his plight. *Galaxy,* the man was big. Aiden was ultra-aware of the man after that little fantasy earlier. He glanced at the big hands he'd imagined wrapped around—

Grinning, Nathaniel crossed his arms over his chest and leaned on the side of the doorjamb. His gaze raked up and down Aiden's body, leaving a tingle of recognition every place it landed. When his gaze zeroed in on Aiden's groin, his eyes widened and his nostrils flared. Finally tearing his gaze from Aiden's cock, he asked, "Yes?" His voice was a husky whisper.

Oh Galaxy, how embarrassing. *Please don't let me be blushing.* This was the second time—the third actually, but his clothes had hid it well enough while they were dancing. He had to get out of here before he made a complete fool of himself. Make that more of a fool. "Good night, Lord Deverell." Aiden turned to leave, cursing himself.

Nathaniel grasped his wrist, turning him back around. "Not yet."

Chapter Seven

A small surprised sound escaped, but the younger man didn't pull away. Slowly, Aiden's cheeks turned bright red.

Real fucking smooth, Nate. He was going to have to remember the prince was not used to people being forward with him. "I wanted to ask you some things."

"Me?" Aiden's eyebrows shot up.

"Yes." Tugging Aiden's arm, Nate tried his best to keep his gaze on Aiden's face. Nate would never get any answers if he started ogling Aiden again. He'd scare the man off. And damned if he wasn't reluctant to relinquish Aiden's company. Being attracted to him was a very bad idea, but Nate couldn't seem to get his body to understand that. Heck, his mind didn't want to see it either.

Nate walked them back into the study. "Jeffers, please give us some privacy."

"I'm sorry, milord, I cannot do that with Lord Aiden in the room. I must act as his chaperone."

Aiden's blush actually darkened.

Galaxy, what would the man do if Nate were to— Nate sighed and let go of Aiden's wrist. There he went again, thinking things he shouldn't. This society may be a bit foreign to him, but he respected it and the basic principles it was founded on.

Looking for something to put Aiden at ease, he spotted the painting above the fireplace. It was doubtful that it was Aiden's but it *was* art, something Aiden enjoyed. It was an unusual but very pleasing composition, the little girl, Muffin, was dressed in white lace, standing in front of a window, with the moonlight peeking through the dark curtains. She held a bouquet of black roses up to her nose. Her blue eyes sparkled over the petals. With her rosy cheeks and pale skin, she looked like an angel. The child was innocent in contrast to the ebony flowers with their deadly looking thorns. The highlights and shading were incredible. It was crisp superrealism, the texture so well done it beckoned the viewer to touch it. "That is one of the best fantasy pieces I've seen in a long time."

"Thank you, but it's not a fantasy piece. Those are Regelence Roses. They bloom at night and are found only on Regelence. It's not one of my best, but it's one of my favorites. If you like, sometime I'll take you out one night while you are here to see them."

Nate was stunned. Not that the roses were really black or that they bloomed at night, but the painting was amazing. Aiden was an even better artist than he'd assumed. "You're very good."

Aiden smiled, the blush gone from his cheeks. "Thank you." He didn't pretend to be bashful about his talent—he knew how good it was. The confidence was very sexy. "Why do you want to talk to me?" Aiden went around the desk, peering toward the monitor. The light from the monitor and the fireplace highlighted his high cheekbones. He cocked his head at the screen, contemplating it.

Fuck, the man was beautiful.

"Lord Deverell?" Aiden looked up, meeting his gaze.

"Nate."

"I shou—" He grinned. "Okay. Nate, what do you want with me?"

What don't I want with you? Nate walked to the other side of the desk, regarding the screen. It was a video of the hall leading to the basement and the storage. "Tell me how Payton shut Jeffers down."

Aiden shook his head. "Why would I do that?" Breaking eye contact, he dragged his fingers across the surface of the desk. "Why are you here? What was stolen?" He looked back up, peering directly into Nate's eyes.

Nate studied him, nearly getting lost in the cool gray, looking for any indication that the prince was playing him. He didn't see any, and he was damned good at reading people. Nate gave Aiden the same calculated stare he used to intimidate junior officers into confessing their sins. But the young man never faltered. Aiden never blinked, his eyes didn't leave Nate's. It impressed the hell out of Nate. Innocent and naïve Aiden may be, but the man didn't intimidate easily and damned if that didn't make him even more appealing. Nate's cock filled. What would that defiant mouth taste like?

Stepping closer, Nate caught Aiden's chin with his fingers.

Aiden licked his lips. He swallowed, making the barely noticeable Adam's apple move, but other than that he stayed rooted to the spot.

"Lord Deverell, please put distance between yourself and Lord Aiden or I'll be forced to alert their majesties," Jeffers said.

Letting go of Aiden's chin, Nate stepped back. It was a contest to what he wanted to do most, thank Jeffers or try to give him a virus, maybe rip out his damned plugs. For the first time in a long time, Nate found himself in the awkward position of not knowing what to do. He was attracted to Aiden, no doubt about it, but he also had a feeling Aiden knew stuff that would help him figure out who took the weapons. If his instincts were wrong he was fucked, but he couldn't help feeling that Aiden had nothing to do with the actual crime. His instincts were almost always right.

Swiveling the chair around, Nate offered Aiden a seat. "I'll make you a deal. You tell me what I want to know and I'll tell you what you want to know."

Aiden's lips quirked, then he nodded and took a seat. "Turn around."

"I beg your pardon?"

"Please." Aiden raised a brow. "If you want to know, turn around."

What was he up to? *The hell with it.* He was going to trust Aiden until Aiden gave him a reason not to. Nate narrowed his eyes a little bit to let Aiden know he wasn't thrilled about the request.

Aiden glared right back.

Damn, the man was something. Nate turned around. He listened for any sudden movement, anything to indicate Aiden was up to something. But he didn't hear anything other than the clacking of fingertips hitting the keyboard. What was he doing?

"Okay, you can look."

Nate turned. Nothing looked different. "What did you do?"

"I bypassed security on this room and the surrounding rooms manually."

Wonderful, another of the Townsend offspring who knew way too much about castle security. "You turned Jeffers off?"

"No, I tossed him out of here so we can talk. Shutting him down would compromise the castle's safety, not a good idea with everyone asleep. Talk."

Did he just give me an order? Nate's lips twitched. The more he learned the more he liked. His dick got harder. "How did you do that?"

Aiden smiled, his eyes wrinkling at the corners. "It wasn't hard—you were already in the system—but I can't tell you. Not until— Give me a reason to trust you, Nate."

If Nate hadn't been watching carefully he might not have seen Aiden biting his lower lip then releasing it. Nate couldn't look away. He couldn't help but notice everything about the younger man.

He sat on the edge of the desk, trying to ignore his idiot libido. "I work for the IN. I'm captain of the IN Destroyer, Lady Anna. I'm here to investigate a stolen weapons cache. As soon as I figure that out, I'll be out of your hair and back to my ship." Nate studied Aiden's expressions intently.

Aiden's mouth opened then closed and his brow furrowed. After a few seconds he nodded. "I should have thought of something like that. Regelence has always had a good relationship with the IN, but I had no idea we were storing weapons." A lock of hair fell into his eyes. "They were stolen when Payton took Jeffers offline."

Nate itched to reach out and brush the black hair off Aiden's pale forehead. "Yes."

Aiden blew at the hank of hair, getting it out of his face. He stared at Nate, his eyes wide. "How is that possible? No one knew but the four of us."

Closing his eyes, Nate took a deep breath. Yes, this is exactly what he needed to know. If Aiden were lying, he was one hell of a liar. He opened his eyes, letting the last bit of doubt go.

Aiden's face was a study in confusion. "One of the servants had to have done it."

"That's what Raleigh thinks. But that takes an awful lot of planning. Are you sure no one else knew?"

"Only Payton, Colton, Tarren and myself."

"Not Rexley?"

Shaking his head, Aiden stood. "No, Rexley is a tattletale." He began pacing back and forth in front of the desk, the white nightshirt molding against him as he moved. With the light from the fireplace behind him, the shirt was nearly see-through. The man had a hell of a body. He was slim, but very fit. His leg muscles were solid and clearly delineated through the thin fabric.

Nate groaned. The man had a great backside. Wide shoulders in comparison to the rest of him, narrow waist and hips, nice round ass. Trying to relieve the pressure on his cock, Nate shifted.

"What's that?" Aiden turned around.

Instead of staring at his very delectable ass, Nate was now faced with a picturesque front view. Nate gazed up, looking into the handsome face. "What?"

"You made a sound."

"I did?"

Aiden nodded.

Come on, Nate. Business. Think. "How did Payton get past the security cameras?"

Aiden sighed and stepped forward. "Okay, what I'm about to tell you—" He put his hand on Nate's chest.

Covering Aiden's hand and keeping it there, Nate leaned forward, aware of the heat emanating from the young man. Galaxy, he'd love to hold those slim wrists captive above his head as he— "Yes?"

"The cameras in the upper halls are on a loop. It's a glitch, left over from when the security system was updated. The main rooms are on constant surveillance now, but the private rooms are not. They reprogrammed Jeffers to watch outside the castle and the family rooms continuously, but they forgot to change over the private halls when the video equipment got changed over. No one knows about it but Payton and myself." Aiden's gaze rested on Nate's lips and he stepped closer. "You can't tell any—" Aiden touched Nate's beard tentatively at first, then his fingers dragged across it, exploring. Parting his lips, Aiden tilted his head, his gaze still following his fingers.

Damn, just damn. Nate let go of Aiden's hand and slid his own around the younger man's waist, pulling him even closer until Aiden's hips were cradled between his thighs. Slowly, he leaned forward, his mouth searching for Aiden's.

Blinking several times, Aiden closed his eyes and brushed his lips against Nate's.

The kiss went straight to Nate's cock. Leaving a hand around Aiden's waist, Nate brought the other up and caressed one smooth cheek with his thumb as he nuzzled the corner of the younger man's lips. "Open your mouth, boy."

When Aiden's lips parted, Nate deepened the kiss.

Aiden stood there, stiff at first, but soon his tongue was making timid touches to Nate's. In no time, the prince was kissing back, his tongue tangling and exploring. He tasted sweet, like strawberries and chocolate and like...Aiden?

Moaning into Nate's mouth, Aiden pressed even closer, bringing his very evident erection into contact with Nate's stomach. He drew away, looking down. "Oh." His eyes met Nate's again and he dove right back into the kiss. Aiden's hand cautiously slipped between them.

Oh, was right. Nate clutched a handful of the delectable ass and mashed Aiden against him. He worked his hands under the nightshirt, meeting skin and a lovely firm ass. An ass that would probably look even better with Nate's handprint on it.

Aiden grabbed Nate's prick through his trousers and squeezed. Moving his hand, Aiden explored, nearly blowing Nate's mind in the process. Finding the ring through Nate's cock, Aiden gasped, his eyes wide. He let go. "Uh..."

Regardless of the nice tight little ass in his hands, this time when Aiden pulled back he might as well have thrown water on Nate because it had the same effect. Nate let go and scooted back on the desk, trying to distance himself from the heat of Aiden's body. What the fuck was he thinking? He should have considered how shocking his piercing would be to Aiden. Hell, in comparison to the things he wanted from Aiden, the Prince Albert was mild.

Aiden started walking backwards. "I—I—"

Nate let him go. He could not dishonor this young man. Aiden was intelligent and spirited. He'd make some man a great consort. *Why not you, Nate? You could get used to being in this type of environment again, it'd be good for Trouble.*

"I— Good night, Lord Deverell." Aiden turned and fled.

Damn.

Nate sat in the computer chair and tried to ignore his conscience. He had to see if he could reverse what Aiden had done to the computer. It was surprisingly easy, but Nate would have never figured it out if Aiden hadn't left the screen up. "Jeffers, show me audio and video outside the princes' corridor right now."

"Yes, milord."

A light slapping sound could be heard seconds before Aiden ran down the hall, white nightshirt billowing behind him.

Stopping outside his room, he heaved in a breath and rested his head against the door with a soft thud. He rolled his forehead against the wood, then banged it a few times before turning the knob and going inside.

Nate sat there, staring as the screen changed to a different hallway. He should go after Aiden and talk to him. But to what end? Putting himself in the same vicinity as Aiden and a bed was not a good idea. He was proving to have very bad willpower where the prince was concerned.

Ↄ

Nate was up bright and early the next morning. He was determined to keep things professional between himself and Aiden, but he was going to request that Aiden be allowed to help him with this case. And it had nothing to do with the intense attraction they shared, or so he kept telling himself. Raleigh and Steven were too busy to sit around helping him and he needed someone who knew the servants. Besides, he could easily pretend to court Aiden. On Englor it wasn't unusual for an out-of-town visitor to show interest in his host's daughters. Sometimes the father even invited foreign business associates over to see if their daughters suited before an actual betrothal was announced.

Upon walking downstairs, Nate took a deep breath, inhaling the scent of brownies, his favorite. He looked around the foyer, amazed. A table with an emerald green tablecloth that hadn't been there the day before sat in the entryway, covered with white bakery boxes. There were calling cards attached to the boxes, and the hum of people talking came from the parlor.

Nate looked through the French doors. The parlor was filled to the brim with lords vying for the young princes' attention.

Nate had expected flowers and visitors. On Englor it was customary for gentlemen to pay ladies a call and bring flowers after a ball. But the baked goods...that was new. Apparently, on Regelence they took to heart the ancient saying "a way to a man's heart is through his stomach". He chuckled, heading toward the breakfast room.

If those men wanted to win Aiden's hand, they'd be better off buying him some canvas and paints. The smile froze on his face and he backtracked, going back to the parlor doors. Rexley, Tarren and Colton all sat side by side on a couch, with Steven to their left. Aiden was nowhere in sight. How had he gotten out of entertaining?

A rustling sound brought Nate's attention back to the baked-goods table. A slender hand came out from under the green cloth, reaching on top. When the pale hand found a box, it latched on and slowly moved it, pulling it under the table. Nate frowned. *That better not be—* He crossed the hall and lifted the emerald linen. *Damn it.*

A headful of platinum curls bent over the now-opened box. The head rose at the intrusion and a set of big aquamarine eyes met Nate's.

Trouble grinned sheepishly, chocolate on his lips and nose. He fluttered his icing-covered fingers. "Hi, Hawk." Trouble held up a chocolate-chip cookie, offering it to him.

Closing his eyes, Nate counted to ten, then kept right on going. He was going to strangle the kid this time, he was. And there was no one here to stop him.

Laughter rang out behind him and he turned to find Raleigh standing there. The king-consort sauntered forward. "Your son?" he asked quietly once he was beside Nate.

"For the next few seconds."

Raleigh bent and took the cookie Trouble was now presenting to him. "And after that?"

"He's going to be dead."

Trouble blanched, swallowing audibly.

Taking a bite of cookie, Raleigh held out his other hand to Trouble. The pest took the offered hand and unfolded his willowy form from under the table.

Raleigh ruffled Trouble's hair, grinning ear to ear, and finished off the dessert. "He's adorable, you shouldn't kill him. What's your name?"

Trouble beamed at the man. "Jeremy."

"Trouble," Nate growled.

Raleigh's brow furrowed. He stared at Jeremy for several seconds then shook his head. Nate was about to ask what was wrong when Raleigh chuckled and spoke again. "Ah, well, we should keep him away from my Terror, something tells me they could likely bring the entire castle down about our ears if they combined their efforts."

Strange. What was that odd look about? Nate narrowed his gaze on his son, but decided to let it go. He was fairly certain Raleigh would tell him if Trouble had been into something...make that something else besides cookies. Then it occurred to him that Raleigh knew about the staff's nicknames for the princes.

Raleigh retrieved the box Jeremy had left under the table and handed it to the kid. "You are supposed to be a servant, remember?"

"Yes, sir," Trouble said.

"Yes, Your Highness," Nate corrected.

Trouble darted a glance at Nate then back to Raleigh, batting his eyelashes. "Yes, Your Highness." The little flirt's voice was as sugary as the box of cookies he held.

Pinching his cheek, Raleigh fought his mirth. He bent close to the kid's ear. "Go upstairs before Nate throttles you, Trouble."

Trouble glanced at Nate, then back to Raleigh, then back at Nate. His eyes twinkled with mischief.

Nate opened his mouth to tell the pest that he better behave when Trouble went up on tiptoe and kissed the consort's cheek. Giggling, he fled up the stairs.

Raleigh threw his head back and laughed long and loud. "Oh boy, you have your hands full."

Nate shook his head, trying not to be amused, but the kid *was* cute. It was the only reason Nate hadn't beat him to death over the years. "Yes, I do. Sorry about that."

"Quite all right. Believe me when I tell you I understand." He clapped Nate on the shoulder. "Breakfast?"

"Sure. I was on my way there."

"Me too. I've two children to browbeat. Come along. I'll glare, and we can both grab a plate and go to the study."

Nate and Raleigh entered the breakfast room. Aiden and Payton sat slumped at the table with piles of food in front of them. When they noticed Raleigh and Nate's appearance, they bolted upright, attaining perfect posture in the blink of an eye.

Looking up at Nate, Aiden turned three different shades of red before averting his gaze.

Nate grimaced. He'd gone to bed last night harder than stone and unable to get Aiden out of his mind. He'd finally jerked off so he could catch some sleep, but that had proved to be even more disturbing, because he couldn't quit picturing Aiden.

Glancing between Nate and Aiden, Raleigh lifted a brow. He shook it off and leaned his hands on the end of the table, glowering at his sons. "Are the two of you going to sit here with the pretense of eating until the callers leave?"

Payton took a bite of food, and Aiden grabbed his drink, both feigning interest in the meal.

Suppressing the urge to smile, Nate wondered how long they'd been sitting here. These two really did not like being in the public eye. He pondered if it was just the idea of marrying, or if it was the attention in general. Aiden didn't seem to mind attention so long as it had to do with art, so it was probably the adoring lords he objected to. Not that Nate could blame him. It would make one feel like a piece of meat. It gave him a new appreciation for what women everywhere had gone through for a millennia.

Raleigh sighed. "If the two of you insist on keeping this up all season, you're going to get fat. I'll expect you both in the ballroom at noon, starting tomorrow."

Payton frowned. "Whatever for, Cony?"

"Exercise." Raleigh crossed to the sideboard and began filling a plate.

"What kind of exercise?" Aiden wanted to know.

"Running mostly. Nate?" Raleigh turned. "Grab a plate."

Both the princes groaned, but Aiden sought out Nate's gaze, his cheeks still pink.

Could the man look any more adorable? And since when did adorable make him hard? Nate shifted, willing his cock to behave.

"Ahem." Raleigh handed him a plate.

Nate realized he was staring and turned his attention to the food. He had to quit staring like some love-struck fool. He had priorities. Food, business, kill Trouble...in that order. Aiden didn't fit anywhere in that picture, except in regards to the case. He filled his plate and followed Raleigh to the office without another glance at Aiden, even if it did take all his willpower.

After retiring to the study with breakfast to ensure their privacy, Nate and Raleigh discussed everything Raleigh had discovered so far. Sadly, it wasn't much. Nate had actually discovered more talking to Aiden last night.

"Why do your children call you Cony?"

Rolling his eyes, Raleigh took a sip of his juice. "It's a nickname. Most children call their parents Father and Sire. But thanks to Steven and his penchant for irritating me, my children call me Cony. It started because Steven used to call me Consort Dear to annoy me. Rexley was a baby at the time, and altered it to Cony. It stuck." He smiled, shook his head and took another drink. He may not like the name Steven had tried to stick him with, but apparently he didn't mind the one the children had given him.

Nate thought about it for a minute. What would it be like to have your kids give you a special name? Trouble had always called him Hawk, like everyone else on the ship. It didn't matter, he had no plans for more children. "Raleigh, I need to talk to you about Aiden."

Frowning at his orange juice, Raleigh set his glass down. Crossing his hands over his beige waistcoat, he leaned back, giving Nate his undivided attention. "You have my blessing, but he will have to choose you himself, Nate. I won't force him to take a consort he doesn't want."

"What?" Nate's mouth dropped open before he caught himself. For half a second he considered going with it and pretending to court Aiden. It would enable Aiden to help him, but Nate didn't want to lie to Raleigh. He honestly liked the man. "Since you and Steven both have other duties to attend to, I wanted to see if Aiden can help me. He knows the castle and its occupants. He can tell me things only an insider can. I need that if I'm going to figure out who took those weapons."

Raleigh stared at him for several minutes. His gray eyes, very much like Aiden's, seemed to see everything.

Nate got the distinct impression the man could see through him. It was chilling. He couldn't remember the last time he had the urge to squirm under such scrutiny.

Finally, Raleigh nodded. "If anything happens to him, I will hold you personally accountable."

"Nothing is going to happen to him while he's in my care."

"Just so that we understand each other. Your military record is exceptional and quite impressive, I've no problem with that. You are more than a worthy suitor for any one of my boys and Admiral Jenkins says you really are an earl. If you compromise him—"

Without hesitation, Nate held up a hand. "I swear I will propose marriage immediately." The ease at which that came out should have been scary. He wondered briefly if he was getting in over his head. "And before you give your final consent, you should know that I'm no longer an earl. That honor now belongs to my brother. I'm an IN captain, period."

"As I said before, we are a military-based society. Your record as a solider and your rank makes you more than an acceptable match for my son." Raleigh was quiet for several seconds. He stood and stared down at Nate. "He may be rebellious, but make no mistake, he is innocent, and I don't mean that in just the most literal sense. I will not have him hurt." The warning was clear. And the cold ease at which Raleigh delivered it had Nate nearly squirming again.

Raleigh smiled, dissipating the tension in the room, and held out his hand. "If you leave the house with him, you will take an appropriate chaperone. Other than that, you have my blessing. Take care of him, that's all I ask."

Nate gave him a crisp nod and shook hands. Why did he get the feeling he just agreed to a betrothal contract?

Chapter Eight

He had fifteen seconds to make it to the end of the hall and through Nate's door. If Nate's door was locked...he might even be able to make it into the next hall over undetected. Two minutes ago, Jeffers had said he'd heard Nate in the shower. Aiden sure hoped *The Spy*'s info was correct. Looking at the pocket watch one last time, Aiden began counting in his head. Ten seconds to go. Putting the pocket watch into his waistcoat, he secured his grip on the sketch pad and artist's pencil he'd brought for this expedition. He'd have rather had his sketchscreen, but the sketches on the screen were stored in Jeffers' memory and for what he had in mind he didn't want to chance one of his nosey family members hacking into his files and discovering it. *Three, two, one...*

Opening and closing the door silently, Aiden took off down the hall. His shoes slid on the wood floor, making him wish he'd ditched them and the hose. Thankfully, no one but Nate had a room in this hall, so he didn't worry too much about the clacking sound his running made. The video loop Jeffers was on in the hallway included audio but it too was off at the moment.

Much to his relief, when he reached Nate's door and turned the knob, it opened. He hurried inside and closed it as quietly as he could. Jeffers had audio function in the bedrooms, whether the hall video was off or not. He didn't record in the bedrooms, but he could still notify Aiden's parents of his presence. Leaning against the door to catch his breath, he did a quick survey. The room was empty and he could hear the water running in the other room. *Thank you, Jeffers.*

Smiling, he looked around for a place to hide. He couldn't remember being in this room before. The big four-poster bed was against the wall on his left as was the door leading to the washroom. A window was positioned high up on the opposite wall. To the far left of the window next to the washroom was an armoire. A fireplace and bookcase dominated the wall to Aiden's right. The room was lit only by the lamp on the nightstand and the sun coming in from the window. Good, it wasn't overly bright. The décor was dark and bold with heavy mahogany furniture and deep jewel tones, so the light didn't reflect very well.

There was a large upholstered chair with a skirt on it in front of the window facing the bed. It looked like the best hiding spot.

Crossing to the window, Aiden dropped his pencil at the foot of the bed. It rolled toward the far wall. As Aiden bent to pick it up the doorknob on the washroom door turned. *Dust.* He dove behind the chair, leaving the graphite utensil where it landed. His sketchbook slipped as his butt hit the floor, but he caught it and even managed not to make a sound while getting himself all the way behind the big chair.

The door opened. Nate came into the room, his hair damp, wearing nothing but a white towel. A drop of water dribbled down the powerfully built chest, to where the hair narrowed and disappeared under the white cloth. The man was so big and masculine. His legs, thickly muscled...and look at the size of those feet. *Good Galaxy.*

Biting his lip, Aiden stared at the artist's pencil. Now what was he supposed to do?

Going to the armoire next to the washroom door, Nate opened the doors.

Aiden's attention narrowed on the man's butt. The white cloth was pulled tight enough Aiden could make out a nicely defined rear end. His prick had been half hard at the idea of sneaking in here to see Nate. Now, it was almost painfully hard. Aiden closed his eyes and leaned his head against the back of the chair. *Note to self, always carry two graphite pencils from now on.*

Nate removed something from the cabinet and tossed it onto the bed. He started to turn back toward the open chest but stopped, his head down.

Aiden followed Nate's gaze to the pencil. *Dust!* He was caught. Any second, Nate would say something or look around.

Shaking his head, Nate turned back toward the armoire. He paused again then shut the doors.

Aiden swallowed the lump in his throat, knowing darn well he was blushing. That had been close. His palms were sweating at the fear of being caught, but he couldn't tear his eyes away from the object of his desire.

Sitting on the bed, Nate ran his fingers through his hair and took a deep breath, his chest moving in and out.

Aiden's stomach clenched, and his heart pounded harder. His mouth was dry. Licking his lips did little for his parched mouth. He wanted to see Nate so badly, see what he'd felt the other night.

Unwrapping the towel, Nate pulled it off and laid back on the bed, until his shoulders were against the headboard and his feet on the mattress. As Aiden got his first good look at Nate, he exhaled and his lungs seized, refusing to take air back in.

The man's cock was in proportion to the rest of him, and it wasn't even fully erect yet. A heavy gold ring peeked out of the foreskin. Even though it wasn't all visible, he assumed it looped through the head and out the tip, but it was definitely gold. It glimmered in the lamplight, beckoning. Nate's cock was beautiful.

Leaning back on the pillows, Nate wrapped his hand around the foreskin and tugged. "Mmm..." He pulled on it again, making his cock even harder, as he leaned his head against the headboard and closed his eyes.

Aiden barely held back a whimper as Nate's hand slid down the shaft. Drawing the skin back and exposing the fat pink head, he groaned. "Can't wait to feel your mouth on me, your teeth. Yeah, that's it, lick under my foreskin and around the head, boy. Pull the foreskin down with your teeth. Damn, that's good." He began stroking, the skin bunching around the top then moving back down. "If you're a real good boy, I might even let you taste me." Nate pulled one hairy leg up, bending it at the knee, giving Aiden a better view of his testicles. "Then again, maybe I'll just come on those pretty little lips. You'd look incredible with my cum all over your face."

Oh man. Aiden's prick twitched, leaking from the tip. He was going to die. Who was Nate thinking about?

Nate's hand kept pumping. His cock had become fully erect, and *oh he was big.* He used the other hand to tug on the ring while he stroked himself. "Ah, shit yeah, Aiden."

Biting his lip, Aiden froze, even trying to hold his breath. Panic raced through him. Could Nate see him? No, no, of course not, his eyes were closed. Aiden made himself relax. Nate didn't know he was here. Which meant... *He wants me.*

Aiden was hard and throbbing. He should be shocked, and he was, but he was more excited. Everything Nate said went right to his head, making him need. He wanted Nate, he wanted to taste and touch and he—

"You like this? Want me to fuck your sweet, hot little ass with this big piece of uncut meat, boy?" Nate's hand squeezed, drawing forth clear drops on the pink tip around the base of the gold ring. "Want my cock in your ass?"

Aiden tried to imagine it. *Could he?* No, no that wasn't...was it? His mind might not be sure but his body didn't seem to have the same objections. His ass and thigh muscles tightened. He was very close to coming without even touching himself.

Stilling his hand, Nate brought it to his mouth and spit into it before wrapping his fist around his prick once more.

Licking his lips, Aiden stared. He'd never even considered doing something so crude as using saliva. His heart pounded and his cock felt like it was going to burst. Why did Nate's vulgarity turn him on this much?

Nate moaned, his hand moving faster, his voice husky and rough now, breathy. "Oh, hell yeah, I'm going to own your ass, boy. Not only my dick, but my fist. First one finger, then two, then three and four, till my whole fucking hand is in your tight, slutty hole. Would you like that? Are you man enough? Stretched out on my bed taking my fist and pleading for me to go deeper. I'll be able to feel your fuckin' heart, Aiden. Will it belong to me? Can you handle it? Can you give me all I want from you, Aiden, what I'll demand?"

Aiden's ass squeezed tight at the scandalous words. Shocked to the core, he knew he should leave, run, but he couldn't. His body tingled, begging for release. Reaching down, he rubbed himself through the fabric of his trousers.

"Oh, fuck yes, come for me, Aiden. Give in to me, boy." Nate's voice was a hoarse whisper.

Balls drawing impossibly close, Aiden's whole body tensed. Rubbing harder against his cock, he let the slap of skin and smell of sweat permeate his senses.

Nate stroked faster, his hips lifting off the bed. "Mine, I'll fucking take you, Aiden. All of you. Body, mind and soul."

Yes. Thrusting his hips against his hand, Aiden's muscles contracted sharply. He came staring at Nate, trying not to pant for breath.

A trail of sweat ran over Nate's abs, getting caught in the thick, dark hair above his prick. Groaning, Nate followed him. "Mine. Aiden." Nate shot. Semen landed everywhere, coating the heavy gold ring, running down his hand, over his knuckles. It trailed up his belly and chest—there was even a spot on Nate's cheek, by the corner of his mouth. His tongue darted out and licked it off.

Nate grabbed the towel and wiped down. He laid there for a few minutes, then sighed and heaved himself up. Taking the clothes off the bed, he went back into the washroom, shutting the door behind him.

Aiden sat there for several seconds. What just happened? He scrambled up from in back of the chair. Clutching his sketchbook, he looked back at the pencil, before he turned and ran. He didn't stop until he reached his room and got inside. Leaning against the door, he dropped his sketchbook and slid to the floor. He dragged his trembling hands down his face and took a deep breath. He knew he was in way over his head with Nate, but darned if his prick wasn't still harder than a rock, despite having the orgasm of his life.

CsquareicroInfinitySymbol

Groaning, Raleigh sat back in his chair and ran his hands over his face. Having a traitor in his house was beginning to grate on his nerves. There was no doubt in his mind that whoever stole those weapons had inside information, he just didn't know who or how. Even with Nate helping him, they hadn't learned much. Only that there was a hover truck missing from the carriage barn.

Jeffers had been instructed to inform him of any staff members acting unusual or snooping around. So far the computer hadn't noticed a thing out of the ordinary. "Jeffers, has *anything* strange happened the last few days?"

"Only Lord Aiden running down the guest hall, milord."

Raleigh frowned. Why was that unusual? Sure, he'd instructed the kids not to run, but they all did it from time to time, well all except Rexley, that boy had been born mature. "Show me the video."

The hall outside of the boys' rooms flashed on the screen, then seconds later it switched to one of the guest halls where Aiden stood outside of a guestroom. His hand jerked away from the doorknob and he took off running down the hall, away from the camera.

Raleigh sat forward, watching until Aiden disappeared around the corner. "Play it again, Jeffers."

Again the video started in the princes' hallway and looped to the guest hallway. The one where Nate was staying. And that had been Nate's door.

Raleigh's teeth ground together. Taking a deep breath, he pushed back from the chair. He had trusted Nate, something he rarely did on such short acquaintance. Raleigh had even started to wonder if Nate would approach Steven to officially offer for Aiden. He had never thought the man would compromise Aiden on purpose. Nate's military record had been above reproach and painted him an honorable man.

By the time he got to Nate's room, he was silently fuming, feeling like a first-class idiot. He opened the door without even knocking.

"What the—" Nate's son, Trouble, sat up on the bed.

Raleigh continued into the room undeterred and looked around.

"Whoa, hey, what's your problem?" Trouble got up and followed him toward the washroom door.

"Where is Nate?"

"He isn't here. He went shopping with the princes."

Damn, he'd forgotten all about that. Payton had even poked his head in the office door to tell him they were leaving. It was rare he got so mad he couldn't think straight, but no one messed with his kids. "If he took Aiden's virginity, I'll kill him."

He'd said it under his breath, but Trouble stiffened noticeably beside him. Taking in Trouble's appearance for the first time, Raleigh frowned. The kid was wearing a pair of loose flowery pants and white bunny slippers, no shirt. All the boyish charm had fled from his face. It was the look of a predator, a killer. Shocked at this new discovery, Raleigh stepped out of reach and watched the boy.

Standing by the bedpost, Trouble appeared for all the world like a carefree teenager, but Raleigh wasn't fooled. The kid's eyes sized up Raleigh. He'd kicked off his slippers and given himself room to maneuver. When he spoke, his voice was low and very clear, deadly. "I can assure you Nate would never take anything he was not willfully given. I will also swear to you, even though I personally disagree with your whole idiotic no-sex-before-marriage crap, Nate always does the right thing. So if he corrupted your son, he will marry him."

"My son was seen running out of here yesterday. What am I supposed to think?"

"Nate is far too honorable. That man found me in a space station stealing and killing to survive after my parents decided to ditch me. If it weren't for Nate I'd probably be dead now myself. So, let's make something very clear, Mr. IN Assassin, if you lay a hand on Nate, I'll kill you."

"How do you... Does Nate know?" Raleigh was even more shocked, making his heart race. A knot formed in the pit of his stomach. He tensed, ready to spring. "How did you find out?"

Trouble shook his head slowly, still watching Raleigh. "Nate doesn't know. He's good with computers like Jeffers, but *I* can break IN encryption in my sleep."

"And you're telling me this why?"

"Because I want to make sure we understand each other. Nate and I are here to help you. I know you are as in the dark as Nate is about what happened with the weapons. We are supposed to be working together. You should remember that."

Standing there letting that sink in, Raleigh scowled. He had kept that secret for years and here was this fifteen-year-old child who had discovered it with a few keystrokes. "You realize I am more than capable of making sure you will never say anything?"

"You can try."

Giving the kid the same steely gaze he'd given Raleigh minutes ago, Raleigh made his point. "Make no mistake, Trouble, I am very capable of carrying out the threat."

"I don't underestimate you, Raleigh. But you need to understand that Nate is like a father to me, and I will not have you or anyone else threatening him. I may not have your IN training, but I have experience. If you so much as dare to hurt Nate, I will make a formidable enemy, one you cannot afford to make right now. I think you need to give them room to decide their own minds on this subject. I'll keep your secrets and you'll keep mine, that way things will not have to get messy." Trouble glared.

Raleigh hadn't run into an opponent as worthy as this mere slip of a boy in a long time. Trouble may be small and untrained, but the kid was highly intelligent and had great instincts. "I'll take your word then, Nate had better do the right thing. But you know my feelings should Aiden get hurt." Raleigh watched Trouble for a minute. Taking his measure. He had no doubt the kid would try to kill him if he hurt Nate, nor did he doubt Trouble would keep his secret. The kid was cut from the same cloth he was, and since Nate had chosen to make Trouble his son then the boy had obviously had more than a chance to learn his father's military sense of honor and integrity.

Raleigh offered Trouble a hand. Raleigh had a feeling this kid could come in handy one day. Trouble was someone Raleigh had misjudged and that did not happen often.

Trouble took his hand reluctantly, his eyes watchful.

Raleigh pulled the boy's arm up when he would have let go. He thought he saw somethi— Yes, under his right arm was a small Regelence Rose birthmark. A birthmark that was placed on only the sons of Regelence. Which explained the deadly aggression Trouble showed. Regelens were made to be topnotch warriors. Their regency society and their rules of propriety helped to temper them, instill self-control. Trouble hadn't had that. "What do you remember about your parents?"

"I don't. I told you, Nate found me on a space station. I'd been there since I was a toddler. I guess my parents decided they didn't want a kid and dumped me there." He sat on the edge of the bed, blinking big aquamarine eyes up at Raleigh.

Raleigh stared into the pale eyes that looked like they belonged to an innocent kid once more. They also looked vaguely familiar. "We'll talk more later." Maybe Steven could help him remember where he'd seen eyes that color before.

Chapter Nine

He was obsessed, completely and utterly. Aiden frowned at the screen. The shading was off. He filled in the shadow by the nose and hit the save button. Drawing Nate was becoming an addiction. Watching him masturbate and say those wicked things should have nipped his fixation in the bud. Instead it had the exact opposite effect. He wanted Nate, even if only for a night. He yearned to be with Nate, discover the things Nate spoke of.

Rexley stopped in front of Aiden again. "Oof." The screen smashed against his chest and he drew a line through his rendering.

"Aiden, put that thing away."

Aiden growled and hit the undo button to get rid of the gigantic streak across Nate's forehead. "If you wouldn't just stop."

"I stopped because we have arrived at the hatter's." Rexley wheeled around to glare at him, then looked past him and began shaking his head. "Muffin. Behave or we won't go to the toy store."

What did Aiden care about hats? Or toys for that matter? He'd already gone to the art store and bought another large sketchscreen—he was done shopping.

He turned, seeking one of their two escorts. Maybe he could persuade them to let him go sit inside the lift while everyone else finished shopping.

Christy was right behind him, tugging on Muffin's hand as the little girl grumbled about not liking hats. Thomas was still putting purchases from the last shop in the lift. The rest of Aiden's brothers rushed past him, chattering amongst themselves, and into the shop. Rexley took Muffin's hand from Christy and walked off toward their loud siblings.

Grinning at him, Christy squeezed his arm as she went by. "Come along, love." Christy had been his and all his brothers' nurse before she became Muffin's and had never stopped calling them by pet names.

Reluctantly, Aiden followed everyone inside the shop and headed toward the back where the shop owner was coming from the stockroom.

Promptly, he found a secluded spot in a back corner of the shop and turned on his screen. Leaning against the wall, he tuned his brothers out. They were all talking to the hatter at once and trying on hats. They would likely look at hats for hours or until Christy forced them to leave. At which time they'd look for him to make sure he was among the group, thus he wasn't overly concerned about being forgotten.

He was about to start adding color to his current portrait of Nate when someone whispered in his ear.

"That's amazing. You've done it from memory?"

"Ah." Aiden jumped, his stylus skidding across the screen again. *Star dust.*

Nate leaned on the wall not even a foot away from him, his arms crossed over his chest, studying Aiden's sketch.

As usual, the man's presence had the undivided attention of Aiden's body. He swore he could hear his heart beating harder. Why were his palms getting sweaty?

Trying to hide his embarrassment, Aiden hit the back button on the screen to erase his foul up. He didn't bother trying to hide the sketch, Nate had already seen it. It didn't keep him from being self-conscious, of course, but hiding it was a moot point. The man was well aware of Aiden's interest in him. How could he not be? At least he didn't know about Aiden spying on him. "Yes, thank you. You surprised me."

"Sorry. Didn't mean to sneak up on you."

"Can you pretend you did not see me off in my own little world?"

"Like I didn't see you fall out of the tree?"

"Exactly."

Nate pretended to think about it for a few seconds. "I might be persuaded to." He winked. "Why do you want to keep it quiet? Everyone knows you're an artist."

Aiden got the distinct impression he was being flirted with. Turning off the screen, he put his stylus in its holder and gave Nate his full attention. "When I get into my work, I sort of forget everything else. It's been backfiring on me lately and Father and Cony have given me an ultimatum."

Nodding, Nate took the screen from him and turned it on. "What's the ultimatum?"

Aiden watched as Nate examined his sketches. Normally he'd have already made a grab for it. He didn't like people seeing his work before it was done, but it didn't bother him this time. He wasn't sure if it was the look of awe on Nate's face or what, but he let the man look through the three sketches he'd done this afternoon since getting the new screen. "They said if I get into one more tight spot they will find me a consort and have me married off, whether I like the man or not."

Eyebrow raised, Nate grinned slowly, almost sensually. "Maybe I should go make certain the consort they find is likable. You do enjoy my company, don't you?"

Aiden could only gape. He started to ask if Nate were serious, but all that came out was a sputter. What if Nate did offer for him? He hadn't planned on a consort, but the idea was anything but unpleasant. It made him practically giddy, thinking about it. "I—I do." Oh Galaxy, that sounded like a vow. *Okay, relax, Aiden, he was teasing. He wants to go back to his ship.* Nate had made that clear the other night. "It's an empty threat. They wouldn't force me to marry someone I didn't choose. And they offered me an incentive. They said if I can get through the season, they'll hire Contenetti to teach me."

Nate stared at him for several seconds, the expression practically scorching, before looking back at the sketchscreen. "I don't know that Contenetti could teach you anything. He's good, but then so are you. Maybe I could find a thing or two to teach you."

Aiden shivered. Nate had already admitted to not being able to draw. There was no doubt in Aiden's mind that Nate could instruct him in any number of things and none of them had anything to do with art. "What would you teach me?" Aiden's gaze narrowed on Nate's lips.

"What would you want me to teach you, boy?"

The low, gravelly voice resonated through Aiden, making his cock harden. A tingly feeling started where his shoulders met his neck, like his body was begging for Nate to kiss him, run his beard over Aiden. He closed his eyes, feeling Nate's breath on his face. When had they moved closer? Remembering

Nate's lips on his, his tongue in Aiden's mouth—Aiden opened his eyes, staring at the full, practiced lips inches from his.

"Damn," Nate whispered. "You make me forget myself." Groaning, Nate pulled away and held the screen up again. After several seconds, his breathing seemed to even out.

Aiden's eventually did as well, but not without an inner struggle. The connection between them just got stronger and stronger. Aiden had only meant to flirt back and instead he'd nearly kissed Nate in public.

Nate ran a hand through his hair. "Seriously, these are very good. You have a lot of talent."

"Those are nothing. That's from this afternoon. Those were all done in less than thirty minutes. It's a new screen—my other large one got stolen."

"Maybe I should commission you to paint a portrait of Jeremy." Nate's voice was still a little rough.

"Jeremy?" Aiden mentally patted himself on the back for being able to sound normal. Now, if he could get his body to comply...

"My son."

Aiden's eyes widened. "Your son?" His heart climbed up into his throat, then fell to his feet.

"He's adopted, but yes. My son."

"Then you aren't married?" *Oh please let him say no.* Aiden had no idea why it mattered so much but...

Nate frowned and shook his head. "No. An IN destroyer is no place for a family. I shouldn't even have Jeremy living on the ship, but I don't really have much of a choice."

The fact that Nate didn't want a family aboard ship didn't make Aiden feel any better but he wasn't sure why he cared. He hadn't harbored any hopes that Nate would offer for him.

"Did you say someone stole your sketchscreen from the castle?" Nate's brows drew together.

"Okay, maybe not stolen, but definitely misplaced. Jeffers couldn't locate it in the castle. I'm not sure what happened to it. I brought it back with me the day I went to the docks by myself and gave it to Thomas to put in my—"

Nate turned off the screen. "You went where?" His voice was tight, strained, and it put Aiden's hackles up immediately.

"The docks, it was the day Jeffers was shut off." *The day the weapons were stolen...*

"What in the bloody hell were you thinking? You went to the docks without a chaperone? You could have been raped or murdered or Galaxy knows—"

"Lord Deverell, will you be joining us? Lord Raleigh said you might be." Christy walked toward them, Muffin on her hip. "We're going to the toy store next. It's only a few blocks over and their highnesses have decided to walk."

Aiden was relieved at the intrusion. Nate thoroughly confused him. Making himself relax his shoulders and balled up fists, he took his screen from Nate's hands. He didn't know what to think about Nate's tone. On one hand he didn't like it at all—he hated being told what to do—but on the other... Nate sounded like he was honestly concerned.

Christy turned and left them to follow.

He didn't dare look at Nate, but he felt the man staring at him. As he stepped forward, Nate touched Aiden's elbow and offered up his arm.

Hesitating only a second, Aiden looped his arm under Nate's.

Nate smiled, relieving the tension between them, and for a second Aiden thought he'd apologize for losing his temper, but he didn't.

Amazingly, Aiden was glad. Most men would have groveled and tried to backtrack to make sure they were still in Aiden's favor. But not Nate. Nate didn't make apologies for what he felt. It would have been out of character with what Aiden knew about the man. Nate had clearly been agitated at Aiden for having gone to the docks, and he had no qualms about telling Aiden. And that directness went straight through Aiden.

He held his sketchscreen against him, trying to hide his renewed erection, and allowed Nate to escort him. He felt a little shaky, but it wasn't a bad feeling, only different, kind of scary and new.

Looking over Christy's shoulder at them, Muffin pointed at Nate. "Pretty."

Aiden spoke without thought. "Yes, Muffin, very. But the word is handsome. He's very—" He stopped, aware Nate was staring at him.

Fortunately, he was saved from further embarrassment by a round of greetings from his brothers. After a summary of what hats they all bought, they exited the shop.

Walking on the sidewalk, following his siblings and chaperones, they garnered a few stares. For once, Aiden didn't mind the attention. He liked the idea of showing Nate off, letting people know Nate was with him. He'd never had anyone act as his escort, but Aiden was sure the looks were due to the big man walking to his left and not him. With Nate's arrival in town, he had suddenly become the beau of the ball. Not only was it nice that someone other than Aiden and his brothers were getting all the attention, but it was sort of neat being envied for walking with the man the ton was dying to be formally introduced to.

"I'll make you a deal. That's why I came looking for you." Nate turned his head toward Aiden as he tipped his hat to a couple of gentlemen passing them going the opposite direction.

Nate had come looking for *him*. Aiden's heart rate kicked up a notch and he got that weird fluttering in his stomach. "A deal?"

"I won't tell your parents about the tree incident or today in the hat shop, if you help me with the investigation."

"Really?" He said it a little louder than he intended, but he couldn't help it. He was excited. Nate wanted *his* help. Not only would he get to spend time with Nate, but how often was he going to get the opportunity to do something like this?

"Yes, really." Nate laughed and tugged on his arm.

Aiden hadn't even realized he'd stopped. "Throw in posing for me and you've got a deal."

"From what I've seen you don't need me to pose for you."

Maybe he could even talk the man into posing nude. And how scandalous was that? But Aiden couldn't get the sight of Nate naked on the bed touching himself out of his mind. He wanted to see it again, wanted to participate this time. The thought of it had his own prick throbbing.

Nate's arm tensed under his hand and he leaned close to Aiden's ear. "Aiden, why are you blushing?"

The question did nothing for Aiden's blush, he could actually feel the heat in his face. He tried to change the subject, hoping that would help. "Tell me about your ship. What's it like being an IN captain?"

"It's hard to describe. I wanted to have my own ship since I was a little boy. Which made me a bit odd among my peers, they all wanted to be Marines." Chuckling, he shook his head. "The Lady Anna is amazing. I still remember when she was given to me." He grinned fondly. "It was probably the best day of my life. The Lady Anna makes me proud. I worked hard to make captain, harder than I've ever worked for anything in my life. And she's a constant reminder of that. She makes me feel like I can do anything." He looked down at Aiden, still smiling. "To me, she's probably very much like your art is to you. She's my first love, I guess." Nate groaned. "That sounds strange I know, but—"

"No, not at all." It did sound like how Aiden's art felt to him. It was a part of him. Something that he would never give up. He felt a kinship to Nate, yet he also felt a bit disappointed knowing he could never compete with Nate's ship. Not that he wanted to, but if he did... It explained a lot, that boyish grin Nate got when he said "Lady Anna". Aiden grinned. "You'd never give her up, would you?"

"Not without a fight." Dipping his head toward another person passing them, Nate tipped his hat. "Look, there is a bakery. How about a lemon ice? Or something to drink?"

Aiden looked to make sure they weren't too far behind the others and nodded. "Sure."

Nate stopped and turned to him. "Stay here so that I can see you out the window. I'll be right back."

"Okay."

Aiden watched Nate open the glass door and go inside. The man had an amazing backside and those trousers were just tight enough to show off the heavy thigh muscles. He even had a naval officer's scabbard with sword on his hip, reminding Aiden of Nate's military background.

"Lord Aiden."

Having been caught ogling Nate's arse, Aiden flinched.

Lord Braxton tipped his hat, stepping close to Aiden's side. "Whatever are you doing here alone? This is no place for a young lord to be un-chaperoned." Braxton slid his hand beneath Aiden's arm and began trying to maneuver him.

Aiden's stomach dropped to his feet. Something wasn't right. Braxton didn't seem right. The man had a gleam in his eyes Aiden hadn't noticed before. His pupils were huge.

Gripping Aiden's arm so hard it hurt, Braxton crowded him with his body. All the while the man was smiling and going on about how Aiden needed a chaperone and how he'd protect him to make certain nothing happened.

Aiden dug his heels in, looking around. He didn't want to cause a scene, but Braxton wasn't getting the hint. Panic set in. When Aiden spoke it was low and not as adamant as he intended. "I'm not alone, Lord Braxton. Please, let go of—"

There was a growl, sounding like the words "hands off", and a tug on Aiden's arm as Braxton flew backward, jerking Aiden's shoulder hard. It spun him around and he nearly dropped his sketchscreen. An arm wrapped around his middle, flattening his back against solid muscle.

"I don't know who the fu—who you think you are, but you had better keep your da—your hands to yourself," Nate hissed as he nestled Aiden closer to his side.

Breathing a sigh of relief, Aiden got a better grip on his screen. Nate's nearness was comforting and the alarm that had held him in its grip earlier subsided. He turned his head toward Braxton.

He gazed at Nate, his top lip turned up slightly before he snarled. "Lord Deverell, wasn't it?"

"It was." Nate rubbed Aiden's stomach. "And you owe Prince Aiden an apology."

Aiden winced at the steely thread to Nate's tone and put his hand on top of Nate's, stopping it. He wondered if Nate even realized he was trying to soothe him.

Braxton blanched, his gaze darting to Aiden's. He reached toward Aiden. "Lord Ai—"

In a flash, Nate sidestepped with him and ushered Aiden behind him, drawing his sword.

A chorus of gasps sounded from all around them and Aiden noticed the crowd they'd attracted for the first time. Galaxy, Father and Cony were going to blame this on him.

Scoffing, Braxton backpedaled. "Forgive me, sir, but I think you are quite overreacting. I was merely seeing that Lord Aiden was properly chaperoned. A young lord should not be on the street by himself. I was going to escort him back to his party."

A loud clap of footsteps came from in front of them and Christy pushed her way through the small gathering. "Excuse me, Lord Deverell, what is going on?"

Nate nodded crisply and stepped aside. "Nothing."

Lord Braxton tipped his hat and bowed to Christy. "Now that you have arrived, madam, and Lord Aiden is once again being properly watched, I will take my leave." He walked past, then turned back, dipping his head. "Lord Aiden."

Growling, Nate took Aiden's arm and got him and Christy moving again. They walked in silence until they met up with Thomas and his brothers. He was still a little off kilter from Braxton, but Aiden couldn't deny the happiness rushing through him at Nate's actions.

"Aiden, are you all right?" Nate's face lost the tension, his gaze searching Aiden up and down.

The protective gesture made a quiver race up Aiden's spine. He smiled, trying to alleviate Nate's concern. "Yes, thank you. I—he was insistent."

"I noticed." Nate pulled him to a stop, frowning. "Listen, I have got some things I need to look into. Will you be all right with Christy and Thomas?"

Was Nate mad at him? "Sure." His unease returned, but this time it was different. He wasn't afraid of Nate. Did this mean Nate no longer wanted him?

Grabbing Aiden's hand, Nate brought it to his lips and grinned, while peering directly into Aiden's eyes. "I want the first waltz tonight at the ball." Kissing Aiden's gloved hand, he let it go. "Stay out of trouble and stay close to your chaperones."

Before Aiden could respond, Nate took the sketchscreen from him. "Just so your attention will be on your surroundings, I'll take this back to the castle for you."

Aiden stood there staring after Nate's retreating back, trying to ignore the warring feelings of excitement and disbelief crashing through him.

03

Nate pulled on his boxers and his pants before walking to the mirror. For several seconds he stared blankly, trying to come up with answers. He'd spent most of the afternoon—after nearly beating the hell out of a lord of the realm—thinking about Aiden.

Closing his eyes, he rested his forehead against the cool glass. Practically since the first day he'd come here, he'd been trying his damnedest to be good and keep his hands off Aiden.

He'd tried like hell to distance himself from Aiden, but the more he tried, the harder it got.

Seeing that horse's ass Braxton with his hands on Aiden had sent Nate into a rage like he'd never before experienced. And the day before when he'd tried teaching Aiden a lesson to scare him away? Man, had that ever blown up in Nate's face. He'd never expected the prince to show interest...to get excited. Aiden was supposed to have been appalled and run. It was supposed to have made Aiden's infatuation with him disintegrate, not make Nate's intensify.

Nate had been pissed off at seeing that pencil and thought of nothing but shocking Aiden and scaring him away...for both their sakes. Furthering their connection had never been part of the plan, but that's exactly what had happened. Nate had seen the sheer excitement play over Aiden's face as he watched and listened. Then Aiden had come and— Nate was getting hard just thinking about it.

"Hey, Hawk, you in here?" Trouble knocked on the door before opening it.

Well, that took care of his growing erection. Nate groaned and moved his head from the mirror. "Yeah." Turning on the faucet, he stuck his hands under the cool water and splashed his face.

"Ready for the daily servants' gossip? Tarren's valet and Aiden's valet are having an affair. And one of the footmen knocked up the— What's wrong with you?" Plopping himself up on the vanity, Trouble grabbed the towel from the rack next to him and handed it to Nate.

Nate took the towel and blotted his face. "I've lost my damned mind."

"I was talking about right now. You lost your mind some time ago." Grinning, Trouble pulled his feet up onto the black granite vanity top and rested his head on his knees. "What's up, Hawk?"

Turning to lean his hip against the counter, Nate looked at Trouble. "Aiden."

Trouble's brow furrowed. "Okay, can you be a little more specific? What about him?"

"I want him." Somehow saying it out loud gave it credence. He did want the man, could see building a life with him. And now that he thought about it, he couldn't see any real reason to deny himself.

"Uh..." Trouble blinked several times. "The man *is* hot, but—"

Nate reached out and flicked Trouble's ear.

"Ow. Whaaat? I'm just saying..." Glaring at Nate, Trouble dropped his feet back down and leaned against the wall, crossing his arms over his chest. "Let me finish before you go smacking me around. I was going to remind you that you told me hands off the princes. Do you really want to end up leg shackled for a roll in the hay?"

That was exactly what he wanted. Nate ran his hands down his face. *Fuck it!* He was tired of fighting it and thinking it to death. He knew what he wanted and he wasn't likely to change his mind. "Yes."

"I didn't think s— What?" Trouble's mouth fell open.

Nodding, Nate swiveled around, looking for his shirt. He'd talk to Raleigh and Steven later.

"Whoa, wait a minute, Hawk. Have you taken complete leave of your senses?" Jeremy grabbed his arm, trying to turn him.

Nate gave in and focused his attention back to his son. "Probably. But it doesn't change the fact that I've made up my mind and I've decided to keep him."

"You can't just decide to keep someone. They sort of have to agree. Besides, what the fuck are we going to do with him after we go back to the Lady Anna?"

Nate picked up his shirt. "Watch your mouth. He'll agree. And I don't know. I'll figure out something." Putting his arms into the shirt, he waited for Trouble to protest. When he didn't say anything, Nate started to get worried. It wasn't like the kid not to voice his opinion. "Trouble?"

Trouble was quiet for several minutes. He resumed pacing while Nate continued dressing. "I don't want to leave the ship. I don't care if you bring Aiden with us, but I don't want to leave the Lady Anna." Moving to face Nate, he bit his lip, his eyes practically pleading. "It's home."

Nate stopped in the middle of tucking in his shirt. He hadn't planned on it. There was no reason Aiden couldn't come with them.

Trouble nodded and resumed pacing. "Try sticking me in a boarding school and you will live to regret it."

What? Where had that come from? He'd never even considered putting the pest in a boarding school. Trouble could be a real pain sometimes, like all kids Nate supposed, but Trouble was the only family he had. Nate had raised the kid since he was nine, adopted him and made him Nate's legal heir. He couldn't love the pest any more if Trouble had been his own blood.

Focusing his attention on his surroundings, Trouble looked everywhere but at Nate. He wrung his hands and worried his bottom lip. Stopping to lean against the vanity, he turned his feet in. His left foot covered his right and he stared at his toes.

Uh-oh. Nate had always thought of that position as Trouble's insecure pose. Not a stance that showed up very often. In fact, Nate hadn't seen it in years.

"What's wrong?"

Trouble shrugged. His bottom lip quivered, even caught, as it was, by his teeth.

"Jeremy... For crying out loud you look like you did when I first met you when you stopped those boys you were hanging out with from slitting my throat." Nate grinned at the memory. He'd turned on Trouble after those kids had run off. The kid had looked so helpless and innocent, despite having just taken on a group of boys twice his size. He'd been half starved, yet he'd respected Nate's uniform, enough not to want to steal from him. Nate shook it off. It was a long time ago. Trouble wasn't the same kid anymore. He had a nice, sheltered life now. Hell, Nate spoiled the boy.

Trouble was silent for all of ten seconds, then everything came spilling out in a babble Nate could barely understand. "What if he doesn't want me around? You should have married when I was a kid and cute, now I'm not little and no one wants a grown kid, he's going to want his own kids not some orphaned bastard you picked up in a space station, I wanna stay with you. I don't wanna leave, please don't make me leave."

Whoa. Nate blinked, stunned. "Jeremy Hawkins." Nate finished tucking in his shirt and buttoned his pants as he made his way in front of his son. He lifted Trouble's chin to make him look Nate in the eye. "How could you think that?"

Trouble shrugged, turning his head away.

Taking the kid's chin in hand again, Nate made Trouble look at him. "Even if I thought Aiden was the type to have a problem with you being around—which I can't imagine—I'd never abandon you. You are my son and whatever happens nothing can change that."

Trouble worried his lip for a few more moments then nodded slowly. "'Kay. But for the record, I don't want to stay here, this planet is too stuffy." Trouble snuffled a little, then mumbled, "I love you, Dad."

Nate hugged him and patted his back. "Love you too, Son." *What a day.* He'd never been very good with this emotional crap. But he did not like seeing the pest upset. He smiled and tried to lighten the mood. "No way am I turning you loose on the galaxy yet."

"Afraid I'll take over and become some evil dictator?"

"Absolutely."

They both chuckled.

Nate ruffled the kid's hair. "Then you aren't going to freak if I marry Aiden?"

"Nah. I still think it's a little extreme for a piece of ass, but if that's what you want..."

Nate rolled his eyes and stepped back, pointing a finger at Trouble. "Watch—"

Trouble waved his hand. "My mouth, I know." He hopped back up on the counter.

After putting his shoes on, Nate went back to the mirror, found his hairbrush and ran it through his hair. He was actually excited about this ball and he wanted to look nice. It wasn't every day a man declared himself.

Chapter Ten

Aiden stared out over the crowd of military uniforms, his fingers itching to draw. The ball was being held in honor of veterans and most men in attendance were Regelence Naval officers. There were also a few Regelence Marines and three or four IN officers, including Nate.

Aiden hadn't realized Nate was attending in the capacity of an IN officer, but before leaving the castle Cony had informed them Father and Nate had gone to the ball early for The Fallen Warriors ceremony. Since then, Aiden had been dying to see Nate in uniform.

All day Aiden's mind played over the scene this afternoon and Nate's flirting with him. He didn't quite know what to make of it, but he was excited nonetheless.

"Lord Aiden, how are you this evening?"

Aiden turned to find the Duke of Keithman's second son, Christian Morris, standing next to him, all decked out in his black and silver dress uniform. Aiden bowed. "Lieutenant Commander Lord Christian."

Christian smiled and gripped Aiden's hand. "I'm sorry to disturb you." He wasn't conventionally handsome, but he was attractive in a rugged way—the Regelence Navel uniform only enhanced that. He brought to mind an avid outdoorsman, with his tanned skin and reddish-brown hair.

"You didn't. I was only watching the dancers while I wait for the next dance."

"Were you stood up?" Christian frowned. "I'd love to dance with you. It's such a shame you should have to sit out. Whoever your dance partner is, they must not be very smart giving up the chance to dance with such a fine young man."

"I've no partner for this set, but thank you for the offer. I'm catching my breath, waiting for the next one." Aiden spotted his friends Rupert and Bannon heading toward himself and Christian. Dipping his head in greeting, he realized Lord Christian was doing the same.

After pleasantries were exchanged, Bannon turned to Aiden. "Do you mind if I ask you a question?"

"No, of course not." He may not have seen Bannon for a few days, but they *were* friends. Like Aiden and Rupert, Bannon was a fellow artist.

"The gentleman staying at the castle, Lord Deverell? What is his given name?"

Aiden had no right to feel pride, but he did. "Lord Deverell's name is Nathaniel Hawkins."

The lieutenant commander smiled. "I met Captain Hawkins during my service with the IN. Surprising to find out he's an earl. The man is practically a legend. His war record is phenomenal."

"Oh yes, I've been meaning to ask you..." Rupert's grin should have warned Aiden what was to come. "What happened on Platt Street today? I've heard everything from fisticuffs to a marriage proposal."

Aiden's eyes widened. They were saying he and Nate were engaged?

Lord Casey, one of Christian's acquaintances, stepped up beside the lieutenant and answered before Aiden got the chance. "My brother says he saw you and Lord Deverell walking together this afternoon. He said Deverell called Lord Braxton out for trying to kiss you."

Good Galaxy, the gossip had made the rounds already. Aiden shook his head. "No, that wasn't it at all. It was a misunderstanding. Braxton was trying to rescue me thinking I'd lost my chaperone. And then Na—Lord Deverell rescued me from Braxton." At least according to Braxton that was the story. Aiden wasn't convinced. Braxton had seemed...different today, threatening.

"Speaking of rescues. I heard Lord Deverell rescued a Regelence ship that was under attack and in flames," Bannon stated.

"My father told me he's a mustang captain, that he was promoted the first time every time. He was one of the youngest men to make captain in IN history," Lord Casey said.

Christian nodded. "Yes, he got his commission while he was enlisted, worked his way up the ranks."

"Amazing considering he's an earl, surely his family could have easily bought him an officer's commission." Rupert touched his chest dramatically.

Aiden was fascinated. He'd already surmised that Nate was an honorable, noble man, but he had no clue that Nate had such a well-known reputation here on Regelence. Nate may not be an earl, but his rank and status as an IN captain made him more than acceptable consort material. Keeping quiet, Aiden soaked it all in. A man like Nate would never leave his career as an IN captain for marriage. It made Aiden's spirits drop a little— which was ridiculous, Aiden didn't want a consort—but he could not help but admire the man even more.

Bannon grabbed a drink off a passing tray. "Captain Fitzgerald said it was his ship Captain Hawkins saved."

Leaning close to Aiden's ear, Rupert whispered, "He's so handsome."

Aiden was about to agree when an opening formed directly in front of him, and through a chasm of people, a vision appeared.

Nate. Aiden's heart began beating so hard he was certain it could be seen through his waistcoat and evening coat. Like tunnel vision, his entire focus centered on the man walking toward him. Whispers and gasps sounded all around him, but Aiden barely heard.

Nate was covered head to toe in brilliant almost blinding white. The uniform hugged his body as he strode forward. It accentuated his powerful frame, making him seem even bigger somehow. Which was something, because Nate was a very big man. He wore gold cords over his shoulder and under his arm proclaiming him an Admiral's aide, likely the Admiral in command of Aries Fleet, the fleet in charge of protecting Regelence's system. That and the colorful ribbon bars on his chest marked him as the highest decorated officer at the ball, out of IN and Regelence officers. He was the most beautiful and masculine thing Aiden had ever seen.

Aiden would have given almost anything to have had his sketchscreen at that moment. He had to capture Nate like this. *This* was Nate. He was the embodiment of military authority and strength. He took Aiden's breath away.

When Nate finally stopped in front of him, Aiden just stared. He wanted to touch Nate, yet at the same time he was afraid to. Nate was so...perfect.

Looking up into the chestnut eyes, Aiden caught Nate's gaze. It was like the entire assembly disappeared and the two of them were alone. They stood there for several seconds, neither of them saying a word—they didn't have to. It was then that Aiden knew exactly what he wanted. He wanted Nate.

The side of Nate's mouth turned up, as if he knew, then he offered Aiden his hand.

Aiden got the distinct feeling if he grasped it he was accepting much more than a dance. Which was fine by him. He inhaled deeply and took what he wanted, seizing Nate's hand.

Arching his right brow, Nate gave Aiden a full-fledged smile. "You promised to waltz with me."

"I did indeed."

Aiden's group of friends began murmuring at once.

Bending over Aiden's hand, Nate kissed the knuckles. "Forgive me, but after seeing you tonight, I must command all three."

Aiden's hand trembled in Nate's. Surely Nate knew what he'd just done. That was akin to a proposal. No, he probably didn't. He wasn't really an earl, he was an IN captain.

Silence surrounded them, followed by whispers.

Nate squeezed his hand, his gaze never faltering.

Aiden wondered briefly what he'd do after Nate left. How would he deal with the rumors? He didn't care, he let happiness bubble inside him until he couldn't hold it back any longer. He laughed and nodded. He'd deal with Nate's leaving and the rumors of a broken engagement when it happened. "The saying is your wish is my command but tonight your command is my wish, milord. Let's dance."

Nate knew he had it bad when he found himself spending the only free moment he'd had at this ball staring at Aiden. He was getting anxious for the last waltz. It was a little Neanderthal of him, but he didn't care. Having decided Aiden was his, he wanted to make sure everyone else was aware of it. Nate took a swig of his scotch and continued to watch Aiden. He was dancing with one of the Regelence Marines Nate had met earlier. The man seemed a decent sort, but Nate was watching the marine like a...well like a Hawk. Funny, Nate had never considered himself a possessive man.

The song came to an end. The marine escorted Aiden from the dance floor where they parted ways. The marine went to the punch bowl and Aiden toward the hallway outside of the ballroom. There was a bit of a break before the waltz began, so Nate made himself relax. He knew Aiden hadn't forgotten their dance—the man had been ogling him off and on all evening. It made Nate want to drag him to the nearest dark, secluded corner.

"Enjoying yourself?" Steven strolled up beside him with a drink in hand.

"Yes, actually."

Steven leaned close. "I think we need to talk."

Nate nodded. He'd known this was coming. He should have already sought Aiden's parents out, but the entire situation had besieged him. Give him a ship of people to command and he was in his element, but throw a pretty little artist in his path, his head was spinning. "I apologize, I should have spoken to you first."

Steven's smile was radiant. "I only wanted to make certain we were of a like mind. I assume you will join me in the study tomorrow to discuss a betrothal contract?"

"Name the time." Nate took another sip of his scotch then set the glass on the tray of a passing waiter.

"Eight a.m."

"Done. But I can save you the hassle. A dowry isn't necessary."

"I like hearing that. But nevertheless, you'll get one. I want to discuss living arrangements too."

Damn. Was Steven going to give him grief about Aiden living with him on his ship? It wasn't at all unheard of in the IN for captains to bring their families aboard. No way was he going to debate this with Steven in the middle of a ball. He gave a crisp nod.

That seemed to please the king. He was quiet for several seconds then he chuckled. "Three waltzes?"

Nate smiled. "Too much?"

"No. It's a bold statement, it fits you. Besides, haven't you heard the whispers? It's wildly romantic."

"Guess that explains all the young lords sighing at me."

"No, the sighing is probably due to the uniform."

"The uniform is supposed to be intimidating."

At that moment a couple of young lords walked by, doing nothing to conceal their interested gazes.

Steven laughed and took a drink out of the glass he held.

Nate groaned. He'd gone from being fawned over by a bunch of women on his home planet because he was a duke's heir, to being sighed over by a bunch of men because he was a war hero. Well, he was being sized up for being an earl too, but these men seemed much more impressed with his military status. They hadn't been quite so demanding of his time when they thought him merely a titled gentleman.

Steven's mirth faded, his gaze thoughtful. "How is the investigation going?"

"I'm still trying to figure out how the thieves got away with it. I think if I can figure that out, it will make finding them much easier."

"Have you questioned Thomas and Christy yet?"

"I haven't."

Steven swirled the contents of his glass. "I wish I had more time to help you with this. Sometimes being king really rains meteors. I miss the times when my father and sire handled everything and Raleigh and I could play all day...take the children hunting and things like that."

His parents must have died recently if the princes were old enough to hunt. Nate knew what it was like to lose loved ones. He'd lost his mother when he was a boy and, in a sense, he'd lost his father and brother when he left Englor. "I'm sorry for your loss."

"Thank you. It was several years ago." After a few minutes, Steven took another sip of his drink and raised an ebony brow. "You will see to it Aiden is allowed to follow his dream?"

"You have my word."

Raleigh sidled up beside them. "If you hurt him, you *won't* live to regret it." It was delivered with such calm assurance that Nate had no doubt the man meant what he said. Whether he could carry it out... Nate didn't question that he would try.

Steven snorted and elbowed his spouse. "Go away, Raleigh."

"I will not." Raleigh turned toward Nate as if to say, "What do you have to say for yourself?"

Nate looked the man right in the eye, just as serious. "He will never want for anything, physically or emotionally, you have my solemn oath."

Raleigh dipped his head, acknowledging the vow for what it was. Which was apparently all the man needed because then he smiled and took the drink from Steven's hand, tossing it back. "Ah, whiskey." He raised both eyebrows. "Why are you drinking whiskey?"

Steven shrugged.

Raleigh's dark brows drew together in a frown. "You were in the card room, weren't you?"

His tawny eyes widening, Steven looked over the crowd and waved like he'd spotted a long-lost friend. "Ah, look there. Isn't that Viscount Foxglove? I haven't seen him in ages." He patted Nate's shoulder. "Enjoy your third dance. We'll talk about a betrothal contract first thing in the morning." He trotted off toward a portly, balding man, the tails of his black evening coat flapping behind him.

"Coward," Raleigh called after him before turning to Nate. "He's terrible at gambling. I don't think the man has won a hand of cards in his life." He shook his head, making the dark curls fall into his eyes. "I don't know where he thinks he's going, he promised me a dance. And that is not Foxglove, it's Stratford."

Nate fought to keep from laughing. He was beginning to see why their children were such a handful.

The beginning notes of the waltz played and Raleigh dismissed himself with a reminder that they'd talk about Aiden tomorrow.

Scanning the ballroom, Nate searched for the prince. It was awfully crowded, and Aiden was shorter than most men in attendance, but Nate didn't think the man was in the room. He studied the crowd for several more minutes and was about to hunt outside when Bannon walked past on the arm of a tall lord dressed in a green waistcoat and shocking purple evening coat, strolling toward the dance floor. Thankfully, all the Townsends had enough sense to dress in sedate colors that enhanced their good looks.

Nate blinked. *Good Galaxy*, the man's color scheme was rough on the eyes. And to top it off the dandy's outfit clashed with Bannon's fiery hair. Nate forced himself not to gawk. "Lord Bannon?"

Bannon paused, giving him a dazzling smile. "Lord Deverell." He scrutinized the area immediately around Nate and frowned. "Might you know where Aiden is? He was looking forward to this set."

"I was hoping you could tell me."

"I haven't seen him." He motioned Nate closer. When Nate did, Bannon leaned in and whispered, "He was going to the water closet, then the refreshment table." He straightened. "Perhaps I should help you find him. He was very anxious to dance with you."

Nate winked. "Go dance. I'll find him. I'm sure he's fine."

Bannon hesitated then reluctantly nodded. "Thank you, Lord Deverell."

Nate headed out of the ballroom after a quick stop by the refreshment table. The estate was huge, but the washrooms were easy to locate. They were just outside the ballroom below the main staircase. Passing several older couples and a group of younger lords on his way, Nate walked the length of the hall, checking doors.

There were several water closets since it would be improper for the young lords to be alone with other men without a chaperone. Most were empty with the door standing open. Knocking on the ones that were locked, Nate didn't recognize any of the voices that called out, "Just a moment." When he got to the last closed door about halfway down the hall, no one answered. Nate knocked again and tested the knob. It was locked and no sound came from within.

He leaned close, listening. These rooms would be perfect places for a lovers' tryst, provided both partners could get in unnoticed. There were no video cameras, microphones or heat sensors inside washrooms—it was against the law. But Aiden wasn't the type to meet someone for a rendezvous. If he were in one of the rooms he was either lost in a drawing or something was wrong.

Nate thought he heard a whimper come from inside the room, but wasn't sure because the music was too loud. Putting his ear against the door, he heard nothing. He was about to leave when the sound came again. He knocked harder and an unfamiliar breathy voice finally called out, "Occupied." Hmm, probably some lovers trying to be quiet as to not get caught. Nate turned to leave but a thud and some moans brought him up short.

He didn't know whether to force the door open or go back to the ballroom. It was probably exactly what he thought, two lovers stealing a moment, but what if it wasn't?

"Hel—" Someone yelped from inside the room and a loud crashing sound followed.

Grabbing the knob, Nate rammed his shoulder into the door. It came open instantly with only a small cracking sound.

A tall, dark-headed man jerked his attention toward the door with a smaller, limp man hanging from his arms. The man had his arm around the smaller man's neck. *Aiden.*

Howling, Nate rushed forward, punching the man directly in the nose.

Blood splattered. With a wail, the man shoved Aiden at Nate and grabbed his wounded face.

Nate caught Aiden's limp body with one arm, keeping him from hitting the floor, as the man darted past him and out the door. Lowering Aiden gently but quickly, Nate sank to the floor next to him. It was as if someone squeezed Nate's lungs in a vise. *Fuck,* he felt lightheaded, like he was going to be sick. His stomach twisted in knots and his chest ached as he searched for a pulse on Aiden's neck. This man had already become a part of Nate's life, his future. He couldn't lose Aiden now. Feeling the heartbeat under his fingers, Nate relaxed and took a deep breath.

Aiden was pallid, his lips almost bluish, but the color was coming back. Nate removed the neckcloth and tossed it aside.

Almost immediately Aiden began coughing and reaching for his throat. He bolted upright, his eyes wide and watery.

Rubbing the prince's back, Nate pulled Aiden's hands away from his throat and kissed his temple. "Shh... Calm down and take deep breaths. Relax, Aiden."

Aiden nodded and did as Nate instructed until the coughing subsided. He sat there for a few minutes, his breath still choppy and labored. Looking around the room, he appeared lost until his gaze landed on Nate. Aiden wrapped his arms around Nate and buried his head against Nate's chest.

Nate enfolded him in his arms, relief finally setting in. Closing his eyes, Nate let his head drop forward, resting his jaw against Aiden's hair, and tried to regain composure. He sat there for several minutes just holding Aiden close, feeling Aiden's warmth. Aiden was still alive. "Are you okay?"

Aiden nodded, jostling Nate's head. When he spoke it was croaky and rough, coming out as a plea. "It wasn't my fault this time. I *was* paying attention."

"Tell me what happened." Kissing Aiden's head, Nate pressed Aiden's cheek against his chest, rocking back and forth slowly.

Snuggling in, Aiden inhaled deeply, still out of breath. "He pushed in behind me and locked the door. I thought it was Payton at first so I didn't even turn around, just called him dust for brains. Then he grabbed me and started choking me."

"Did you know him?"

Aiden shook his head and pulled back to meet Nate's gaze. "I've never seen him before." Trembling softly in his arms, Aiden angled his head upward. His gaze locked on Nate's lips and Aiden licked his own. "I was scared. If you hadn't come in—"

Nate didn't even want to think about that. Aiden was his and he wasn't letting him go. Catching Aiden's face in his hands, Nate kissed him. It was rough and desperate.

Within seconds Aiden was panting for breath, but this time it wasn't from being choked. It was like the man was possessed.

Nate groaned at the arousal that spiked through him. When had he gotten hard? Sliding his hands through Aiden's hair, Nate held his head still and returned the kiss with equal passion. He understood the need all too well. Adrenaline had always been an aphrodisiac, but not like this. This was because of the young man in his arms. He couldn't deny that. There was something special about Aiden and Nate wanted to protect him for the rest of his life. This was all about assuring himself that *his* Aiden was all right.

A loud intake of breath pulled them apart.

Braxton stood in the doorway, his mouth ajar. The sounds of talking and footsteps grew louder behind him and in seconds the hall was packed with people staring into the washroom.

Abruptly, the crowd stopped and the talking ceased except for a few gasps.

Star dust, bloody hell and imploding planets. Aiden scrambled off of Nate's lap and grabbed his cravat. Nate stood and gripped his waist, steadying him.

As he tugged at the collar of his shirt, trying to cover his neck, Father appeared in the doorway. Pushing Braxton aside, the king motioned to them to follow him. "Deverell, you should probably say something before we start getting offers to stand in as our seconds."

Aiden swallowed the lump in his throat, wincing at the pain.

Clasping Aiden's hand, Nate led them out of the washroom into the crowd, behind Father.

Aiden wanted to sink into the floor when he caught sight of all the people in the hallway. To make matters worse, Cony looked like he was ready to explode.

Nate squeezed his hand tighter, then lifted it to his mouth and kissed the back of it. He bowed his head toward Father, then straightened. "Your Majesty, I'm sorry. I know you wanted to announce mine and Aiden's nuptials yourself, but under the circumstances..."

Nuptials? What? Aiden glanced up at Nate.

Nate smiled and winked.

Yep, he's definitely lost his mind.

Nate turned back toward the mass. "Aiden and I took vows as of today."

Aiden blinked, once, twice, three times. Nope, he was still here in a packed hallway holding his dream man's hand. And to make matters worse his own hands were starting to sweat. Could Nate hear his heartbeat too?

Father cleared his throat. "We were going to save the news of their marriage for the ball we were planning to celebrate this news, but since the newlyweds obviously were"—he chuckled—"acting like newlyweds... And I must admit, it's my fault, my apologies everyone, I should have never forced them to come to a soiree on their wedding night. So, if you will all excuse us, I believe we will now retire to the castle." Father grabbed Cony's hand and turned.

Giving Nate and Aiden one last look, Cony let Father lead him away.

Uh-oh. Aiden worried his bottom lip. Cony had had that tick in his jaw he got when he was mad.

People rushed around Aiden and Nate offering their congratulations, patting their backs. There were several snickers and innuendos that Aiden didn't quite catch and someone called him Earl-Consort Deverell. His surroundings were beginning to get a little fuzzy. The only thing convincing him it wasn't a dream was Nate's heat beside him, Nate's firm grip on his hand, steadying him and somehow giving him strength.

Aiden smiled and took the congratulations, never letting go of Nate. Somehow or another they made it outside and into the lift.

As soon as they got in and closed the door, Nate held his hand again and told his parents what happened. After the shock wore off and Cony called the castle ordering the security heightened and an armed escort to meet them, Cony slid across the seat and kissed his forehead. "Are you all right?"

Aiden nodded. "Thanks to Nate."

Looking up, Cony gave a quick dip of his head. "Thank you, Lord Deverell."

"You don't have to thank me." Nate squeezed Aiden's hand. "It was selfishly motivated. I protect what's mine."

The princes began murmuring at once. Father and Cony only nodded. Aiden smiled, feeling all warm and tingly. He was well on his way to being head over heels in love with this man. Taking in every nuance of Nate's expression, Aiden saw the tenderness and affection emanating from it. Scooting closer, he raised his chin, needing Nate's kiss.

Nate caught his chin, running his thumb over Aiden's lips. Shaking his head slightly, Nate whispered, "Later, boy."

Aiden melted as Nate's warm breath caressed his face. His cock was harder than stone and throbbing. He'd never felt like this before. Every time he was near Nate the feeling intensified.

Cony cleared his throat behind him.

Aiden started, realizing where they were and what he'd nearly done. He turned away from Nate, trying to get his body to behave, and caught the shocked look of his siblings. Heat raced up his cheeks. He shifted, hoping his erection wasn't obvious.

Finally, the lift stopped and Father stood. "We're here. Let's get the two of you inside. There is no time stamp on the books or consort license, only the date. If anyone checks, it will give them today's date."

"Where, Father?"

"Regelence Royal Cathedral." Father ordered the door open and everyone out. "Come along. I called ahead, the Bishop is waiting on us."

What? "No, Father, I—" Panic seized Aiden. They were going to force Nate to marry him, and then Nate would hate him and—

Nate glanced over Aiden's shoulder. "Can we have a moment?"

It was quiet for several seconds, then Cony said, "Sure. Everyone else out of the lift, please." Standing, Cony shooed everyone toward the door.

"That means you too, Raleigh." Father reached back inside the coach and caught Cony's arm, tugging him out when he would have stayed.

Cony was still grumbling when the lift door closed behind him.

Cocking a brow at him, Nate smiled.

Aiden's stomach felt queasy. They didn't have a choice. He couldn't decide if it was nerves from Nate smiling at him, or due to the fact that he was facing a marriage ceremony. One he wanted, but nevertheless it was a mistake. Nate was an IN captain, he had to go back to his ship.

Nate touched his cheek gently.

He nuzzled into the touch, loving the feel of the warm, calloused palm on his skin. "I'm sorry, Nate. You rescued me and this is how you're repaid..."

Leaning forward, Nate brushed his lips softly across Aiden's. Nate pulled him onto his lap, his erection pressing against Aiden's hip.

Relaxing into the kiss, Aiden opened his mouth, tangling his own tongue with Nate's. He wanted more, he needed Nate's hands on him, caressing him. Trailing his hands down Nate's chest, Aiden marveled at the hard muscle and heat. He wanted to feel that ring again, wanted Nate's cock in his hand.

Nate leaned back, catching Aiden's hands in his before they reached their goal. "Easy, boy. We both have to go out there in a minute."

Aiden dropped his head forward, resting his forehead on Nate's shoulder. He willed his prick to behave and his heart to stop pounding.

Tears welled up in Aiden's eyes, making him blink rapidly. He lifted his head, catching Nate's gaze. "I'm sorr—"

The door opened and Father stuck his head inside. "Let's go. There will be plenty of time for that later."

Brushing his thumb across Aiden's cheekbone, Nate swiped at the tear dripping down his face. "Shh..."

Chapter Eleven

What the fuck am I going to do now? Nate ran his hands through his hair and let them drop to his side. The sudden realization that Aiden was now his scared the shit out of him. And he wasn't quite sure how to deal with it. He hadn't felt like this in years. Not since he left home.

With trembling hands, Nate unbuttoned his jacket and tossed it on the chair in front of the fireplace. He needed something to do while he waited for Aiden. Having time to think was making him a wreck. Nate chuckled without humor. Half the IN would be busting a gut right now, watching the infamous hard-ass Captain Hawk fret over getting married.

It hadn't seemed like a big deal before. He got Aiden, which is exactly what he wanted. But now what? Aiden was probably going to want kids eventually and...*fuck*. Nate had no idea how to be a father. He and Trouble were different. Trouble had been much older when Nate adopted him.

Taking off his belt, he headed through the master bedroom door. He sat on the edge of the bed and wiped his sweaty hands on his pants. His heart was racing so fast it felt like he'd gone for a run. Why did the thought of kids worry him so much? No, no, it wasn't just that. The thought of trying to work Aiden into his life was scary. Aiden needed a home and a stable environment—he should have a nice big home with a studio to be able to do his art. And there was no way in hell Nate could take him away from his family. Nate missed his own family. He couldn't in good conscience take Aiden from his, but what choice did he have? He couldn't just up and retire, not until his current commission was up in a little under a year.

Seeing Trouble nearly killed last week had made him realize that an IN destroyer was no place for children. He should have retired as soon as he was able after he'd adopted the kid.

The door leading from the valet chamber opened and shut, Trouble came in bitching about something, but Nate didn't look up. He had to make this right. He needed to start providing for his family, more than just financially. He had—

"*Dust*, Hawk. Couldn't you have waited until I could be there?" Trouble squatted in front of him, grabbing Nate's knees and looking up at him. "You, uh, upset?" Trouble cocked his head. Trying to read Nate's mood, Nate supposed.

"Have I been a good father to you?"

Trouble's eyes widened, his mouth opening, then closing. "What? What's wrong, Nate?" Trouble got on his knees, scooting closer. "You're a great father."

Nate took a deep breath, watching the concern play over Trouble's face. Damn, he hadn't meant to do that. He was supposed to calm Trouble's fears, he was the parent, he— Grabbing Trouble, he pulled him into a hug. "I'm sorry. And I'm sorry you weren't at the wedding. Someone tried to kill Aiden tonight and things got messed up. I'd planned on taking more time, getting us all used to the idea." Nate moved back, looking into Trouble's worried aquamarine eyes. "I'm...scared, Jeremy. It just hit me. I don't know how to be a husband or a father. I found you, dragged you onboard and you were just part of my life. I should have given you a home instead of a ship full of sailors. You deserve better than me." Nate's eyes blurred with tears. *Fuck.* He used the back of his hand to brush them away.

Trouble launched himself at Nate, making Nate rock back. He had no choice but to catch Trouble and hug him.

Shaking his head, Trouble bumped Nate's face. "That's not true. You are a wonderful father. If it weren't for you—" His voice cracked a little. "You're a hard-ass, but your kids will never doubt that you love them. I never have. I love you, Dad."

"I love you too, Son." Nate hugged the kid tighter. He was going to do his damnedest to make a good home for not just Aiden but Trouble too. He had to go back to the Lady Anna for now, but as soon as he could, he'd give his family a home. He didn't want to leave Aiden here, but he wanted him in danger even less than he wanted to keep Aiden with him. Hell, for that matter maybe he should leave Trouble here with Aiden but he couldn't do that. Not to Trouble and not to Aiden. Trouble had a fear of abandonment—he could only imagine what it would do to the kid. He had raised Trouble to handle himself so that the ship was less of a danger to him, but he couldn't in good conscience expect Aiden to live on a ship.

All these changes were still a damned scary thought, but he felt better now. Now that he knew who he was doing it for. His family was worth it.

Sitting back on his heels, Trouble dabbed at his eyes and punched Nate in the arm. "Aiden is lucky to have you as a husband. I can only hope I'll find a husband as great as you will be."

"I hope so."

Trouble sniffed and blinked. "Damn it, Hawk, this is twice now with the touchy-feely crap. I hate this shit."

Chuckling, Nate blinked too and wiped his eyes. "Watch your mouth, Trouble." He ruffled the blond locks. "Thank you. You're a good son."

Trouble shrugged, looking around at everything but Nate. The kid never had been very good at shows of affection. Hell, Nate wasn't either for that matter.

Nate considered telling Trouble what he planned, but he didn't think he was up for another emotional display at the moment. Fuck, he didn't want to leave Aiden, even for a year.

"Wish they would have waited for me to be there."

"Yeah, me too." It had felt odd without the kid there, but there was nothing he could do about it now.

Scrunching his face a little, Trouble grinned. "It's a nice room, though. Did you notice there are fireplaces in every room, even the bathing room?"

"I saw that." It *was* a nice room with dark, masculine colors and very cozy furnishings. The whole suite was essentially two suites joined by a sitting room. Which was pointless in his opinion. He had every intention of sharing a bed with Aiden. They only needed one bedroom. "You want the other bedroom?"

Trouble hopped up, grinning ear to ear. "Heck, yeah." He slugged Nate in the arm again as he got up and wandered around.

Nate stood and stretched. Nate hadn't looked over the room before, he'd been too busy lost in his own fears. The bedroom was romantic, with its heavy burgundy curtains on the window and bed. Aiden's pale skin would look heavenly against the velvet coverlet.

Trouble had crawled across the bed and was fiddling with something a few inches above the headboard. He held his hand under what looked like a spigot and a glop of clear liquid dropped into his hand. "Oh wow. It's automatic and heated."

What the... Nate snatched Trouble's hand, dipping his own finger in the goo. *Lubricant.* That was neat. Bringing it to his nose, he sniffed. It smelled like vanilla. He touched it to his tongue. Tasted like vanilla too.

Trouble wiped the rest of the lube on his pants. "I want one of those in my room."

Nate rolled his eyes. He didn't want to think about lube right now. That would lead to thinking about sex, which would make him think of Aiden and... "Where in the hell is Aiden?" Nate walked around the room and debated pouring himself a scotch. Shouldn't he be there by now? Frowning, Nate crossed to the door, intent on going across the suite to the bedroom they'd given Aiden.

"He's not in there."

Nate turned. "Where is he?"

"Raleigh and Steven's suite. There was some mention amongst the servants of a wedding tradition, but according to gossip Raleigh doesn't like it, so no one knows if it will happen or not. No one seemed to know if you'd insist on it or not. I kept my mouth shut."

Nate lifted a brow. "Wedding tradition?"

"Uh-huh." Trouble laid back, stretching out on the bed, and wiggled his slipper-clad feet. "I wonder if I'll ever get married. You know I never really considered it before, but now..."

Sometimes Nate was positive the kid changed subjects just to annoy him. "Trouble."

"Whaaat? I'm just saying..." He held his hands up, all wide-eyed innocence.

"Wedding tradition?"

"Oh, yeah, that. Now, that is absolutely fascinating. Apparently, it's customary for the young lords to be fit with a butt plug before sending him to his new consort on the night of their nuptials. To get them ready as it were. But it's generally the best man who does this, and since Aiden's best man was his sire... Well, that's kinda gross, and—"

"What? That's terrible."

"Terrible?" Trouble shook his head. "Are you kidding me? That is neat as hell." Then under his breath he murmured, "I want a plug."

Nate groaned and walked back around the bed. Those idiots were going to ruin his wedding night. "Take me to the king's suites." He pulled his son up by the arms, practically dragging him out of the room. No way was he letting them do that to Aiden. It was Nate's privilege to teach Aiden such things, if Aiden wanted to know about them, not theirs. What were they thinking? Nate growled.

"Hey, Hawk, wait. Why are we going there?"

"To rescue Aiden. Lead the way."

Jeremy frowned, but he kept walking. "You're going to deprive the man of a plug?" He tsked. "You're so insensitive sometimes."

Nate gave him a pointed look. "Would you want something being shoved up your ass *without* your permission to be your first sexual experience?"

"Okay, okay, you're right. Follow me." Trouble picked up his pace, leading Nate through the hall and up a set of stairs.

They made several turns, but Nate recognized their destination when they arrived because the three younger Townsend siblings were crowded around the door with their ears pressed to it.

J.L. Langley

Nate stopped, motioning for Trouble to be quiet, watching them for a minute.

Tarren groaned and straightened. "I can't hear a thing."

"Me either," Colton complained.

Payton shook his head. "The door must be soundproof. Maybe if we sneak into the—"

Nate put his hands on his hips, striving for intimidating, even though he was highly amused. "Ahem."

They all jumped.

"Ack." Tarren was the first to respond.

"We, uh..." Payton pointed at the door. "Uh..."

Colton grabbed his brothers by the arms. "We were leaving."

The three of them fled without ever looking back.

Trouble cocked his head, watching the three of them scurry away. He finally let out a long whistle. "I hate that they left, but watching them go was nice."

Nate stifled his mirth and elbowed him. "Go back to our room."

"Oof." Jeremy frowned at him, then walked away. "You're always smacking me around."

A chuckle sounded from behind him, making Nate turn.

Steven strolled up the hall, smiling. "Thanks for running the boys off. What brings you here?"

"A rescue attempt."

One of Steven's ebony brows lifted, a smirk on his face. "Rescue, huh?"

Heat suffused Nate's face.

Steven laughed and pushed the door open just in time for them to hear Raleigh say, "Remember to use lots of lube and watch your teeth."

Nate nearly groaned. Good Galaxy, the thought of Aiden having a reason to be aware of his teeth and use lube. His cock twitched, threatening to harden again.

Steven chuckled. "That's the best you could come up with?"

Raleigh arched a brow. "I don't see you in here trying to talk to him."

Nate met Aiden's gaze.

Aiden beamed at him, his gray eyes twinkling. He took Nate's breath away and put his libido into hyperdrive. Raleigh and Steven continued to talk, but Nate tuned them out. He was standing in front of Aiden holding his hand out, before he even realized he'd done so.

"Hi." Aiden clasped his hand and stood. His hand was warm and perfect, with long elegant fingers. The hand of an artist.

"Hi, yourself. I came to make sure everything was all right."

The hand not in his touched his chest as Aiden stepped closer. "Thank Galaxy. Think we can sneak out without them noticing?"

Nate sure hoped so, because he was now sporting another hard-on. "We can try. I only have one small problem." Well, two if he counted his sex drive.

Aiden blinked. "What's that?"

"I don't know if I can remember how to get back to my new—our new suite."

Chuckling, Aiden tugged on his hand. "Come on, I know the way."

They were almost to the door when Raleigh stopped them. "And just where do you two think you're going?"

Nate turned, but didn't let go of Aiden's hand. "To our room. I hope the wedding tradition wasn't followed here."

Raleigh glowered. "You're damned right it wasn't. As far as I'm concerned that custom will never be performed under my roof."

Steven gave Nate an exasperated look that spoke volumes. "Thanks for reminding him, Nate." Steven threw his hands in the air and let them fall.

The look Raleigh turned on Steven would have felled a weaker man, but Steven just sighed and flopped down on the spot Aiden had vacated. "It was twenty-two years ago, Raleigh, how many times do I have to tell you I had no idea they were going to do that?" While the king-consort's attention was focused on him, Steven waved the newlyweds on, silently mouthing the word, "Go."

Without hesitation, Nate hurried out, pulling Aiden with him. No way was he going to stick around and listen to the two of them hash it out. He had a virgin to debauch.

Aiden wrinkled his nose. "Tradition? What tradition?"

"Oh, this is going to be interesting." Nate chuckled, squeezing his hand. "Trust me, boy, you'll find out later."

They walked most of the way in silence. Aiden kept an eye on where they were going but felt Nate watching him.

Aiden couldn't decide whether to be nervous or thrilled with the attention. He was a little of both. This had to be the strangest, most confusing night of his life. Someone had tried to kill him. He was now married. It was like a dream or a nightmare, he couldn't decide which. On one hand he could now give into his desires for Nate, and he would have his freedom when Nate went back to the IN, yet he couldn't help but feel it wasn't as good a deal as he first thought.

"Are you all right?" Nate stopped as they neared their door.

"Yes."

Opening the door, Nate stepped aside, motioning for Aiden to continue into the room. Once inside, Nate took Aiden's hand and escorted him to the bedroom.

When they reached the bed, Nate loosened Aiden's cravat. Tossing it away, he caught Aiden's chin and turned his head from one side to the other.

Nate narrowed his eyes and his fingers touched Aiden's neck. "The bruises are darker." Nate's jaw ticked. "I should have killed that guy when I had the chance, but I was anxious to get to you and make sure you were alive. Are you sore?"

He was having problems breathing, but it wasn't due to being strangled. Aiden nodded.

"Good." Nate brushed a quick kiss across his lips. "I've been dying to get your clothes off since I first met you. Strip, boy."

Swallowing the lump in his throat, Aiden tried to relax as Nate sat on the edge of the bed. The thought of baring himself had his prick hard. "You have?"

"Hell, yes." Nate leaned back on his elbows, his gaze on Aiden.

The uneasiness tried to creep to the surface, but Aiden pushed it back and fumbled for the buttons on his waistcoat. He was nervous, but he was excited too. In no time, he had it and his shirt off. After unbuttoning his trousers, he remembered his shoes. Kicking them loose, he bent and took off the hose.

Catching Nate's gaze, he hooked his thumbs through the waistband of both the trousers and his short pants, pulling them down. His prick bobbed free, leaving a wet spot on his lower belly below his navel, as he stood and stepped free of the fabric. *Please let Nate like what he sees.*

Nate lounged there for several seconds, a predatory gleam in his eyes. "Damn, I knew you'd be beautiful." He offered his hand to Aiden as he sat.

Exhaling the breath he'd been holding, Aiden took Nate's hand and let him draw Aiden closer and position him astride Nate's lap. He moaned at the starched fabric rubbing the backs of his thighs and his arse cheeks. Being naked while Nate was still mostly dressed felt deliciously naughty.

"Fuck, boy." Nate traced his sides, his back and finally cupped his arse, pulling him forward.

"Oh." His cock brushed against Nate and he pushed closer, trying to get more friction. Knowing Nate wanted him as badly as he wanted Nate was taking care of his anxiety of the unknown.

"So damned hot." Gaze roaming everywhere, Nate touched Aiden's chest. He flipped the pebbled nipples with his thumbs then pinched, making Aiden ache and moan again.

From the very beginning Nate had stirred something in him. And hearing Nate calling out his name the other day while he touched himself made the sensation even more intense. Aiden craved Nate. He longed for all the things Nate could teach him, do to him and with him. The man was an addiction which got worse with everything Aiden learned.

Slipping his hands around Aiden's hips, Nate grabbed Aiden's arse cheeks and kissed Aiden's lips. "You make me want, Aiden." Trailing down Aiden's jaw, Nate nuzzled his neck.

Goose bumps spread like wildfire over Aiden's arms and back. As if the feel of Nate's beard on his skin wasn't enough to send his senses reeling, Nate raked his teeth over the spot where Aiden's neck met his shoulder.

Aiden groaned and shuddered. His prick throbbed, leaking precome. He kissed Nate's beard, his neck, anywhere he could reach. He loved what Nate was doing but he wanted to touch too, he wanted to make Nate feel as good as he was making Aiden feel.

Dragging his hands over the hard body, Aiden found Nate's prick. The memory of that heavy gold ring taunted Aiden, making him desperate to examine it closer. He barely got his fingers around Nate's cock because of the pants and the thickness.

"Open my pants, boy," Nate rasped against Aiden's neck before kissing his shoulder and touching his arsehole.

Aiden froze.

Doing it again, Nate licked a long line up Aiden's neck. Nate's other hand slipped further back, caressing the ridge between his testicles and his anus, while he continued to circle Aiden's hole.

It felt strange. He'd never been touched there before. It tickled, yet not quite.

Undoing Nate's pants while Nate was doing that wasn't easy, but eventually he did and got one hand inside and around Nate's hot prick. Finding the ring with the other hand, he pulled back a little so he could see.

Nate was hard, his foreskin already retracted and the ring clearly visible. Aiden ran his fingers over it, then tugged gently as he squeezed Nate's shaft. The smooth metal was such a neat contrast to warm velvety skin.

"Oh, shit, boy."

Aiden whimpered, a thrill going through him as he continued to play with the ring. "I like that."

"Like what?"

"When you call me boy and how you curse when you get excited."

One side of Nate's mouth turned up, his eyes flashing. He tapped Aiden's hip. "Up. Get your ass in the middle of the bed, boy."

Crawling off Nate's lap, Aiden laid down in the middle of the mattress. As soon as he moved, Nate stood and undressed. Aiden gasped. He'd seen Nate naked before, but it was still a feast for the eyes. He was so muscular and hairy.

The firelight cast shadows over Nate's tanned skin. His shoulder and arm muscles flexed as he moved. It was hypnotizing. He made Aiden's mouth water and at the same time gave him butterflies. Fear and lust competed within, but before he could work up too much apprehension, Nate positioned himself next to Aiden. His warmth and nearness was comforting, erasing Aiden's doubts.

"Damn, baby, the way you look at me." Nate lay on his side with his head propped on his hand. He dragged Aiden so close their skin brushed, the hair on Nate's body caressing his skin.

His cock touched Nate's and Aiden bucked, mashing them closer together. Aiden ran his fingers over Nate's beard, along his throat and chest.

Grabbing Aiden's top leg, Nate positioned it over his hip. He leaned forward and devoured Aiden's mouth at the same time, his tongue pressing and stabbing between Aiden's lips.

Aiden moaned and stroked Nate's hip. Working his hand further down, he wrapped it around Nate's cock, stroking. The foreskin slid over the ring and Nate made a rumbling sound in his throat.

Nate's fingers rubbed Aiden's hole again, making him push back into the touch. Abruptly, the finger disappeared and Nate reached over their heads. Seconds later the finger was back, circling Aiden's hole with a slippery warm substance. It felt good until Nate pushed inside.

Aiden gasped, breaking their kiss. It stung enough to make his erection soften.

"Shh... It's okay. Relax. Let me in, boy."

Taking a deep breath, Aiden forced the tension to recede, trusting Nate. He concentrated on what he was doing, trying to ignore the foreign feeling. Stroking Nate's cock, his fingers brushed the ring. He caught the ring, moving it back and forth, but was still aware of the digit inside him.

"So fucking tight," Nate growled and took his mouth again.

The finger in his ass still felt strange, but it no longer hurt. Aiden was beginning to have a tough time concentrating on Nate's prick. His attention was divided between discovering the unknown of his consort's body and feeling the new sensations Nate wrung from him.

Moving his finger deeper, Nate hit something.

Aiden's eyes widened, his balls drawing closer to his body, and his cock got harder, fully erect again.

Pulling back, Nate smiled. "That's it, boy. So fucking hot. Just relax and feel."

Nodding, Aiden loosened his grip on Nate's cock as Nate rolled him to his back and leaned over him.

Nate devoured Aiden's mouth, making his head swim and his heart beat faster. In no time, Aiden's prick was once again dripping.

Aiden was so caught up in the kiss that when another finger joined the first, he didn't even tense. The burn came again, but he knew what to expect and when Nate hit that place inside him, it disappeared entirely. Another finger followed quickly after.

Aiden moaned as Nate pressed further in. It felt so good. Lifting his hips, he pushed down on the fingers in his arse.

"That's it, boy. You like that?"

He nodded. "Yes, oh yes."

Nate moved then, positioning himself on his knees between Aiden's legs. Thrusting his fingers in and out, Nate groaned and his eyes met Aiden's. "Ready for my cock? Want my big prick in this tight little hole, boy?"

His belly clenched and a whimper escaped. The thought of Nate's prick in his arse had his own cock throbbing.

"You're going to love it. Going to beg me to fuck you."

"Please..." Aiden lifted his knees, his hands tangling in the covers. The constant rhythm of Nate's fingers, the heat in his eyes, it was too much. Aiden tried to stop it but he couldn't. His back arched, his muscles tensing. And with a shout he came without so much as a hand touching his cock. Heat splashed on his stomach.

Nate practically purred, pulling his fingers free, and reached above Aiden's head again.

Before Aiden's body even stopped convulsing, Nate pushed into him. It was wider, more intense than his fingers, but it wasn't painful. He closed his eyes, the reality of it hitting him. Nate's cock was in his arse.

"Open your eyes, boy."

Aiden blinked his eyes open as Nate moved slowly forward. There wasn't any friction, only the stretching as the head made its way inside. Aiden swore he could feel every inch sliding further in, until the ring hit— "Oh! Nate. Please." His cock jerked, still filled with blood.

Staring into his eyes, Nate grabbed his legs under the knees and looped them over his arms. "Please what? Tell me."

Aiden stared into Nate's eyes, panting for breath. It suddenly occurred to him that he still had his hands twisted in the comforter and there was a cooling puddle on his stomach, running down his side. But he didn't care. He tried to shift his hips, wanting to feel that again.

Nate held him in place. "Say it. Tell me what you want."

Biting his bottom lip, he squeezed his eyes shut then opened them. He needed Nate to move. His entire body was on fire, begging for release, even after having climaxed. He took a deep breath and said it, knowing exactly what words were going to get him what he wanted. "Fuck me, please."

Nate growled and thrust. He pounded into Aiden without hesitation. The whole time he held Aiden's gaze. Sweat dripped down his temples and a fine sheen covered his chest, shining in the firelight when he moved.

Soon Aiden was teetering on the edge again, his whole body screaming for release. "Nate."

Nate thrust into him harder a few more times then stopped. A hoarse groan left his throat and he tensed.

No. No, not yet. He was so close. Aiden did his best to propel Nate's cock into him. He was almost there, just a little more. He grunted, trying to move, but Nate held perfectly still. "More, Nate. I don't want it to end. Please." His head thrashed back and forth. "Please."

Nate's chest heaved as he took a deep breath. Nate set his legs down and dropped on to one hand, his face close to Aiden's. Sweat dripped, mingling with the semen coating Aiden's belly and chest. Nate's beard and mustache tickled his ear. "Shh... It doesn't have to." He moved slowly forward as his tongue probed Aiden's mouth.

Turning his head to catch his breath, Aiden panted. His whole body tensed, fighting for his release. He was going to lose his mind. All the nerves in his body tingled, reaching for sensation, anything to bring him over the edge. He couldn't think, all he could do was feel.

Nate's hot breath fanned across his cheek, over his neck and then pain flared through his shoulder as Nate bit down.

Aiden jerked. A tingle raced through his spine as Nate's tongue caressed his skin.

"Come on, boy. Come for me again. Now."

A warm gush filled him and Nate sighed above him. He could almost— His eyes widened in shock. "Nate, oh fuck, Nate!" It felt like every one of his muscles contracted at once, and pleasure assailed him. White lights danced behind his eyes and Aiden came, shaking violently.

Nate's hand came up, brushing the sweaty hair off his face. "That's it, boy. Give yourself to me."

Chapter Twelve

Aiden lay there, his eyes closed, with semen trickling down his sides as his abdomen rose and fell. His body was thoroughly sated, but now his mind was in turmoil.

What if he couldn't handle what Nate wanted from him? That had been intense. He'd loved it, but... What if he wasn't enough for Nate? When this mission was over Nate would leave and go back to his ship. What then?

Nate kissed him one last time then got off the bed. "You still alive?"

Nodding, Aiden licked his dry lips. He opened his eyes and turned his head toward Nate. Seeing the handsome man he'd married somehow made him feel worse. He was going to miss Nate when he was gone. How often would he come back to Regelence? Did Aiden even want him to? Maybe it would be best if they just parted ways. Something told Aiden it was going to get harder and harder to let Nate go.

"You're dripping, boy." As he held Aiden's gaze he bent over and rubbed his beard through the cum on Aiden's belly, sopping up some of the mess.

Hissing out a breath, Aiden tensed, his head coming off the bed. He reached down, raking his fingers through Nate's beard. For all his refined manners in public, the man had very little in private. It was extremely arousing. Groaning, Aiden dropped his head, fingers still combing Nate's wet whiskers.

Kissing Aiden's belly, Nate swiped his tongue over it, tasting. He stood, patting Aiden's hip. "Stay there. I'll be right back."

"'Kay."

Nate went to the washroom.

Aiden lay on top of the covers, arms and legs thrown out. He was getting a headache. He was mourning Nate's loss before the man even left. It was a waste of time. He'd wanted this. Granted, he hadn't really thought it out. If he had he might not have been so anxious, but he'd made the decision and now he would live with it. He should be enjoying the time he had. It was an experience he'd probably never get again. Or if he did it would be for short intervals over the years.

Lost in thought, Aiden started when Nate came back in and slid his arms underneath Aiden, lifting him. Nate held tight and went to the washroom.

Willing his heart to quit pounding, Aiden smiled and wrapped his arms around Nate's neck. He was going to stop worrying and deal with Nate's absence when it happened.

Nate carried him to the tub and climbed in. The big, black marble tub was plenty big enough for both of them. Nate turned him, pulling Aiden between his legs and pressing Aiden's back against his chest. Aiden closed his eyes, enjoying the feel of naked skin against his own and the warm, relaxing water.

Nate's lips trailed over the back of his neck as he ran a soapy hand over Aiden's cheek. "Boy, how do you feel? Are you sore?"

Aiden shook his head. He was aware of his body, but it didn't hurt—it was a nice reminder of what they'd done. He'd never dreamed that physical intimacy would be so intense.
190

Something told him it wouldn't be that way with just anyone. He and Nate had a connection. *If only that were enough.* Aiden snuggled back into Nate's chest. He promised himself he wasn't going to fret.

Turning a little, Nate caught Aiden's chin, lifting it. He smiled and kissed Aiden's lips. The look he gave Aiden, the tenderness in his eyes, was nearly Aiden's undoing. He wanted to cry and beg for Nate to stay with him, but he couldn't. Nate would never respect such a show of weakness. And Nate did respect him, he had no doubt about that. Nate's actions spoke volumes. He may be rough and domineering, but he was considerate and gentle at times too. Nate cared what Aiden thought and about what he did. He brushed his lips across Aiden's one more time before letting go.

Aiden settled back against his lover, caressing Nate's arms where they wrapped around him. Closing his eyes once more, he stayed there reveling in the feel of the strong arms around him and the thick masculine chest against his back.

Finally, Nate reached for the sponge on the side of the tub, his hairy chest touching Aiden's skin. Nate took his time washing Aiden, exploring his body.

It was exhilarating and soothing at the same time. Aiden felt cherished, pampered. He could go right to sleep if he wanted. There wasn't a single doubt in his mind that Nate would take care of him. What was it about this man?

They lay there quietly for several minutes while Nate's hands roamed over him, washing and loving. Nate's prick began to harden against his back and just like that, Aiden's body responded in kind. He no longer wanted to fall asleep. He wanted to spend as much time with Nate as he could.

Turning, he straddled Nate's legs so he could look at him. He was such a handsome and virile man. Nate was tough. He made Aiden feel protected, yet he made him want to be able to fight at his side and make him proud as well. Cupping Nate's cheeks in his hands, Aiden pressed his lips to Nate's. The whiskers on Nate's face tickled and caressed his own face, making him remember the feel of it on his neck when Nate thrust into him. Aiden moaned, his cock jerking against Nate's belly.

Grabbing his ass, Nate hauled Aiden up against him. With his hands gripping each ass cheek, Nate pulled Aiden closer, making their pricks slide together.

Aiden groaned and moved on his own. The water sloshed, threatening to spill out of the tub, but he didn't care. The only thing that mattered was making certain Nate knew how much Aiden wanted him, how much he'd miss him.

"Whoa, slow down, boy." Nate pressed Aiden against him, not allowing him to move.

He loved the way Nate called him boy. It made him feel special. But even still he had to fight the urge to groan. His body was aching for attention. He didn't want to stop.

Nate used one hand to slide up Aiden's back and force his head down on Nate's shoulder, while the other moved into Aiden's crease. Nate pushed one finger inside his hole.

"Ahh..." Aiden was still loose from earlier and turned-on. There was only the feeling of pleasure.

"That's it, boy, just be still." Nate thrust his finger in and out a few times before inserting another. His beard rubbed Aiden's shoulder as he nibbled and laved Aiden's neck. Nate continued to fuck him with his fingers shallowly.

Aiden couldn't seem to help himself. He pushed back, wanting those fingers deeper. They ended up practically laying down in the tub, with only their heads above water. Aiden rocked back on Nate's fingers, then forward, mashing their pricks together. His breath huffed across Nate's face accompanied by small grunts and moans. But it was to no avail, he was learning quickly that Nate did things at his own pace. He decided when and how much.

Stopping, Nate pulled his fingers from Aiden's arse and sat up, taking Aiden with him. "Come on, boy. We're going back to bed before we end up drowning each other."

Blinking at him, Aiden frowned a little, but he stood and climbed out of the water. He handed Nate a towel from the rack and reached for the other.

"Jeffers, are the servants done changing the bedding and straightening the room?" Nate stopped Aiden, using the towel to dry Aiden.

"Yes, milord."

Aiden closed his eyes, taking pleasure in the way Nate cherished and massaged Aiden's muscles beneath the towel. Nate showed him how special he was without words. Aiden knew Nate was as anxious to get to the bedroom as he was, but Nate took his time. When he was done, he draped the towel over Aiden's shoulders and retrieved the other and dried himself. "To bed, boy."

Aiden practically ran to the bedroom. Nate smiled and shook his head, following at a slower pace.

His boy was gorgeous, that tight little body, the firm muscles. "No nightshirts from now on, boy."

Watching Nate's every move, Aiden nodded. With his gaze focused on Nate's cock, he licked his lips. "Yes."

Damn. Nate's prick jerked. He was dying to feel that sweet mouth on him. Tossing his towel away, Nate joined him on the mattress. As soon as he was in the bed, Aiden pounced, landing on top of him. He attacked Nate's mouth, kissing him, and ground his hot, hard cock against Nate's thigh. Nate laughed and pulled back. He rolled them over so that Aiden was on the bottom and pinned his hands next to his head. "Slow down."

"Please."

He bit down on Aiden's shoulder, the one he'd marked earlier.

Aiden practically purred, his back arching a bit.

For a few minutes Nate nibbled on his neck, licking and sucking, before making himself stop. He pushed up and off Aiden and sat with his back against the headboard. The boy was making him crazy.

Crawling between his legs, Aiden peered up at him, then his eyes flicked down to Nate's cock. "Nate?"

Nate groaned and reached for him, pulling him closer. "Oh hell yes. Suck me." Grabbing his dick, Nate held it toward Aiden's full lips.

Aiden tentatively flicked the heavy gold ring with his tongue, his hand wrapped around the base of Nate's cock over Nate's hand. He did it again a few more times, then took just the very tip of Nate's cock into his mouth, flicking and stabbing his tongue at the ring.

Every nerve ending in Nate's body screamed out. He stroked Aiden's cheek with the back of his fingers, feeling so overwhelmed he thought he'd explode. It wasn't the most skilled blowjob he'd ever had, but the connection he shared with Aiden made it the best. Dropping his hand, Nate let go of himself and Aiden's cheek before leaning back to watch.

It wasn't long before Aiden caught the ring between his teeth and tugged a little. Aiden was obsessed with the Prince Albert. He kept pulling back and looking at it.

It was nice, but Nate wanted more. "Boy, quit playing." Nate spread his legs further apart and cupped the back of Aiden's neck, leading his head down toward his balls. "Lick."

The gray eyes widened as Aiden's mouth slipped down further on Nate's dick, licking. He squeezed Nate's prick in his hand and turned his head sideways, running his lips along the base of Nate's shaft. He played there too. Then he stopped, looking up at Nate. "What should I call you?"

Damned if Nate's cock didn't jerk. He'd been so afraid he'd pushed too hard. He knew Aiden was having some doubts, but that made some of Nate's own misgivings disappear. And it was sexy as hell. "You can call me sir, boy."

Aiden smiled, his tongue flicking out to swipe Nate's balls again. He drove Nate crazy, laving and sucking. Moving down, he nuzzled his face into Nate's balls, licking behind them, his tongue caressing.

Nate growled, his balls drawing tighter. *Fuck, that felt good.* "Boy, get up here and suck my cock."

Aiden lifted his head, his cheeks shiny with saliva, his eyes heavy lidded. "Yes, sir." He brought Nate's cock to him and covered it with his mouth. He couldn't seem to help himself, his tongue went right to the ring, but pretty soon he began to go further down and sucked on the way up. It was awkward to begin with, but quickly enough he started getting braver and going farther down. He pulled back, gagging the first several times, the ring tickling the back of his throat, no doubt, but he kept going back for more.

Tangling his fingers in Aiden's hair, Nate maneuvered his head, thrusting up a little. "That's it, boy. Use your teeth."

Holding Nate's gaze, Aiden dragged his teeth up Nate's cock, then nibbled and chewed at the foreskin. Aiden moaned and sucked him in again. Spit dripped down his chin and over

Nate's balls. He began using his hand, pumping it up and down as he sucked.

Nate planted his feet on the bed, moving his hips, fucking his boy's mouth.

Aiden took it all, feeding him little moans and grunts along with the wet sucking sounds.

It wasn't long before Nate's whole body felt like it was on fire. His balls were so tight, his cock incredibly hard. His ass and thigh muscles contracted. "Fuck, boy." He grabbed a handful of Aiden's hair with one hand and his shaft with the other. Pulling Aiden off his dick, he came.

Spunk hit Aiden's smooth pale cheeks, his chin, his nose and lips. It was one of the hottest things Nate had seen in a long time. Aiden blinked, his tongue darting out to clean his lips.

Nate groaned and sat forward. He caught Aiden's face in his hands and tugged him to his knees. Slanting his mouth over Aiden's, he kissed him hard and deep before stopping to lick the semen from his face.

Shivering, Aiden's leaking prick jerked against Nate's stomach. *Oh hell yeah.* Nate groaned and maneuvered Aiden on to his back. He kissed his way down Aiden's chest. Now it was his turn to drive his boy insane with lust. When he got to the red swollen tip of Aiden's cock, he slowly engulfed it between his lips, feeling it slide over his tongue and into the back of his throat. He swallowed, his throat constricting around the head.

Aiden moaned, his thighs contracting.

"You like that?"

Nodding, Aiden practically whimpered.

Doing it again, Nate varied his technique, trying to discover what Aiden liked. He caressed with his tongue, probing at the slit. He sucked hard, then backed off using his teeth. "Do you like that, boy?"

Again Aiden nodded.

Turning his head to the side, Nate ran his mouth up, then back down. He tongued Aiden's balls. "Do you—"

Aiden's head came off the mattress. "Sir?"

Nate arched a brow.

"Just shut up and suck my cock."

଼ଃ

Something jostled Aiden out of sleep. He didn't have to pee and his stomach wasn't growling. How long had he been asleep? Was it morning? Aiden listened for a minute before opening his eyes. The crackle and pop of wood burning in the fireplace nearly drowned out everything else. Even so, he could barely discern a clock ticking. The sheets rustled faintly as Nate moved, bumping his side. *Mmm... Nate.* Warring emotions rose up inside him again, but he pushed them away.

Cracking open an eye, he turned his head, looking for Nate. He rolled over, or tried to, but there was a heavy arm draped over his middle. His stomach fluttered and his already hard cock jerked, begging that he wake Nate to play. He groaned. Just a day and he'd become a wanton.

Ignoring his prick, he lifted Nate's arm and sat up. What was that tapping sound? He didn't see anything. They were cosseted in the bed with the side curtains pulled. Light radiated from the fireplace, casting shadows on the canopy.

"Hawk? Hawk, let me in. Jeffers won't listen to me."

Aiden frowned. The voice and knocking came from the sitting room that connected the suite. "Jeffers, unlock the door and open it please."

"Yes, Lord Aiden," Jeffers answered immediately and the door clicked and opened.

A handsome young blond practically fell inside the room. He stumbled several steps before righting himself. He spotted Aiden and waved. "Oh, hi."

"Hello."

Nate grumbled something inaudible and rolled onto his side. He reached out with his arm again and wrapped it around Aiden's thighs, nuzzling his face into Aiden's hip, making a smacking sound.

The closeness of Nate's face to his groin made the memory of the night before come rushing back. Nate's lips around him, sucking. Aiden pulled his knees up, making the covers tent over him, and turned his attention back to the boy. "Are you Nate's valet?"

"I'm...Jeremy." The last word came out hesitant.

Aiden frowned. "Nate's son?" Why hadn't Nate told him his son was here on Regelence?

"Yes. You know about me?" Jeremy's gaze darted to Nate's sleeping form.

Nodding, Aiden tried to calm the unease inside him. He felt almost betrayed that he hadn't known Nate's son was here. Jeremy obviously knew about Aiden. It brought back his importance in Nate's life with alarming clarity. Aiden's heart sank. "I thought you were still on Nate's ship."

"Nope. I'm here. Well, I'm sort of here. No one realizes I'm me. I'm posing as Hawk's valet."

"Why do you call him Hawk?"

"'Cause his last name is Hawkins. I've always called him that." Jeremy shrugged and held up what appeared to be a newly starched cravat. "Listen, I'm starving, do you know how to tie this damn thing?"

Nate groaned, rolling onto his back. "Watch your mouth, Trouble."

Starting at Nate's voice, Aiden looked down. "You call him Trouble?"

"Trust me, it will become obvious why in no time." Nate pushed himself up and kissed Aiden's lips. Nate crooked his fingers at Trouble. "Come have a seat, Trouble."

Jeremy padded over and crawled up onto the foot of the bed. Crossing his feet over his legs, he sat, looking at everything but Aiden.

For the first time, Aiden noticed that Jeremy, or Trouble as Nate referred to him, was fully dressed except for the cravat. Aiden felt like an outsider, but it wasn't the kid's fault. Holding out his hand, Aiden smiled. "Nice to meet you, Trouble. I hope you will forgive us for having the marriage ceremony without you."

Trouble's mouth dropped open, and he looked at Nate then back at Aiden. Finally, he shook Aiden's hand. "Nice to meet you too, Aiden."

Nate tugged his arm, pulling Aiden into his chest, and kissed his forehead. He whispered the words, "Thank you," against Aiden's skin.

Aiden burrowed closer, feeling a little better.

"Ahem."

They turned, looking at Jeremy, still hanging on to one another.

"I came in here for a reason."

Nate groaned. "What?"

Trouble grinned, showing off even white teeth, and held out the cravat. "I need you to tie this so I can go downstairs and get something to eat."

Nate motioned for Jeremy to come closer. "Bring us some while you're at it."

Trouble crawled forward, perching on his knees in front of Nate.

Taking the neckcloth, Nate proceeded to tie it in an intricate knot.

It was very impressive. Aiden couldn't tie a cravat. "How did you learn to do that?"

Nate's long fingers slid on the white linen, reminding Aiden of what else those fingers were capable of. Heat filled his lap, his prick stirring again. Following the bare muscular arms to the burly chest, Aiden licked his lips.

"I had a valet show me when I was younger."

So? Aiden's brow furrowed. "I have one now and *I* can't do that."

"If you want, I'll teach you the next time I try to teach Trouble again." Nate finished, patting the cloth, then leaned back. "Trouble, bring us some breakfast back with you, please."

Trouble immediately started tugging at the cravat. "I'm a fake valet, not a fake butler."

Nate knocked the kid's hands away. "Stop it. You're going to mess it up. And it's a footman who brings the food, not the butler."

Growling, Trouble hopped off the bed out of Nate's reach and tugged on the neckcloth again. "Well, I'm not a fake footman either."

"Trouble..." Nate grumbled.

Aiden bit his lip to keep from laughing. Nate was right, the nickname Trouble fit this kid to a T. It amazed Aiden that the kid was brave enough to back talk Nate. He imagined even grown men were reluctant to cross Nate.

Nate chuckled and threw his pillow at him.

Laughing, Trouble tossed the pillow back. "Fine."

Aiden laughed too. He liked seeing this playful side of Nate. The contrast of the commanding naughty sailor in bed and the attentive lover and...well father, was intriguing, sexy. It gave Aiden hope that maybe Nate would eventually decide to retire and stay here with Aiden.

As soon as Trouble left, Aiden reached behind Nate's neck and pulled his head down for a kiss. He sealed his lips to Nate, his tongue probing.

Moaning, Nate opened for Aiden. His hand clutched Aiden's shoulders. Slowly he kissed down Aiden's neck and just as he got there, he stopped and pulled back.

Tracing Aiden's neck with his fingers, Nate growled. "Aiden?" Nate tugged him forward, making him straddle his lap.

Aiden's cock jerked at the contact and he leaned in, flicking his tongue over Nate's lips, his fingers playing with the hair on Nate's face. "Huh?"

Nate made a low rumbling sound deep in his throat and clutched Aiden's shoulders. "Can you draw the man who attacked you last night?"

Chapter Thirteen

Aiden lay on his stomach with his feet curled over his back in the middle of the bed. His pencil flew over the paper with sure, even strokes. Every now and then he'd stop, his head tilting to the side. He'd make a hmm sound then grunt and go right back to sketching. The passion and intensity was astounding and arousing in the extreme.

It had to be one of the sexiest things Nate had ever seen. It shouldn't have been erotic at all, but it was, and damned if Nate's dick wasn't hard. He groaned and adjusted himself again before pacing back around the other side of the bed.

Sadly, his arousal went completely unnoticed. Hell, he wasn't even sure Aiden realized he was still in the room as caught up in his work as Aiden was. Nate was tempted to make his presence known, but this was important. They needed to find out who and why someone had tried to murder Aiden.

Nate dragged his attention from the sweet little linen-clad ass and the constantly moving bare feet above it. He'd never seen anyone as deeply immersed in their work. He could certainly see why Aiden's parents were concerned about his safety if Aiden was always like this, but Nate still didn't understand their ultimatum. It didn't matter now, but why didn't they just assign him a guard to follow him around and watch after him while he concentrated on his art? The man was an artistic genius. Nate was probably a tad partial, but—he took another peek of the sketch Aiden was working on—no, it wasn't his bias, Aiden *was* amazing.

It astonished Nate the detail Aiden was able to recall and add into the picture. He couldn't possibly have seen the attacker for very long—he claimed to have only glimpsed the assailant in the mirror as he was being choked—but he had specifics down that most people would have missed. Nate had noticed Aiden studying things before, but he had no idea the extent of his observation skills. Aiden had included minute things, like a faint scar at the corner of the man's left eye and a freckle on the side of his nose. Nate hadn't taken note of either of those things, but looking at the drawing, the thug appeared exactly as he remembered. *Incredible.*

Aiden sat, dropping his pencil. "Done." He stretched his arms in the air and tilted to each side. "Nate?"

"Here."

Turning his head, Aiden smiled, his face softening from the intense expression he'd worn while working. "Oh." He motioned toward the paper, then held out his hand to Nate. "What do you think? Is it how you remember him?"

Nate took his hand and sat on the bed behind Aiden. Wrapping his arms around Aiden, Nate pressed his face into the back of Aiden's bare neck and inhaled his scent. "Mmm..."

Aiden laughed, reaching up and running his fingers over Nate's beard. Last night and this morning, Aiden had kept stroking his beard and mustache, trying to tangle his fingers in it. Nate didn't think he even realized he did it. Not that he was complaining. He liked Aiden touching him.

Resting his chin on Aiden's shoulder, he glanced at the sketch again and the hair on the back of his arms stood up.

Even in black and white it looked very lifelike. The sketch was both beautiful for all the skill put into producing it and horrible for its likeness to the person it represented. Nate felt as though he could wrap his hands around the man's throat and choke the life from him just as he'd tried to do to Aiden. The reminder took some of the edge off Nate's desire. His hand moved up to Aiden's throat, rubbing absently. He hugged Aiden tighter with the other arm. "You are unbelievable."

Turning his head, Aiden smiled and kissed his cheek. "Thank you."

Oh, he still liked that, the self-confidence. It was every bit as sexy as Aiden drawing. "Why did you do this on paper?"

Aiden shrugged, jostling him. "I can't find any of my screens."

"Any? How many do you have?" That didn't sound right to Nate. Had it been anything else he might have considered that Aiden misplaced it, but not his art.

"Three. A large, a medium and a small one." Aiden shook his head, bumping Nate. He touched the side of Nate's face and began playing with his beard again. "Actually, I have four if you count the new large screen I bought yesterday to replace the other one that was stolen."

Grabbing Aiden's waist, Nate turned him so he could see him better. "Maybe they're still in your old room?"

"Hmm..." Aiden began fiddling with Nate's mustache. "No, the trunk I keep them is in the other bedroom, the one Trouble is using. That's where I found that." He pointed to the sketchbook. "My paints, charcoals and easel are still there."

Nate frowned, catching Aiden's hand to still it. "Does this happen a lot?"

"No never." Aiden's eyebrows pulled together and he began running his thumb over Nate's fingers. "The first time was the day the weapons were stolen."

It was too strange to be a coincidence.

Apparently, Aiden came to the same conclusion. Still looking at Nate, he bit his bottom lip. "Jeffers, are any of my screens in the castle?"

"No, milord."

"Who took them from the castle, Jeffers?" Nate asked.

"I do not know, Lord Deverell. I did not see them leave, I only sensed them."

"What?" How the hell was that possible? Nate frowned. "That doesn't make any—"

Aiden nodded and squeezed his hand, bouncing a little. "Yes, it makes perfect sense. After Rupert dropped his screen a couple of years back without updating his data on Myron—his house butler—he lost all his sketches. No way was I going to end up in the same predicament. So I instructed Jeffers to update my files whenever one of my screens left or came into the castle. If Jeffers can't see them he wouldn't know who took them, but he knows when they cross a threshold leading outside and he can download information from them until they exit the gates."

Then all of Aiden's sketches were saved in Jeffers' memory. Nate grabbed Aiden's hand and the sketchbook. "Come on, we need to look at your drawings." He suspected they were about to find not only Aiden's attacker but who stole the weapons.

It never occurred to Nate that they were both barefoot and missing cravats and waistcoats until they got to Raleigh and Steven's hallway. He should have realized they weren't going downstairs. "Why are we here?"

Aiden raised his hand to knock on his parents' door. "Because the access screen in Cony's private study is larger than the one in the library."

Wonderful. They were half naked—by Regelence standards anyway—and judging from the looks Raleigh gave him last night, Raleigh already thought Nate was taking advantage of Aiden.

"Father? Cony?" Aiden knocked on the door.

The door flew open. Raleigh immediately started fussing over Aiden. He was dressed much the same way Nate and Aiden were, with his shirt un-tucked and no cravat. "Aiden, are you—"

"We need to access Jeffers from your study, Cony." Aiden pushed right past his sire and waved at Steven without breaking stride. "Hello, Father."

"Hello, Son."

Raleigh caught sight of Nate, his eyes widening. "Nate? What's going on?"

Nate and Raleigh watched Aiden round the corner into a room in the suite as Steven came to the door. "Nate."

"Steven." Shrugging, Nate handed Raleigh the sketch pad and followed his consort. "That's the man who attacked Aiden."

Raleigh scrutinized the sketch.

The private study looked more like a command center. There was no actual desk, only chairs and a huge screen along one wall. Nate felt like he'd just stepped into a war room. It was all very high tech and didn't fit with the rest of the castle.

Aiden was already standing in front of the display barking out orders. After a few seconds, he turned around. Spotting Nate, Aiden grinned. "Do you want to see all of the sketches before the weapons were stolen?"

He stepped up behind Aiden, still taking in the room. "No. Start with the ones you did on that day, then we'll go back if we need to." He wrapped his arms around Aiden's waist, pulling Aiden flush against him, and looked at the display panel.

The picture changed, going through sketches of the docks. They were all very nice. Once again Nate was awed by Aiden's talent. Nate kissed Aiden's ear and whispered, "These are good."

Aiden reached up, his hand absently going to Nate's beard. "Thank you."

"What are you two doing?" Raleigh demanded.

They turned their heads to find Raleigh standing in the doorway, his hands on his hips, scowling at them. In his hand was the sketchbook Nate had given him.

Steven came through the door behind Raleigh, his attention on the screen. He pointed. "There. Stop." He rushed forward, standing next to Aiden and Nate. "Look at that."

On the monitor was a sketch of the weapon crates being loaded onto a Cargo Hydro-Space Craft.

ᘓ

Aiden closed his eyes and rested his head on Nate's shoulder. Riding in a lift hadn't made him sleepy in years. But then he'd never spent all night making love either. "What was your childhood like?"

Touching his cheek, Nate held Aiden's head against his shoulder. "Probably a lot like yours, actually." Nate's voice was soothing, relaxing.

It was nice being able to spend time alone with him during the day, even if they were on a mission of sorts. "Really?"

"Yes, really. I was raised on Englor. It's very similar to Regelence."

Englor? It was another Regency planet, he remembered that from his schooling. Did that mean— "Are you really an earl?"

"Earl of Deverell." Nate turned sideways in the seat, resting his back against the side, and pulled Aiden in between his legs. "And heir to the Duke of Hawthorne." Wrapping his arms around Aiden's waist, Nate nuzzled his neck.

Oh, that felt good. Aiden closed his eyes and relaxed. He loved Nate's beard. Loved just being near Nate.

Aiden's eyes flew open, and he turned his head slightly. "You're heir to a dukedom?" That meant Nate had known what their society would think of them dancing three waltzes together. But why would he do that?

"Not anymore. I was disowned."

"Why?"

"Why?" Nate settled Aiden back against him. "I killed my father's best friend's heir in a duel." He said it very matter-of-factly, but Aiden wasn't fooled. There was a story here.

Nate tightened his grip on Aiden's waist and kissed his cheek. "Daniel's fiancée accused me of compromising her. I tried to go talk him out of the duel. When he wouldn't listen, I decided to shoot over his shoulder, but he shot first and clipped my arm as I pulled the trigger."

"But you didn't compromise her." Nate was way too honorable for that.

"No, I didn't. I caught her leaving a rendezvous in the garden at a ball. I'd heard her saying goodbye to her lover right before I rounded the hedge. She wasn't about to let me go, knowing I'd overheard that. She ran to Daniel and said I attacked her."

What a witch. Aiden touched Nate's cheek, where it rested beside his, and combed his fingers through the hair. "Why didn't you tell him the truth anyway?"

Practically purring, Nate leaned into his touch. "I didn't have an alibi. Or rather I didn't have one I could share. I was with Daniel's younger brother."

Aiden didn't like the idea of Nate with another man. Which was utterly ridiculous, it was in the past...and probably their future too. Aiden frowned, really not liking that idea because he was beginning to think of Nate as his and he didn't like sharing.

"Englor does not approve of same-sex relationships. It's not illegal, but it's not acceptable either. Had it been only myself to consider I'd have told the truth, but Presley was my friend and I was not going to jeopardize him."

That didn't surprise Aiden one bit that Nate had sacrificed himself to protect someone else. It seemed to be a habit with him. It's what made him such a wonderful captain. Aiden had heard numerous accountings of Nate's bravery and altruism at the military ball.

Aiden turned to face Nate, straddling Nate's thighs. Catching Nate's face in his palms, Aiden kissed him. "I'm sorry you lost your family over it."

"So am I, Aiden, so am I."

"Did you have a large family?"

He shook his head. "No, only me, my younger brother Jared and my father. My mother died when I was young."

There was a longing to his voice when he spoke. Aiden's heart ached for him. He couldn't imagine not having his parents and brothers even if they were pains in the neck sometimes. "You have me now, if that helps. And Trouble."

Nate's eyes flashed, his demeanor changing to one of certainty in an instant.

The look almost made Aiden feel treasured. Mashing his mouth against Nate's, he controlled the kiss all of a second before Nate made a growling sound and took over.

Nate plunged his tongue into Aiden's mouth, finding his. Wrapping his fingers in Aiden's hair, he tilted his head back.

The tingle in Aiden's scalp went right through him, making his prick fill. He loved how demanding Nate was, how he always took over. It made him feel desirable, like Nate needed him. It seemed as though Nate was out of control to have him, but Aiden knew it was an illusion. Nate was very in control. Everything he did was designed to drive Aiden crazy. And it worked. Aiden couldn't get enough of him. Being the center of such concentrated attention was becoming a craving.

Tugging on Aiden's hair, Nate broke the kiss. He nipped Aiden's jaw, his other hand sliding to cup Aiden's arse. "Boy, you have horrible timing, you know that? We're almost at the docks."

Aiden whimpered. *Oh Galaxy*, his cock was so hard, it was throbbing. He loved how Nate's voice got deeper and rumbled with passion. It made his body tingle, gave him goose bumps. He tried to scoot his hips forward to rub against Nate.

Nate nipped his jaw again. "Raise up."

"Sir?"

Nate's face softened and he took Aiden's lips in a brief kiss. "Lift up on your knees for a second."

Hurrying to comply, Aiden moved his arse off Nate's legs. He didn't know what Nate had in mind, but he sure wanted to find out.

Unfastening Aiden's trousers, Nate slipped his hands inside the back of them. He grabbed Aiden's arse, pulling him forward, and kissed him.

Fingers slid over Aiden's crease, his hole. "Mmm..." Nate's hands on him, anywhere, was a sensual delight. Nate had such big, strong, calloused hands.

Moving one hand from Aiden's arse, Nate pushed a finger into Aiden's mouth. "Suck, boy. Get it good and wet."

A shiver raced along Aiden's spine at the realization of what Nate intended to do. His arsehole clenched and relaxed. He sucked, gathering saliva in his mouth.

Nate moaned, his lips going to Aiden's jawline. His tongue traced down and then up behind Aiden's ear, wringing another tremor from Aiden. Nate drew his finger out and worked his hand into the back of Aiden's pants.

A wet fingertip rubbed over his hole before pressing inside. Aiden groaned, his cock jerking. It was strange for only a second then his whole body relaxed. It felt very good.

Pushing his finger in and pulling back out, Nate teased. He did it again, barely touching Aiden's prostate.

"Oh." Shuddering, Aiden closed his eyes and dipped his head backward. He would have never thought he'd like such a thing. Clutching Nate's shoulders, he tried to move, to impale himself. He should be embarrassed at his own actions, but he wasn't. He wanted Nate so badly, wanted Nate to fuck him instead of using his finger. Aiden whimpered. "Please..."

Nate rubbed his gland several times before taking his finger out and tapping Aiden's lips with it.

Aiden engulfed the digit. A warm rich slightly bitter taste filled his mouth and it occurred to Aiden what he'd done. He should have been horrified, but instead his balls drew tighter, his belly tensed. *Oh.*

"You like that, boy? Like the taste? I'm going to eat this sweet little ass out, tonight. You're going to love the feel of my tongue fucking your ass."

Aiden shuddered at the thought of Nate's face buried between his cheeks. The things the man said to him. His cock got even harder.

A second finger forged into his mouth. Nate's tongue circled Aiden's ear as he wet the fingers.

Sliding them free of Aiden's mouth, Nate bit Aiden's earlobe. Not hard enough to hurt, but enough to distract Aiden when both fingers pressed into his arse. Going deep, they nudged his gland. Over and over, Nate stroked relentlessly as he kissed Aiden deeply, sharing the flavor. "Mmm, you like my fingers in your ass, boy?"

Moaning, Aiden tried to thrust down and his eyes flew open. His hole squeezed Nate's fingers. He was close, his prick leaking, just a little—

Nate pulled out. "Un-uh, no coming. You have to wait until later." Pushing the two digits he'd used into Aiden's mouth again, he groaned.

No, no, no. Aiden sucked greedily, hoping to entice Nate to continue. Dust, the things Nate did to him, made him want. Aiden moaned. "Fuck me, please."

Nate moved his fingers, sliding them over Aiden's cheek, and ground his mouth into Aiden's. He kissed him deep and hard, ravishing his mouth. "Oh fuck, boy."

Aiden squeezed his eyes shut, resting his forehead against Nate's. Why did this man make him so out of control with need? He'd always been a bit of a hedonist, it was the artist in him, he supposed. But this trust and passion that flared between them surprised even him. And oddly, as new and almost scary as it was, he didn't want it to ever stop.

Nate tucked Aiden's shirt back in and buttoned up his pants. "We've got to go. The lift stopped several minutes ago."

Panting for breath, Aiden tried to ignore the need for release. Knowing this was only a postponement, he stood.

Nate stood too and immediately adjusted himself.

Good. Aiden was glad he wasn't the only one suffering. "Are you sure you don't want to stay here a little while longer?"

"Behave, boy." The fondness and sexy growl in Nate's tone made it less of a chastisement and more of a plea. "C'mon. We have a ship to find. If it's in port, we shouldn't have any problem identifying it." Nate exited the lift and waited for Aiden to join him before ordering the door closed.

That much was true, he'd had the details down so well that he'd even gotten the "Property of the IN" on the side of the crates. Unfortunately, the ship numbers had been on the other side and he hadn't gotten them. Jeffers hadn't found the attacker in any of the crew lists of the ships in port either. Therefore, he and Nate were taking a trip to the docks to see if they could locate the freighter.

Aiden reached for Nate's right hand, trying to get his mind on business.

Shaking his head, Nate stepped around Aiden and took his hand. "Left side. We're at the docks."

Aiden must have looked as confused as he felt, because Nate chuckled. "I'm right handed. If I need my sword in a hurry..."

"Ah." That was a good point. Aiden sure could have used a sword when he was here last time. "I want a sword."

"You don't have one?"

"No." They walked down the small slope between buildings to a wood pier. "Unmarried men don't carry swords."

Aiden stared in awe as they got closer to the ships. They were huge. Much bigger than they'd seemed up on the cliff. And the smell. He was right, it was much worse closer to the water.

"Can you use one?" Nate jerked his arm, making Aiden slam into his side.

"Oof."

A sailor rushed by, a barrel over his shoulder. "Wotch out, guv."

He'd have run over Aiden if Nate hadn't pulled him out of the way. Aiden turned to watch the sailor hurry past. Man, this place was much busier than it had seemed from above. Everyone seemed to be running about. And it was loud, with people shouting out orders. It was all very interesting.

"Aiden?" Nate squeezed his hand.

"Huh?" He looked back at Nate. "Oh! Yes, swords. I can use them. It was part of my schooling. I'm proficient in several firearms as well. But they can only be used for sport on Regelence so I'd need a sword to carry instead of a fragger." His gaze drifted to the other side, past Nate. The buildings were dingy and rough, like they'd seen better days. The atmosphere itself was dull and gray. There was no green anywhere, unless you considered the murky greenish water. Yet the place was teeming with life.

Nate chuckled. "I asked if you were all right."

Aiden nodded. "Yes, just taking everything in." He sure wished he had a screen right about now. Normally, this setting would have made him uncomfortable. He was definitely out of his element, but he also had Nate. And he had no doubt Nate would keep him safe. Likely walking close to Nate would deter most people from messing with him.

This was different than watching from above. Here in the midst of things he could see better. He could feel what it was like. It was much more real down here. Even his skin felt different, clammy. The air was thicker, harsher. Capturing this on screen would allow others to experience it too.

Squeezing his hand again, Nate laughed. "You should see your face. And the answer is no you cannot stop and sketch."

Turning toward Nate, Aiden laughed. "Am I that transparent?"

"Yes."

Aiden smiled. Nate didn't seem to mind one bit that he was in "artist mode". Nate liked that part of him too. Amazing really, no one else did, it annoyed most people. He bumped his head into Nate's arm, chuckling. How had he gotten this lucky?

They continued down the pier, listening to the boards squeak and clack beneath their feet, silently enjoying each other's company. At least Aiden did. It felt right to hold Nate's hand and walk beside him, sharing the experience with him.

Nate jostled his hand, getting his attention. "Aiden, look in front of us."

Turning his head away from a pair of squawking seagulls fighting over a fish, Aiden spotted the ship. His stomach plummeted to his feet and jumped for joy at the same time. He'd half expected not to find it today. "Do you see the numbers or a name yet?"

"Not yet."

Aiden inspected the Cargo Hydro-Space Craft from top to bottom and side to side, trying to burn the details into his brain, and he knew Nate was doing the same. It didn't look like the other ships. It was much nicer, newer. He hadn't noticed that before. Or maybe he had, but seeing it next to some of the other ships, up close, made it very apparent.

As they approached the ship, Nate hailed a passing sailor. "What's the name of this ship? Do you know if she takes on passengers? Where can I find the captain?"

The man shook his head. "That there is the bloomin' Marchioness, guv. Ain't she a beaut? Far as me knows, she's a cargo ship now, guv. At's 'er cap'n there." The man pointed.

Nate tightened his grip on Aiden's hand and jerked him in between two stacks of wooden crates right next to them. He pushed Aiden against the wall of crates, grabbed Aiden's shoulders and shoved him to his knees.

What the—?

"Suck, boy. I did not pay you good money not to have your mouth doing something besides flapping." Nate spoke loudly, unhooking the placket of his trousers.

Oww. His knees. Aiden frowned up at him. What in the Galaxy was he doing? "I—"

Nate's prick smacked his cheek. The sound seemed much louder than it should have from the feel of it. "Don't make me punish you, boy. Do you know what I do with naughty little boys who don't do as they're told? You want to be stripped bare and tied up in my dungeon? Want me to whip the insolence out of you, boy?" Nate wasn't even hard.

Despite their location and the fact that he was certain Nate had just lost his mind, Aiden's prick hardened right up. The ring peeked out from the foreskin, glimmering in the light, and made his mouth water. He leaned forward, taking Nate all the way in. Being careful, he sucked, pulling the foreskin.

When Nate grunted, there was a little hitch in the sound like he was surprised. His fingers threaded through Aiden's hair, hesitating slightly before clenching.

The feel of Nate hardening in his mouth was amazing. Aiden used his tongue, running it around the head underneath the foreskin. He found the ring with his teeth and tugged gently. In no time Nate was fully erect. Aiden's own cock jerked. "Mmm..."

Relaxing his throat, he took more in. He liked the way Nate felt sliding over his tongue. The ring that had caused him to gag the night before felt like a part of Nate to him now. Holding the base of Nate's cock, Aiden held it down and really got to work. He wanted Nate's pleasure. Wanted to taste it. He did everything he knew Nate liked, really throwing himself into the moment, forgetting everything but Nate and how Nate made him feel.

In no time, Nate was groaning and fucking his face. Aiden was so turned-on his own prick was leaking. He was very close to an orgasm himself.

Suddenly, Nate thrust into his mouth hard and stilled, his thighs tensing. The tangy taste of Nate filled his mouth and just like that, Aiden came too. He closed his eyes, resting his forehead on Nate's abdomen. Cleaning Nate's prick, Aiden inhaled the masculine smells of sex and sweat found in Nate's pubic hair.

Stiffening again, Nate grabbed Aiden's face in his hands.

Glancing up, Aiden realized Nate wasn't even paying attention. He was staring out of the alleyway.

Aiden turned his head, letting Nate's cock slip from his mouth. Nate turned him back, mashing his head against Nate's hip, but not before Aiden saw the man who'd attacked him the night before walk by.

Chapter Fourteen

They had a name. *Halle-fucking-luiah.* Nate sat in front of the computer feeling much better than he had when he and Aiden left for the docks. He was afraid the ship wouldn't be in port. Not only had they found the ship, but they found Aiden's attacker, Felix Chapman. "Jeffers, search the port guards' records for a ship by the name of The Marchioness."

Aiden stuck his head around the door. "Nate?"

He smiled. Just the sight of the man made him happy. How fucked was that? He'd only left Aiden in the dining room a few minutes ago. "Yes?"

"Want company?"

"Yours? Always."

Aiden smiled and came into the room, empty-handed.

Nate frowned. He knew damned good and well after the trip to the docks his boy was itching to get everything he'd seen immortalized in art. *Damn.* He'd forgotten someone had stolen Aiden's screens again. They were going to have to find out who. Not only did it piss him off that someone was taking them from Aiden, but whoever it was had a hand in Aiden being attacked.

"Find anything yet?"

"Not yet. Jeffers is looking for the ship info now." Pushing himself back from the desk, he patted his thigh. "Is Thomas here?"

"Yes, everyone went to a ball. I imagine Thomas is in his room or playing cards with some of the other servants or something. Why?"

"I was going to have him go buy you some new screens."

Aiden kissed his cheek. "Thank you, but the art store is closed. I've already asked Thomas to go first thing tomorrow morning. Besides, I have several sketchbooks upstairs. I came to help you." Turning toward the computer, he cocked his head. "Although I shouldn't. Once you solve the crime, you'll go back to your ship." Aiden frowned, intently studying the screen. "Hmm..."

Nate ignored the comment. He didn't want to think about leaving, not when he had Aiden here, in his lap. He fought the urge to suck on Aiden's earlobe and looked at the monitor. There was a list of the dates and times The Marchioness was in the bay of Pruluce harbor, as well as a list of the ship's cargo. The weapons were not on the list.

"The port guards are in on it."

"Not necessarily." Wrapping his arms around Aiden's waist, Nate read through the list again and found the date the weapons were stolen.

Aiden scoffed and pointed at the screen before turning to look at Nate. "Why doesn't it say weapons? Aren't they supposed to search the cargo?"

"Technically yes, but I imagine if they were really busy, as they appeared to be from your sketches, it might get overlooked, especially if they were paid. Happens all the time. Doesn't mean they are necessarily guilty of anything but expediency versus greed."

"We need better commerce laws."

Nate chuckled. "Are you going to lobby for them?"

Aiden groaned. "Good Galaxy, no. I'm actually thankful you aren't a Regelence lord, so I don't have to sit in parliament. I've much better things to do. I'll mention it to my father, but that is the extent to how involved I want to be in politics, thank you very much."

Aiden looked so horrified at the idea, Nate laughed harder. "What if the government starts encroaching on your rights?"

"Then I'll make a political statement with my work and get the public riled. Don't underestimate the power of art."

Apparently, he'd thought this out. Nate was impressed. "You do realize your own family is head of the government?"

Aiden grinned, and his eyes practically twinkled. "Oh yes, that makes it even better. I know their weaknesses. My father is easily swayed by gore."

Nate raised a brow. "Oh? How exactly did you find this out?"

"I painted a lovely piece for the dining room in celebration of liver." Aiden shook his head and sighed. "Father didn't like it. What a shame too, it was such a lovely representation of the inside of a slaughterhouse. And I thought the dead bloodied cows looked peaceful..." He shrugged. "Everyone's an art critic."

Nate started laughing before Aiden even finished talking. He laughed so hard his sides hurt and he had tears in his eyes. "Remind me not to piss you off."

Aiden kissed his lips and stood, chuckling. "Just don't try to make me eat liver. I'm going upstairs. You coming?"

Wiping the tears from his eyes, Nate shook his head. "No, I need to call the admiral. I'll be there shortly." He would have loved to see that. They got along so well together, Nate had nearly forgotten how defiant Aiden could be.

"Okay, I'll draw until you come up."

Aiden turned to leave and Nate caught his hand and tugged. "I'll be up as soon as I check in with Admiral Jenkins."

Aiden looked like he wanted to say something but he didn't. Nodding, Aiden squeezed Nate's hand and left.

Resting his head on the desk, Nate sighed. He would rather follow his spouse upstairs. *Work first.* "Jeffers, can you get Admiral Carl Jenkins for me? He's on Regelence Space Station."

"Yes, milord."

Nate sat with his elbows resting on the desk and waited. It wasn't long before Carl came on the screen.

"Hawk, how's it going? I trust you've settled in and gotten things moving with the investigation?"

"It's going good, Carl. The investigation is going a little slowly, but I've got some leads to check out."

"Do you have some information for me?"

"I do, yes. And I have a favor to ask. I need you to check someone for me. I need you to look into a man named Felix Chapman. I'll have Jeffers send you the sketch Aiden did of the man. Regelence only logs criminals and registered voters. Apparently, Felix Chapman is neither." Nate would investigate the ship more tomorrow.

"Done." Carl nodded. "Anything else? I bet you're anxious to get back to the Lady Anna."

Nate was surprised to find that he wasn't. He'd decided to stay here and he had no regrets, but he'd expected to miss the ship, miss his life as an IN captain. He smiled at his old friend. "I married Prince Aiden."

"What? It sounded like you said you married Prince Aiden."

"That is exactly what I said."

Carl smiled reluctantly. "Is this a good thing?"

"It's a very good thing." Nate chuckled at Carl's disbelief.

"Well, in that case, congratulations, Nate." Carl shook his head. "How in the hell did you manage that, you old dog?"

Nate winked and relaxed back into the computer chair. "With a lot of luck. Shh... He hasn't figured out I'm just a poor sailor yet."

Laughing, Carl slapped his desk. "Somehow I doubt that." After a few seconds he stopped laughing and his face grew serious. "How would you like to impress your prince by becoming an admiral?"

What? A couple of days ago this would have been a dream come true, but now? Nate wasn't so sure. It *would* keep his family off the front line, and it would keep them with him, but still involve taking Aiden from his family.

"Don't tell me you wouldn't love to be in command of Aries Fleet."

Aries Fleet? That was Carl's fleet. It was the fleet that protected Regelence. "What's going on, Carl?" Why would Carl give up his position? The man wasn't that old. Admiral was almost always a position held until the man died or became too infirm to make rational decisions.

Carl waved a hand, but Nate didn't miss the hesitation. The man had to know how surprising his revelation must be. "Nothing. I'm retiring."

Nate frowned. "I'll think about it."

Nate walked upstairs dazed. The IN wanted to promote him to Admiral. It would mean he could keep Aiden with him. He wasn't sure that getting through the year and retiring wasn't a better solution. But Admiral... A few years ago—hell, a few days ago—it would have been an answer to a prayer, but something felt off. Carl wouldn't retire voluntarily, would he? No, Nate didn't think so. Carl lived and breathed the IN. His whole family was IN, his father and grandfather before him, his brother, even his son. Something was wrong, but he didn't know what. Maybe discussing it with Aiden would help. Assuming Aiden was still awake. Nate rounded the corner to the hall outside their suite. Knowing Aiden, he was in bed with a sketchbook. Pushing open the door, he walked in and closed it behind him.

Aiden was right where Nate expected him to be, on the bed, on his stomach, feet in the air and completely absorbed in a sketch. He gave no indication of knowing Nate was there at all.

Nate leaned against the door, watching him for a few minutes. Damned if his prick didn't start filling. Why in the world being ignored was arousing he had no idea, but it was, at least when it was because of Aiden's passion for drawing. He loved how Aiden unconsciously rubbed his feet together and how whenever his pencil stopped his head automatically tilted to the side and the tip of his tongue peeked out from his lips.

As if thinking about it made it happen, Aiden began rubbing the bottoms of his feet together, making the white linen shift further up his pale thighs. Trouble was right, the nightshirts were girly. Nate had hated the damned things even as a teenager. It hadn't taken him long to decide to sleep nude.

Suddenly, it hit him. Aiden had a nightshirt on. Hadn't he told Aiden no nightshirts in bed? Technically, Aiden wasn't in bed, he was on it. But still, Nate wasn't about to argue semantics with himself. This was going to be fun. Nate grinned, his cock getting even harder. "Boy, would you like to explain to me why you have a nightshirt on?"

Aiden gasped, his head jerking toward Nate. "Oh, Nate, you scared me." His gaze traveled over Nate's body, lingering on his groin. His tongue darted out, wetting his lips, and he smiled, meeting Nate's gaze. Dropping the pencil, he rolled onto his side and extended a hand toward Nate.

"And now you're ignoring me. You're begging to get your ass spanked, aren't you, boy?"

"Huh?" Aiden's eyes widened, looking startled, then they softened, glittering with excitement. Biting his bottom lip, he sat up.

Nate stepped forward, already pulling his own waistcoat off. "Nightshirt off, boy."

"Yes, sir." Aiden nearly ripped the thing getting it over his head. Tossing it to the floor, he leaned back on his arms, making sure Nate got a good look at the nice, toned body. He lay all the way down and placed his arms over his head, flexing the lean muscles in his abdomen. His gaze darted to Nate's face and he grinned when he noticed Nate looking.

The little devil. Nate finished undressing and took his time putting his clothes away. The entire time he was aware of Aiden watching him. He even heard an occasional whimper and sigh, letting him know Aiden liked what he saw.

After putting his shoes in the bottom of the armoire, Nate got on the bed. Pushing the pillows against the headboard, he got comfortable, stretching his legs out.

Aiden rolled over to face him. "Sir?"

"Come here."

Aiden crawled to him like an eager puppy, immediately moving to straddle his thighs.

"Over my lap, boy."

Aiden hesitated, but again Nate noticed the spark of excitement flaring in his gray eyes. It intensified Nate's own arousal. He couldn't wait to see that pretty little white ass turn red under his hand.

Aiden draped himself over Nate's legs, wiggling a bit to get comfortable. Finally, he ended up with his ass positioned perfectly on Nate's thighs.

Nate sat there for a minute and let the excitement race through him. *Fuck*, his boy was something else. Aiden had managed to get himself situated where his cock rested against the inside of Nate's leg. "You ready, boy?" Nate put his left hand on the middle of Aiden's back and rested his right over the pale cheek closest to him.

Aiden's muscles tensed under Nate's hands for a second before relaxing again. "Yes, sir?" He said it with a questioning tone, like he wasn't entirely sure.

Lifting his right hand, Nate paused. "You know what this is for, right, boy?"

Bobbing his head, Aiden answered. "Nightshirt, sir."

"Didn't I tell you not to wear a nightshirt in my bed?"

The impudent brat grumbled something, making Nate smile. "What was that?"

"I won't do it again, sir."

"Well, maybe this will help you remember next time." Nate swatted his ass and received a shocked gasp and an automatic tensing in response. He did it again, slow and hard at first then a little quicker. The slapping sound of skin and Aiden's writhing went right to his cock. That pretty little ass pinkened up nicely.

Something nudged his leg and it took him a few seconds to realize it was Aiden's cock. *Damn.* His boy was hard from the spanking. Nate continued to rain down smack after smack, beginning to work up a sweat. Nate watched for Aiden anticipating the blow and adjusted to keep him off balance.

At first Aiden only squirmed, yelping occasionally, but when the yelps grew into sobs, Nate stopped. Aiden was still hard and hot against his thigh but— "Aiden?"

"Don't st-stop, please don't stop, sir." His voice was rough with tears from the sound of it.

Nate sat there, a knot forming in his stomach. *Shit.* He hadn't meant to hurt Aiden. Aiden said don't stop, but... Nate started to pull him up, then he noticed it. A drop of something warm ran down the inside of his thigh right at the spot the tip of Aiden's dick nudged his leg. *Oh fuck. Precome.* Nate groaned and slapped his boy's ass again, several times.

Aiden writhed some more. "Oh, th-thank you, sir. Ple-ase don't st-op, sir. More." His rough, broken voice made Nate ache.

"I'll decide when and if we stop, boy." Sweat dripped from Nate's temple and his lungs labored for air. Whether it was due to exertion or excitement he wasn't sure. His cock throbbed, pressing against Aiden's side. "That's it, give yourself to me. Such a beautiful ass with my handprints all over it. You're mine now, boy." He continued to spank the heated cheeks, watching the rosy glow left by each smack.

After a few more slaps, Aiden tensed, his cock twitching hard against Nate's thigh. He groaned, his hips rocking a little. "Sir—Sir..."

Nate stopped. He was dying to taste, to feel the warmth radiating from the rosy skin on his face. Getting his hands underneath Aiden, he lifted his boy and tossed him on the bed next to Nate. He snagged a pillow and put it under Aiden's hips. "Spread your legs."

Aiden complied eagerly.

Getting to his knees between Aiden's outspread thighs, Nate buried his face in the heated buttocks. He inhaled the musky smell and closed his eyes. *Oh hell yes.*

"Please, sir..."

"Please what, boy?" Nate rubbed his beard against the tender flesh, licking a line up one side then the other. He did it again, letting Aiden feel his beard.

Aiden moaned, squirming at the feel of Nate's whiskers on his tender flesh.

"You want my tongue in your ass? Is that what you want, boy? Want me to tongue fuck you?" Nate spread Aiden's ass apart, his tongue going right for the hole, swirling around and pushing inside.

"Oh, fuck, Nate. Sir." Tensing, Aiden came. His body shuddered and the smell of semen filled the air. He sobbed into the mattress, his voice muffled as his head rocked side to side.

Nate groaned and continued his assault, licking Aiden's crease. The tip of his tongue stabbed into Aiden's hole. He pushed a finger inside, fucking the snug little pucker with it.

Aiden moaned, pushing back toward his finger.

Damn, Nate was so freaking hard, his balls impossibly tight. He rubbed his face against the hot skin again. How had he gotten this lucky? Never in a million years would he have guessed this sweet, innocent man would be his match in bed. No matter how hard he pushed, Aiden took it all and begged for more. What would Aiden look like restrained to his bed while Nate flogged his beautiful, tender back? Nate moaned.

Using another finger, Nate shoved deeper, searching—

The muscles in Aiden's back rippled, his legs shaking. He cried out into the bed and pushed back toward Nate.

Nate gathered more saliva in his mouth. Moving his fingers, he forced the spit into Aiden's ass along with his tongue. Licking down, he nuzzled Aiden's balls. Galaxy, he smelled good, musky like sex and Aiden.

Aiden whimpered.

Nate's whole body clenched at the sweet begging sound. Not only begging, but pleading for *him.* "Fuck, boy." Nate raised up, bracing himself with one hand on the bed. He gave the pretty cheeks one last swat before lining his cock up. The heat of Aiden's reddened skin practically scorched him.

He pushed in slowly until his hips rested against Aiden. Once inside he closed his eyes and dropped forward on both hands. It was a contest to see who moaned louder, him or Aiden.

Aiden gasped. "I can feel it. I feel the ring." His voice came out as a whisper.

Shit. Nate held perfectly still. The tight heat gripping his cock was incredible. The sensation traveled up his shaft and kept going right on to his spine, making him shiver. His abs tautened and his breath caught. Knowing he wasn't going to last long, he took a deep breath and opened his eyes. He became mesmerized by the long pale back and fiery red buttocks shining with sweat. "Good Galaxy, boy, you're beautiful." Leaning forward, he dragged his tongue between Aiden's shoulder blades, tasting the salty skin.

Aiden started grunting at him, thrusting himself backwards. "Sir, move, please."

Gripping his hips, Nate thrust into him. He fucked Aiden hard and deep. Within minutes, Aiden cried out, tensing. His muscles contracted, bringing Nate right over the edge with him.

Somehow, Nate managed to collapse beside Aiden instead of on him.

Aiden stay still, his head turned away from Nate. Nate grabbed his hand and started tugging, trying to get him closer.

Crawling over, Aiden lay down on top of him, making Nate ultra aware of how hot and sweaty he was, how hot and sweaty they both were. His heart was pounding hard against Aiden's chest as he wrapped his arms around Aiden and kissed his forehead.

After a few minutes, when they were both breathing easier, Aiden raised his head. His gaze caught Nate's and he blinked, his big gray eyes shiny with tears. Aiden rested his head on Nate's shoulder, inhaling audibly. He rested there for several seconds, then started nuzzling Nate's arm.

Nate grinned and moved his arm. What was his boy up to?

Aiden buried his nose in the hair under Nate's arm and took a deep satisfied breath. His tongue snaked out and caught some sweat dripping off the hair in Nate's armpit.

Then Nate felt it. Aiden's cock was getting hard again against his stomach. *Oh fuck.* Nate groaned and slid his hand up, forcing Aiden's head onto his chest. "Later, boy. You need to rest."

Aiden yawned against him and grinned.

Nate's insides got a fluttery feeling, his chest ached, but not in a bad way. Pulling Aiden up, he sealed their lips together. He'd known from the beginning he'd grow to cherish Aiden. But now? He was such a goner.

Chapter Fifteen

Aiden woke cold and fumbled around until he located the covers at the foot of the bed. He pulled the sheet and comforter up and curled his legs toward his chest to get warm. If Nate wasn't going to let him wear nightshirts the least he could do was cuddle and keep Aiden cozy. Funny, Nate usually *did* snuggle with him. Most of last night he'd slept in Nate's arms.

Aiden grinned. *Last night.* His cock began to stiffen but at the same time his mood fell. Every time Nate pushed him further and further, testing his boundaries and trust, Aiden's resolve to let Nate go cracked a little more. He was now fairly certain Nate would come back often, but Aiden didn't want to let him go at all. Rolling over toward Nate's side of the bed, Aiden reached and came up empty-handed. He tried again and hit the mattress before cracking his eyes open. "Damn." Nate wasn't in bed. "Jeffers, where is Lord Deverell?"

"In the library, milord. He wanted breakfast brought to you when you awoke. Should I order it now?"

"Yes." Aiden sat and stretched. His arse was tender. His prick hardened fully at the nice reminder of that spanking. It had surprised him. He'd never imagined something like that would make him feel the way he had. He groaned. Nate was downstairs, there was no use getting himself worked up.

"Jeffers, do you know if Thomas has had time to purchase new screens for me this morning?

"They are secured in Lord Deverell's space chest at the foot of the bed, milord. He left you a key in the nightstand and instructed that you should keep it and put it in a safe place."

Nate had locked his screens away for safekeeping? It was a little thing, probably anyone would do the same knowing his screens kept getting stolen, but... Aiden smiled, feeling all tingly and warm.

Throwing his legs over the side, he opened the nightstand. There was a note with the key. He picked up both.

Aiden,

Until we figure out what is going on, use my chest for your screens. You and I have the only keys. If someone wants them, they will have to take the whole damned chest.

Nate

He set the note on the nightstand and stood, walking around to the foot of the bed. Crouching, he put the key in the lock.

"Not even dressed and you're already after those screens."

Aiden sucked in air and nearly fell on his arse. Slapping a hand to his chest, he took a deep breath. He hadn't heard the door open.

Nate laughed and closed the door behind him. "Sorry."

He sat, trying to get his heart to go back to normal, and grinned. "It's okay. I didn't hear you."

"Not surprised. You had your mind on drawing already." Nate smiled and walked further into the room. He tossed something on the mattress and leaned against the bedpost at the end of the bed. Crossing his long legs at the ankles and his arms over his chest, he peered down at Aiden. "How do you feel?"

Aiden followed those long muscular legs all the way to the handsome face. Nate was gorgeous and sexy and— Aiden sighed. *Like you should throw me on the bed and ravish me.* "Wonderful. How are you?" Standing, he left the key in the lock and closed the space between them.

Nate engulfed Aiden in his arms as soon as he was within grabbing distance. "I'm fine, thank you. Sore?"

"I don't know, are you?"

Rubbing his back, Nate nipped his chin and chuckled. "Boy..."

"A little. But in a good way." Reaching up, Aiden ran his fingers over Nate's beard.

"I brought you something."

"I know, I got the note. Thanks for putting them in your trunk." He went on tiptoe, kissing Nate on the lips. Oh, the man made him ache. It felt nice having his cock between them. Staying there, he pushed his hips forward against Nate. He slipped a hand between them and—

Nate groaned, pushing his erection into Aiden's hand before stepping back. "Behave, boy. I don't have time for that." He turned, reaching around the bedpost for something on the bed.

Damn. Aiden huffed out a breath, trying to decide how far begging would get him. Probably not far, he'd get the, "I'll decide when, boy." *Oh man,* he whimpered. He loved it when Nate went all dominant and commanding on him, the way his voice actually got deeper and rough sounding. How sore was his arse, really? Could he stand another spanking? Probably not. Trying not to let his shoulders slump, he stepped around the corner of the bed, following Nate.

"I spent most of the morning looking for this." Nate faced him at that exact moment and pressed something to his chest, giving Aiden no choice but to take it.

Aiden jumped. "Cold." He got it away from his bare skin where he could look at it. It was a sword. A sword in a scabbard, with a really cold, really pretty swept hilt. Nate bought him a sword? *Oh! Oh, dust.* Nate bought him his own sword. He caught the handle with one hand and the scabbard with the other and pulled. The polished silver slid free of the black leather, glinting in the light. The blade was wavy, a flamberge rapier.

Grabbing Aiden's hand holding the sword, Nate pushed it aside and wrapped a hand around the back of Aiden's neck, kissing him. "I have to go. I'm expecting a call from the admiral. After you eat and get dressed, come downstairs." Nate let go and turned to leave. "And don't play with that sword naked, you're liable to cut something off."

Nate got me a sword. Aiden stood there in awe, tilting the sword this way and that, catching the light. That's when he noticed the tiny inscription on the center of the blade right below the guard. *To My Boy, For Honor And Duty Until Heart And Sword Break, Love Nate.* He stood there staring at the words, feeling like his heart was lodged in his throat. It was a traditional inscription, but Nate had made it special by adding, "To My Boy". Aiden's eyes got blurry, forcing him to blink. "Sir..."

Stopping with his hand on the doorknob, Nate turned.

"Thank you." Aiden smiled.

Nate let go of the door and crossed the room again. He kissed Aiden hard and deep.

Aiden's toes curled and he nearly dropped his sword. Trying to get closer, he groaned.

Nate stepped back. "You're welcome." He caressed Aiden's cheek with his thumb. "Now, I really have to go. Come down when you get the chance." He left, closing the door quietly behind him.

For several seconds, Aiden stood there staring at the closed door with a goofy grin on his face. He should have told Nate he loved him. Holding the sword up again, he read the engraved words *Love, Nate. Did* Nate really love him? What if he just asked Nate if he could go with him? He didn't want to leave his family, but... Nothing but his art had ever made him feel this way before. He couldn't lie to himself any longer. Losing Nate would hurt.

Laying his sword on the bed, he rushed to get dressed. He needed to talk to Nate. Unsure what good it would do, if any, Aiden had to know what Nate's plans were. He needed to know if Nate was ever going to come back to stay. "Jeffers, cancel my breakfast. I'll go down and get it."

"Yes, milord."

When he had everything on, he realized he had a problem. He couldn't tie his cravat. *Dust.* Well, he could probably tie it, but it wouldn't be fit for public. Could he sneak downstairs? Nah, if Cony caught him... And there were probably visitors since his brothers went to a ball last night. Hanging the starched white cloth around his neck, he opened the bedroom door and went through the sitting area. Noticing the other bedroom door—the one that Trouble was occupying—was cracked open, Aiden peeked inside.

Trouble stood next to the valet's room with his ear pressed to the door.

Rolling his eyes, Aiden pushed the door open, ready to let the kid know it wasn't polite to eavesdrop. "Tro—"

Trouble's finger flew to his mouth, his eyes wide. Shaking his head, he motioned for Aiden to come to him.

Aiden frowned. What in the Galaxy could possible be interesting about Benson? And it had to be Benson Trouble was spying on because this bedroom had been meant for Aiden, and Benson had been given the valet's room.

When Aiden reached Trouble, the younger man pointed to the door. Aiden put his ear against it, although he didn't need to. He could clearly hear Benson arguing with someone.

"I have no idea what you're talking about," Benson hissed.

Trouble's lips curled, a sort of "huh?" expression.

Aiden was fairly certain his face matched. "Who is he talking to?" Aiden mouthed.

"Caldwell," Trouble mouthed back.

"Give me that message I saw you writing!" Caldwell said.

Aiden and Trouble stayed there, their ears stuck to the door, staring at each other. Was it some sort of lover's quarrel? Or was it something more? One of them should go find Nate, but Aiden couldn't move. As soon as he did he was liable to miss something. He was really going to have to talk to Father about having Jeffers record things in the bedrooms. As it was he was pretty much just a voice-activated call button. And calling out to Jeffers to fetch someone would give them away. "Go get Nate," he whispered.

Shaking his head, Trouble pointed at him and mouthed, "You."

Aiden rolled his eyes. No way was he leaving Nate's son here with only a door between him and them. He grabbed the teen's arm and tugged. They were both going to have to go.

Trouble shook his head, glaring.

A series of thuds and grunts sounded on the other side of the door. Something crashed softly onto the carpeted floor. It wasn't loud enough to alert someone unless they were listening for it, but it was definitely the sounds of a struggle.

Freezing, Aiden and Trouble stared at the door. It got quiet. *Shit.* They both took off for the exit.

Aiden grabbed the knob of the door leading to the hallway.

The door they'd just vacated crashed open. "Ah, ah, ah. Let go of the door, Your Highness."

Aiden had no intention of letting go of the door, until he heard a murmur. Turning, he came face-to-face with Trouble.

Caldwell had Trouble around the neck with a fragger to his temple. He crooked his finger at Aiden. Aiden looked around for anything to help them get out of this situation. He spotted Benson on the floor in the other room. Aiden could only see Benson's lower abdomen and legs from where he stood, but it was enough to tell Benson wasn't going to be coming to their rescue. Already a puddle of blood pooled and spread out around the valet.

Swallowing the lump in his throat, Aiden moved. He wasn't about to piss the man off when he had a fragger against Trouble's skull.

When he got close, Caldwell shoved Trouble and grabbed Aiden, placing the pistol to his head.

Trouble stumbled and caught himself on the door, turning to face them. He looked past them toward the valet's room and gasped. "Benson."

"Isn't going to be of any help to you. We are going to take a trip, boys." Caldwell placed the fragger inside his coat and waved it at Aiden, making it clear that he still had the weapon trained on Aiden.

Damn. Jeffers wasn't likely to contact someone on their behalf if he didn't see a gun. Trouble, apparently, realized it too. He gave Aiden a look, glanced at the door, then did it again. He looked lost.

Aiden gave him a wobbly smile. "Open the door." Nate would expect him to take care of Trouble, and probably vice versa. At any rate, if they could stick together they'd have a better chance.

"Basement, gentlemen. And don't forget what I have." Caldwell caught Aiden's arm, tugging him back, making sure he was right in front of him.

Trouble opened the door and led the way, continuing to look back at Aiden and Caldwell every so often.

They made it all the way to the basement without encountering another person. How? Aiden had no idea, but it figured. A castle full of people and where were they when you needed them? If he got out of this alive he was going to see that better security was implemented, personal privacy be damned. "Why did you kill Benson?"

"To settle an argument with him. And unless the two of you want to join him, you best do as I say." Caldwell stopped at the entrance to the door housing Jeffers' Maintenance Room. "Open the door."

Did Caldwell know it would register Aiden's identity? Aiden had no clue how Payton got inside without using his own code and thumbprint, but Aiden couldn't do it.

"Your Highness," Caldwell gritted out, nudging him in the back with the gun.

After pushing in his access code, Aiden scanned his thumb. The door opened.

Trouble must have known what it meant as well. He caught Aiden's gaze, his eyes twinkling.

Maybe they could leave Father and Cony a hint.

ᚒ

"Any idea who took Aiden's sketchscreens?"

Nate glanced up at Raleigh and shook his head. "No. I've looked at the videos of all the castle exits around the time of Jeffers' last download. The only thing that left the castle was garbage. I'm assuming someone threw them in the trash."

"Bloody hell." Raleigh grunted and sat in the chair across from the desk. "Bugger."

Nate arched a brow. In the time he'd been here, he hadn't heard Raleigh use that kind of language. He could certainly understand it though. The idea of a conspirator among them didn't sit right with him either, especially given the attack on Aiden.

Raleigh grimaced. "Sorry. I just hate having a traitor in my house. And whoever keeps getting rid of Aiden's screens..."

He'd thought the same thing. "What I want to know is why they haven't attempted to get the files off of Jeffers. That would make more sense. They have to know that eventually we will get suspicious of all the missing sketchscreens and check the sketches to see what it is they don't want us to see. It doesn't make any sense to me."

"Unless *that* is the point."

"What do you mean?" Nate frowned.

"Unless they want us to look at the sketches." Raleigh frowned and ran his hands down his face. "Why would someone want us to see the ship, if they were responsible for stealing the crates?"

"Guilty conscience?"

"Why not come to me and beg my mercy?"

Nate chuckled. "Do you have any?"

Raleigh grinned. "Only where my kids are concerned."

"Exactly. And in this case, given that it is an IN investigation, they'd be at *my* mercy. My forgiving nature isn't something I'm known for."

"I've heard." Raleigh sighed. "I take it there is no word from Admiral Jenkins on the man who attacked Aiden?"

"Not yet. I'm planning another trip to the docks to see what I can learn."

Raleigh looked away as if he were thinking. He sat quietly for several seconds.

Nate was beginning to think Raleigh was done with their conversation when Raleigh cleared his throat. "You will not take Aiden with you this time." He arched a brow and caught Nate's gaze in a level stare.

Staring right back, Nate silently bristled. He hadn't planned on taking Aiden, but he'd be damned if Raleigh or anyone else dictated what he and Aiden did. The sooner Raleigh understood that the better. "I hadn't planned on it. But if he wants to go, I will not tell him he can't. He's quite capable of making his own decisions. He is not a child."

"I am concerned about his safety."

"So am I." Nate sighed. He appreciated where Raleigh was coming from. Nate would feel the same way if he were in Raleigh's position. Galaxy knew he'd be concerned about Trouble. "The sooner you understand that the better off we'll be. I'm not going to intentionally put Aiden in danger, but I will not have you dictating our actions."

"Does this mean you will not be taking him back to your ship with you?"

Fuck. Nate wasn't ready for this discussion. He had to run it all by Aiden first. He wasn't about to talk to Raleigh about the offer for promotion to admiral, but he knew he wasn't going to endanger Aiden by taking him on the Lady Anna. He could give Raleigh that if nothing else. "I will not take him on the ship."

Raleigh visibly relaxed and gave Nate a crisp nod. "Thank you."

"The decision wasn't made for you, but you're welcome."

"Nevertheless, I'm grateful. And this brings up another topic I've been wanting to discuss with you."

"Oh?" Nate leaned back in the computer chair and crossed his hands over his stomach. So help him, if Raleigh brought up his relationship with Aiden again, Nate was going to strangle the man.

"Your son."

Uh-oh. What had the kid gotten into this time? "Trouble?"

Raleigh nodded. "Have you noticed the birthmark under his arm?"

Nate blinked, taken aback. Jaw clenching, he narrowed his eyes at Raleigh.

Eyebrows pulling together, Raleigh sat forward. "Then you haven't seen it?"

Scowling, Nate sat taller in the chair. "What I want to know is how did you?"

"I spotted it when I came to find you a couple days ago. Jeremy was in your room, half dressed."

When had Raleigh come to find him? Where was Nate at the time? "When was this?" *Damn*, that had come out surly, but Jeremy was none of Raleigh's concern.

"When you went shopping with my boys. I saw the video of Aiden leaving your room the day before." Raleigh snarled his lip ever so slightly. "I came to confront you about it."

That explained a lot about Raleigh's attitude toward him concerning Aiden. Nate relaxed a little, realizing where the man was coming from. "Nothing happened, Raleigh."

Nodding, Raleigh sat back. "It doesn't matter now."

"Just the same. I'm telling you nothing happened."

Raleigh dipped his head in acknowledgment. "Your son is Regelen."

Nate blinked. "Come again?" He practically growled the last bit.

"The birthmark. All artificially procreated babies are born with that particular birthmark under their right arm."

Whoa. Nate felt like someone had knocked the air out of him. He wasn't sure how he felt about this. Jeremy was his son, and nothing was going to change that. If anyone thought different...

Raleigh's gaze drifted. "He reminds me of a couple I used to know. Patrick was very outgoing and personable, very much like Trouble." A barely perceptible smile flitted across his lips. "He was an IN Lieutenant. Marcus, though? Very serious and smart. He—"

"Your Highness, Lord Deverell, there is a transmission from Admiral Jenkins. Do you wish to receive it?" Jeffers asked.

"Yes." Nate sat forward, looking at the monitor, his mind shifting back to the case. He and Raleigh would definitely be discussing Trouble later, but now...

Raleigh came around the desk, pulling a chair over to sit beside Nate.

Carl came on the screen seconds later. "Ah, Nate, Raleigh, hello."

"Hello." Nate tried not to grumble, but he wanted the man to get to the point. Surely he'd had plenty of time to look up Felix Chapman in the IN computers.

"Good morning, Admiral." Raleigh was once again his demure, almost distant self.

"Gentlemen, I'm afraid I was not able to discover much about your attacker. He is a thirty-year-old Regelen with no criminal record. I didn't find a current residence for him. But I did find out something interesting. The Marchioness is not his ship. It's registered to a Chadwick Manche—"

The screen went blank and the lights flickered but stayed on. Everything got utterly still and quiet. What the...?

Raleigh stood. "Jeffers?"

There was no answer. The entire household shut down. *Shit.* Someone had turned Jeffers off. Why were the princes turning Jeffers off again? They all knew Aiden had been attacked. *Fuck.* They wouldn't have done it.

Raleigh raced to the door. "I've got to go find Steven and the boys."

Aiden. Nate was right on his heels. He ran past Raleigh, who was yelling for the king, and started up the stairs.

"Nate, if you find any of the boys keep them with you and meet me back here," Raleigh called after him.

Nate didn't stop running until he got to his and Aiden's suite. "Aiden?"

There was no answer.

"Aiden?"

The sword he'd given Aiden earlier was lying across the bed.

242

Nate searched the washroom. "Aiden? Boy, answer me." His stomach plummeted with each step he took. Aiden wasn't here. Nate crossed the sitting room joining his and Aiden's bedroom to Trouble's. "Trouble?" There was no answer. Not that Nate had expected there to be. Trouble would have come running when he was calling Aiden, if he were here. "Fuck."

He pushed open the door to Trouble's bedroom. The bed was made and Jeremy's reader lay on the bed. The room was immaculate except for the door leading to the valet's room was standing open. *Fuck!* There was someone on the floor—and blood. Nate ran to the door, his heart pounding, dread swelling in his chest. *Benson.* It was Aiden's valet, with a big fucking hole in his chest. The tension inside him eased a little on discovering it wasn't Aiden or Trouble, but now he knew for certain his boys weren't here and they *were* in danger. "Fuck, fuck, fuck!"

Nate noticed a cravat on the floor inside Trouble's room. He frowned. Trouble had had on a cravat, Nate had tied it for him before going downstairs this morning. Picking it up, he brought it to his nose. *Aiden.* It was newly washed and starched, but it smelled faintly of Aiden. *Please let them be okay.*

Nate ran back to his room, grabbing Aiden's sword, and hurried back downstairs. The entire staff was there, all chattering at once from the sounds of it. They quieted when Nate appeared at the bottom of the stairs. He looked around and found everyone but Aiden, Trouble and Raleigh.

Steven stepped forward. "Aiden?"

Nate shook his head. "No. My son is missing as well."

The king's jaw tightened and he closed his eyes for a few seconds before looking back at Nate. "We can't locate Benson and Caldwell either."

"Benson is dead."

Steven's eyes widened, his face paling just a bit, then he turned back to the group gathered in the foyer. "Thomas, Lord Deverell and I are going to help Raleigh get Jeffers up and running. Keep the children here with you and Christy. Everyone else spread out and search the castle. We need to find Aiden, Lord Deverell's valet and Caldwell." Steven turned back to Nate. "Come on."

"Where are we going? We've got to look for them." Nate resisted the urge to yell and destroy something. It was hard, he felt as though his entire world were collapsing around him. "Who is Caldwell? And what do you know about Caldwell?"

Steven shook his head. "Caldwell is Tarren's valet. He has a spotless record or he wouldn't be employed here. Raleigh double-checked every employee after the weapons were stolen. There was nothing that made them stand out." Steven opened the door leading to the basement.

Of course not, or they'd have already caught them. *Damn it.* Nate followed Steven into Jeffers' maintenance room. He had never felt this kind of dread in his entire life. Nothing had prepared him for this. Not the IN, not being disowned by his family. Nothing. He may very well have lost the most important things in his life. He just hoped that Aiden and Trouble stayed together—they'd have a much better chance that way.

Raleigh was typing away on a keyboard on a stand in front of a large screen, like in his personal study. There were racks of computers and different equipment. The overhead lights flickered before going steady again. Raleigh stopped typing and looked at Steven and Nate. "Did you find Aiden?"

"No. But Benson is dead."

"What?"

Nate watched a series of numbers and letters flash on the screen as Jeffers rebooted. "He's upstairs. Someone shot him with a fragger."

Raleigh's fists clenched. "Damn it. Nate, before Jeffers shut off the admiral said the ship was registered to Chadwick Manchester. That is Lord Braxton's given name."

As if that news wasn't disturbing enough a picture of a man flashed on the screen behind Raleigh. Nate had seen the man before. But where? Pointing to the screen he asked. "What's that?"

Raleigh looked but it was Steven who answered first. "That's Caldwell. Raleigh, why is he on the screen?"

Nate racked his brain. He was certain he hadn't seen the man here in the castle, which meant he knew the man from somewhere else. Bringing his hand to his forehead he closed his eyes. *Think, Nate.* Where the hell had he seen the man?

The furious clacking of keys suddenly stopped and Raleigh laughed. "That is our son leaving us a clue. Aiden used his login when he shut Jeffers down. He changed the splash screen."

Nate looked back at the picture of the lean blond man with piercing hazel eyes. Eyes that took on a devious glint when they were cornered and an equally convincing innocent look when they stared back at a panel of officers, requesting a transfer. "Last I knew, that man was IN intelligence."

Chapter Sixteen

They were moving...or maybe not. It could be his head spinning from being zapped with a bio-jet injector full of sedative. Aiden sat, grabbing his head. *Oh, dust.* His head felt four sizes bigger and full of cotton. He groaned and laid right back down.

"Aiden?" Trouble croaked from somewhere to his left.

"Yeah, it's me. Are you okay?" It really felt like they were in motion. Turning his head toward Trouble's voice, Aiden opened his eyes. It was dim, but not so dark that he couldn't see. They were in some sort of a hold. He couldn't see very far, but the room appeared to be empty.

Trouble blinked his eyes open and grabbed his forehead. "I think so. My head feels like it's going to explode. It didn't feel like this when Hawk shot me with a fragger."

"Caldwell must have knocked us ou— Nate shot you?" What in the Galaxy did the hellion do to make Nate shoot him? That didn't sound like Nate. *Nate.* Would he notice they were gone? Aiden sighed. They had to get out of here.

"Yeah, long story. Where the hell are we?"

Aiden looked around from where he lay and pushed himself to a sitting position. Bringing his knees up, he rested his head on them. That wasn't too bad. He was groggy, but whatever Caldwell gave them was wearing off. "I don't know. A ship's hold maybe?" Which completely imploded planets. How were they going to get out of here?

Trouble grumbled but sat. "I think you're right. It looks similar to the hold on the Lady Anna." Getting to his hands and knees, Trouble pushed himself up and staggered to the back of the room. Looking along the bulkhead, he stopped. "Aiden, come over here."

Rising to his feet, Aiden rested his hands on his knees until the wave of dizziness passed. Once he got to where Trouble stood he saw it—a small hatch. "Can we get it open?"

"Uh-huh." Trouble began picking at a panel to the right of the hatch.

"Where does it lead?"

"Access tunnels." His fingernails slipped. "Ow." He shook his hands and went back to work picking at the wall.

"Think we can make it to an emergency shuttle undetected?" All ships had them, right? Aiden dug the little bit of nails he had into the other side of the crevice and in no time the plate popped off. There was a keypad.

Trouble picked his foot up and bashed his heel into the keypad several times. "We can if I can get to a computer." It crunched under his kick, several of the plastic keys falling out, until it cracked in half and hung limply from some wires. He started pulling out wires and crossing them. The three-foot by three-foot hatch slid up into the bulkhead. Trouble grinned and crawled through it. "Just like Hawk's ship. These things never could handle a short."

They traveled through a narrow access tunnel with wires and pipes on each side of them and overhead. They crawled on a grate that covered even more wires and pipes below them. It was harder to hear in here, sounding like air was whishing by them, and their knees banged on the metal-grated deck. And the space was cramped. It was a good thing he and Trouble were both on the small side. Nate never would have fit in here. The thought of Nate made him crawl faster. Damn, he wanted to go home.

Every ten to twenty feet there was a small hatch, like the one they had come through. Finally, they hit a dead end, or rather a closed hatch. It was on the deck and there was no keypad. It was a manual panel.

Trouble bit his bottom lip and contemplated the entryway.

"What?" Aiden asked.

"If there are crewmembers in there, we're fucked."

He nodded. "Where does that lead?"

"The engine room."

It didn't seem to Aiden that they had much choice. Who knew how much time they had. Someone was bound to figure out they'd escaped the hold eventually. And then what? They were, as Trouble said, fucked. "What other options do we have?" He sure as hell didn't want to sit around and wait to be found. There was no telling what the psycho valet had planned for them.

Trouble sighed, ran his hands through his hair and groaned. "Good point. It's now or never, huh?" Trouble slid it open a little.

They both froze. Aiden held his breath. *Please don't let there be anyone in there.*

After several seconds when no one came running to attack them, Trouble stuck his head in the opening and looked around. "Coast is clear." He pushed the hatch all the way open and dropped through.

Aiden followed, looking around. His stomach was tied in knots, but he forced himself to continue. They had to get out of here. Just because no one came rushing at them, didn't mean no one was in there. It was very loud down here so they might not have heard them.

It was colder than in the tunnels, brighter lit too. There were several racks of computers. Blinking red, green and blue lights were all over the place. It was like a maze of computers. He decided they were either very lucky or stupid. It was too soon to tell which.

They turned a corner and were suddenly out of the maze. No one else was in sight. *Lucky, we're definitely lucky.*

An open door. It looked like some sort of command room.

Trouble saw it too. Hurrying over, Trouble waited for him to get inside and closed the hatch. It was a control room or rather control closet.

Rushing to the computer, Trouble started typing. "Aiden. Look around some more. See if you can find anything to use for a weapon."

"Okay. What are you doing?"

"Finding out where we are and where this ship is going. I'm going to try and shut off the ship's cameras and see if I can get us to an emergency shuttle. In the main part of the ship it will be like the main part of the castle. The computer will see us. I have to shut that function down. And make sure it isn't going to give us away to the captain." He continued typing, his fingers flying across the keys.

Aiden was impressed. He knew a hacker when he saw one and Trouble was somewhere in the same league as Payton. It made him feel much better about their chances of escape.

Wandering around, he looked for anything that might be useful. There wasn't much here, it was a small area once you got through the maze of computers. There was a large hatch, which he hoped stayed closed, and little else.

"Aiden." Trouble motioned for him to hurry. "I started nosing around to see if there was any kind of hint as to why we were taken. And I came across the name Lord Braxton. Do you know him? He's in the captain's quarters right now with the captain and Caldwell."

Aiden's jaw dropped. Braxton? "Can you listen in or see them or something?"

Trouble nodded and typed again. Then there were voices. Trouble frowned. "That doesn't sound like Caldwell."

Aiden listened carefully. No it didn't, but it was definitely Braxton. "Who's the captain?"

"Chapman. Felix Chapman."

"That is the man who tried to kill me. We're on The Marchioness."

It wasn't a question, but Trouble nodded anyway, then went back to typing. "I'm going to download everything I can and then we're going to get out of here. I've already disabled the computer's notifications and I sent a distress signal." He reached down and did something with the heel of his ankle boots. The wedge swiveled and he got a small rounded disk-shaped object out before pushing the heel back in. He held it up to Aiden and grinned. "A multifunction drive and holographic camera."

Damn, the kid was good. Aiden's unease let up a little. He wondered if Nate had any idea his son was this prepared for such events.

While Trouble typed, Aiden listened.

"Tell me again why you felt it was necessary to kidnap the prince?" Chapman sounded exasperated.

He and Trouble looked at one another.

"For money. We're going to ransom him."

"I told you I had a buyer already for the schematics we will be obtaining from the deal. That was to help you get away. Why do we need ransom money?" Caldwell said.

"I changed my mind. There is no way they haven't found me out. We left this ship in my name and that little shit has sketches of the weapons on it because you failed to erase them from their damned castle computer. I'm not being hanged as a traitor. We are keeping the money we got from selling the weapons, the schematics and now the ransom for the prince, then I'm taking my share and I'm done. I'm tired of that backward-ass planet and their fucked-up morality anyway. Have you any idea how hard it is to find a decent piece of ass on Regelence? All the women are so inelegant and lower class. Although it is amusing to watch them come crawling back groveling at my feet for a chance at aristocracy even when they know I will leave them bruised, broken and bleeding." Braxton chuckled.

"Are you getting this?" Aiden motioned to the wireless device Trouble had set on the keyboard that now had a steady blue light on the top of it.

Trouble hit a few more buttons. "Yeah. Got *it*, the ship's log and a buttload of encrypted messages."

"They probably would have never noticed the sketches if that idiot Benson had stopped taking the screens. I told him not too, but he did it anyway."

"And where is this Benson now?" Chapman asked.

"Dead."

At the reminder of the dead valet, Aiden and Trouble looked at each other again.

Finally Trouble stopped typing. "We have to go. We've wasted enough time." The blue light on the drive went off.

Picking it up and fumbling with his heel, Trouble put the drive back.

"What now?"

Trouble typed a few more things on the keyboard, grabbed Aiden's arm and took off. "Now we haul ass to the emergency shuttle. Give me a boost."

Aiden put his hands together, letting Trouble step into them and hoist himself back into the tunnel.

Poking his head back out, he held down his hand. "Here."

"Move out of the way." Aiden jumped, caught the edge and pulled himself inside.

After replacing the panel, he crawled back through the maintenance shaft, following Trouble.

"Look for a ladder along the bulkhead."

Aiden began looking ahead for a spot with no pipes. "Where are we going?"

"There is a hatch leading right outside the communications room. If I read it correctly, a few feet from that hatch to the left is the emergency shuttle."

If he read it right? *Great.* If he read it wrong didn't bear thinking on. They would be standing around right outside an occupied room. "There. There is the ladder. Are you sure about this?"

"Not a hundred percent no." Trouble started up the ladder.

Wonderful. Aiden rolled his eyes. "Do you think maybe we should go back and check again?"

"No time. I sort of told the ship to self-destruct."

"You *what?*"

"Come on." Trouble reached the top and glanced down at him. "Okay, we are going to just do it. I'm going to push it open and hurry out and you have to be right behind me. One, two, three, go!"

Aiden didn't have time to panic. He followed Trouble up and out. There was a hatch to their left, one to their right and one directly in front of them.

Trouble hit a button on the wall to their left as the hatch in front of them opened.

An officer stepped out of the communications room, his eyes widening when he came face-to-face with Aiden.

"Shit." Without thinking, Aiden doubled up his fist and hit the man square in the nose. Everything went in slow motion, blood splattered, the man wobbled. Another man came out of the hatch behind the first one, fragger drawn. "Oh shit."

"Aiden!"

He dove for the shuttle as a searing pain flared in his thigh. Falling into the shuttle, he caught himself on his hands. "Go! Trouble, get us out of here now." Another fragger bolt caught his arm and made it buckle. His head hit the deck as a loud popping sound rang out.

"Fuck." Trouble started hitting buttons.

The door closed.

"Aiden?"

"Unh." Lying perfectly still, he stretched out on his stomach. His leg hurt, his arm hurt and he was going to vomit.

"Are you alive?"

He was seeing stars and—where was he? Oh yeah, kidnapped, shuttle escape. He had to focus. He couldn't leave Trouble alone to fend for himself. Nate would expect him to take care of his son. *Nate.* Aiden would miss him terribly whether he was gone for a few months, few years or always. Aiden had gotten his freedom, but he'd lost his heart. "Trouble, tell Nate I love him, 'kay?"

He must have blacked out for a minute, because the next thing he knew Trouble was yelling at him.

"Damn it, Aiden! Talk to me. Please... I can't come back there. They were shooting at us and I have to get further away and..." He sniffled, sounding like he was on the verge of tears. "Aiden?"

"'M here, Trouble. Where are we?" He opened his eyes and tried to sit, but as soon as he put any weight on his right arm pain overwhelmed him.

Trouble let out a big, audible breath. "Fuck if I know. I have no navigational controls. A fragger bolt took out the panel."

"Did you call for help?" Moving himself to where he could see Trouble made his leg hurt, so he gave up and laid still.

"Yes, before we left the ship. You all right?"

"Do it again. Try to get word to the IN and have them send someone to pick us up."

"Okay. The Lady Anna should still be in the area. According to the coordinates before we left The Marchioness, we weren't too far out of The Regelence System. I— Yes! A Destroyer. Aiden, there's an IN Destroyer heading toward us."

Aiden hoped that wasn't a bad thing. He hurt enough without crashing and being blown to bits. "It's not going to run into us since you can't steer, is it?"

"It's the Lady Anna." Trouble sounded relieved.

Forcing himself to lift his head, Aiden squinted toward the viewscreen.

Nate's ship was formidable. It looked like a metal warship of old. Massive gun turrets lined the main hanger deck. The tower, or Island as it was called, stood tall above the flight deck.

The sheer size was intimidating, a sight to send any enemy into a panic. It was easy to see why Nate was so proud of her.

There were a few beeps and then a man spoke. "Please identify yourself. We indicate there are two passengers in your shuttle."

"Oh, thank Galaxy, Lieutenant Taylor. Jeremy Hawkins, sir. I have Prince Aiden of Regelence with me."

There was a cheer from over the speaker, making Aiden grin even through his pain. Then Taylor spoke again, sounding much more cheerful. "Nice to hear your voice, Trouble. Cut the engines and we'll pull you in."

CB

The Lady Anna: One parsec outside of the Regelence System.

Nate stood in front of the hangar bay, trying to look calm and patient when he was anything but. What was taking so long? He, Raleigh and Steven had taken a shuttle to the Lady Anna as soon as Nate realized Aiden and Trouble had been kidnapped. They'd been in pursuit when they noticed the small shuttle heading toward them.

"Are they all right?" Raleigh asked from beside him.

"I don't know." Nate sounded a lot gruffer than he'd meant to, but damn it he was worried. He'd left the bridge as soon as he'd heard Jeremy's voice.

Steven, who was pacing back and forth behind them, stopped beside Raleigh. "I thought you said you talked to them."

"I went to get the two of you as soon as we learned it was them." Nate closed his eyes. Trouble had sounded okay. *Please, let them both be okay.*

"Captain, the shuttle is onboard and another managed to escape The Marchioness before it self-destructed. It is headed away from the Regelence System," Anna's monotone voice stated.

"How many aboard the other shuttle, Anna?" Nate asked.

"My sensors indicate one life form, Captain." The red light above the door changed to green. "The hangar is now pressurized, Captain." The hatch opened.

Nate rushed in with Steven and Raleigh on his heels.

The shuttle door opened and Trouble and Aiden hobbled out together. Trouble looked fine, but Aiden had his arm around Jeremy's shoulder, using him for support and limping badly.

It felt like someone grabbed Nate's heart and squeezed. Running, Nate reached them seconds before the other two men. Nate swooped Aiden into his arms and Steven lifted Trouble, who immediately began protesting.

"Anna, ready the sickbay and let them know we're on our way." Nate ran out of the hanger.

"Yes, Captain."

Aiden looked up and gave him a trembling smile, his eyelids droopy. "Hi."

Nate smiled back. "Hi." The tightness in his chest eased a little. "Steven, how's Trouble?" Hurrying toward the sickbay, he watched Aiden. Aiden's eyes started drifting closed. "Stay with me, boy."

"Says he's fine, but I'm not letting him down," Steven called back.

"Good." Nate could hear Trouble arguing that he was all right. "Jeremy, shut up and let Steven carry you."

They reached the sickbay and four medics met them with gurneys. Nate laid Aiden down gently and was aware of Steven doing the same next to him with Trouble. Nate, Steven and Raleigh followed as the medics wheeled the two younger men into the exam room. After reading the message Benson had on him when he died, Nate didn't trust anyone. He was pretty sure his own ship was safe, but...he wasn't taking any chances.

Aiden reached out and grabbed his hand. "Nate—"

"We'll talk about it all later. Let them check you over." Nate bent and kissed his forehead. Caldwell better hope he died on that ship because if he didn't, he was going to pay for hurting Aiden and Trouble.

The medics started undressing Aiden, but Aiden wouldn't let go of Nate's arm long enough to get the other sleeve off.

"Captain?" The medic hesitated.

"Cut it off." He rubbed his thumb over Aiden's knuckles, staring into the languid gray eyes. "I was afraid I'd lost you."

Aiden nodded. "Me too."

Cutting the pants off Aiden, the medics got to work cleaning the wounds. The wounds didn't look too bad—they looked more like nicks and they weren't bleeding due to being cauterized by the bolts. But Aiden was going to be pretty sore for awhile.

Trouble fussed next to them.

Nate turned to face his son. The kid did seem to be healthy and whole. But Nate would rather be safe than sorry. "Trouble, sit still and let them look at you."

Catching his gaze, Trouble huffed out a breath. "I'm fine. Aiden is the one who needs help. He took a fragger bolt to the arm and leg and hit his head. He lost consciousness in the shuttle once already."

Someone shined a light in Aiden's eyes and started asking him questions. Through it all Nate stayed right there holding his hand.

Wincing at the pain when they probed at the fragger wounds, Aiden met his gaze. "I love you, Nate."

Nate melted inside, his lips turning up into a soft smile. As fucked up as this day had been, suddenly everything felt a little better. He ran his free hand over Aiden's cheek, feeling the warm skin, and noticed Aiden had drifted off to sleep. "I love you too, Aiden."

ᘓ

The medics treated him for the fragger burns—that thankfully weren't serious—gave him some pain meds that wouldn't make him drowsy and told Nate to keep him awake. His concussion, from hitting his head on the deck of the shuttle, was the biggest concern. According to what he heard, he'd lost consciousness again in the sickbay. He barely even remembered being there. The memories of the last few hours were sketchy. He was still a little woozy, but better. He could focus on his surroundings now.

It was his first time on an IN Destroyer—not just any Destroyer but Nate's—and he didn't want to miss anything. This ship was Nate's entire life, it was his rival in a sense, but he couldn't make himself hate it. He was intrigued. Slowly heading toward the bridge, Aiden walked between his father and sire. He had a nice view of Nate's arse in the tight-fitting black IN jumpsuit. It gave him something to focus on instead of his dizziness. "How'd Trouble get one of the cool jumpsuits and I got scrubs?"

Trouble turned his head, grinning. "Because I grabbed one in sickbay. No way I was wearing that stupid noose around my neck any longer. Besides, these are pretty cool, huh?"

"Yeah. I'm feeling way underdressed though." Father and Cony may not have been in the cool IN suits, but they were properly dressed, with cravats and waistcoats.

They turned onto the gangway and Nate stopped before they reached the bridge. He looked every inch the IN captain, aloof and in control. "Let me stop in here and then we will all talk." He gazed at Aiden, his face softening a little. "You all right?"

It made Aiden feel ten feet tall that he could affect this powerful man. He smiled back. "I'm good, sir."

Nate smiled and gave him a crisp nod before preceding them onto the bridge. Cony mumbled something about Aiden not being a soldier and they stepped into the mayhem.

Someone called out, "Captain on deck."

Nate scowled and pointed at the man who said it. "Shut the fuck up, Davis."

Several people laughed and a crewman yelled, "Good to have you back, Captain Hawk."

Trouble leaned in to whisper, "Hopefully this won't take long."

Aiden barely acknowledged him. He was too busy staring in awe and taking the whole scene in. People went back and forth rushing around, and everyone talked at once creating a static buzz. A huge viewscreen up front showed the stars, and what looked like debris of The Marchioness. It was chaotic, and there was Nate in the middle of it all. Officers came to give him reports and verify orders. Every few seconds or so someone was saying, "Aye, aye, Captain."

Watching everything made Aiden feel claustrophobic and his head spin worse, so he focused on Nate.

Nate was big, towering over most of the other officers. He called back orders and looked over reports without missing a beat. It was utterly fascinating and a bit intimidating to see Nate in his natural element. All the gold on his uniform wasn't the only thing that set him apart. His whole comportment was one of authority. Aiden could never take this away from Nate. He'd never ask Nate to give this up. *Deep breath, Aiden.*

Nate finally came toward them, but his attention was still on his crew. "Take us back to orbit around Regelence. Lieutenant Taylor, request proper clearances and notifications. Lieutenant Kindros, give an official report to IN Headquarters and Admiral Jenkins."

Those commands were followed by a barrage of "Aye aye, Captains," then Nate put his hand in the middle of Aiden's back and ushered them all to the left of the bridge. "Please join me in the ready room."

The captain's ready room was subdued, masculine and blessedly quiet. It reminded Aiden a bit of his parents' study. It even had a big oak desk, which Trouble sat on the edge of. Father and Cony took seats in a couple of armchairs and Nate sat with Aiden on a big navy blue leather couch.

Nate put his arm over the back of the couch and Aiden couldn't help but snuggle into his side. This might be the last he saw of Nate for some while. Kissing Aiden's forehead, Nate dropped his arm onto Aiden's shoulder. "Did the two of you learn anything when you were being held captive on the ship?"

"From what we heard, it sounded like Braxton stole the weapons for money to buy some sort of plans to turn around and sell them for more capital. Only he didn't plan on turning over the money for the plans, he was going to steal them, sell them and get richer." Aiden shrugged. "Apparently, kidnapping me and Trouble was an afterthought to get even more cash."

Trouble nodded and took up the tale. "Braxton knew we would figure him out from Aiden's sketches. He wanted to leave Regelence. Caldwell was in on it and so was the captain. I don't know whether Benson was or not, but he knew what Caldwell was up to. He's the one who kept taking Aiden's screens."

Nate and Cony exchanged a look, but neither said anything.

"Was there any mention of Englor?" Steven asked.

Aiden frowned. Englor was Nate's home planet. "No. Why?"

"We found a note on Benson addressed to Colonel Hollister of Englor's Royal Marine corp."

"What did it say?" Trouble cocked his head. "Do you think Englor had something to do with all this?"

Nate shook his head. "I don't know. The note indicated otherwise. Benson was obviously investigating the situation and reporting back to the colonel. It appears that we aren't the only ones trying to figure out what is going on. Benson said they would buy schematics, but he didn't indicate what they were for or who was selling them to Braxton. He did hint that it was someone pretty high up in the government. In his missive, Benson told the colonel that the whole scheme was bigger than it appeared, but again he didn't give specifics."

Cony sat perfectly still, his expression giving nothing of his emotions away. Father appeared very contemplative. He patted Cony's leg. "What are you thinking, Raleigh?"

Looking around at everyone in the room, Cony shook his head. "I believe Benson was right. I think Braxton was a pawn." He stared right at Nate. "Why does the name Hollister sound familiar?"

Running his hand through Aiden's hair and over his neck, Nate sighed. "Because Hollister is the surname of Englor's royal family. Colonel Simon Hollister is the heir apparent to the throne of Englor."

Chapter Seventeen

Nate was dying to go check on his boy again and make certain he was all right. Raleigh had stopped him at the door to his cabin and asked if they could have Trouble's DNA tested. Right after Nate had made the appropriate arrangements with medical, Admiral Jenkins called to discuss what happened and to ask Nate again about the admiral promotion. He'd made certain that Nate knew he could move fleet headquarters anywhere he wanted. He hinted heavily at Regelence. Nate was even more confused. He had a really bad feeling about all of this, but right now, all he wanted to do was see Aiden. Nate knew how close he'd come to losing Aiden today.

Opening the hatch leading to his bedroom, he found Aiden leaning against the bulkhead, staring out the porthole. He was so lost in thought he didn't even notice Nate coming in.

Nate liked the way Aiden looked in his room. It was dark and masculine, much like the ready room. It wasn't luxurious like their suite in the castle. It was plain and simple, decorated in a nautical theme. His elegant prince looked good in this setting. Of course, his boy looked good anywhere, but this room was Nate's, and he liked having Aiden in it.

The hatch slid closed, drawing Aiden's attention. He turned, his face a bit paler than usual, probably from the hellish day he'd had. "I want to go with you."

Nate stopped dead in his tracks. He hadn't expected that. Hell, it was a question Nate didn't have an answer for, but desperately wanted an answer to. He was beginning to think that Aiden was in danger wherever he was.

Aiden paced around the bed, clearly agitated. "I want to stay here on the Lady Anna."

Nate crossed to the bed and sat, patting it and looking up at Aiden. "Come sit down."

"No." Shaking his head almost frantically, Aiden bit his bottom lip. His boy was nervous.

"I haven't managed to rid you of your rebellious streak, have I, boy?" He didn't want to either. He liked Aiden just the way he was. But he didn't like Aiden being upset. It was bound to get worse with what Nate was finding out, but he was going to do his best to make things as easy on his family as possible. "I don't want to put you in danger." Nate dropped his head into his hands and groaned. "I had planned on making you stay on Regelence until I could retire next year, but now I'm not sure what to do. I've been offered a promotion to Admiral. I don't know if I'm going to take it or not. If I do, my headquarters can be most anywhere."

"What are you talking about?" Aiden sounded confused, like this was news to him. It shouldn't. Nate knew damned well he'd told Aiden he didn't think a ship was a place to raise a family.

"Boy. Sit." He tugged, giving Aiden no choice but to sit. He needed to see Aiden's face. "What's on your mind?"

Aiden looked confused. His face was a mix of emotions, like he couldn't make up his mind. "You never planned on leaving me."

"What?" Nate scowled. Aiden thought he was going to abandon him? "Where did you get that idea?"

Aiden laughed. It was a joyous sound and it scared the hell out of Nate because he had no idea what it was about. Aiden must still be suffering from the blow to the head.

Grabbing his face in both hands, Nate made Aiden focus on him. "Boy, look at me."

Aiden laughed harder. "I'm fine." He pushed Nate's hands away and dove at him, knocking him backwards on the bed. "I love you, Nate."

"I love you too. Are you telling me you thought I was going to leave you?" Nate pushed Aiden up, making him straddle Nate's hips.

Aiden nodded. "You love being a captain. You love the Lady Anna and the IN."

For several seconds Nate just lay there staring up at him. He didn't know what to say. They were really going to have to work on their communication skills. Finally, he shook his head, reached up, grabbed Aiden's neck and pulled him down, kissing him. His hands rubbed up and down Aiden's back. He took his time, licking the seam of Aiden's lips, asking for entrance.

When Aiden opened, Nate traced his lips and his teeth. He slowly pushed in, finding Aiden's tongue as hands slid up the back of Aiden's shirt, caressing. He rolled them over, breaking their kiss. "I do, but I love you more."

"That's good. Because I was trying to be understanding and not come between you and your dream, but I'm not above begging."

"And you've proven that repeatedly, boy." Nate caught Aiden's chin, making sure he had his undivided attention. "I don't know what is going to happen yet, boy. But I promise you whatever happens, I have no intention on deserting you."

Aiden wrapped his hands around Nate's neck, nuzzling their faces together. "I'm going to hold you to th—"

"Captain, we are about to dock at the Regelence Space Station. There is a shuttle waiting to take you and your guests down to the planet." Anna's calm melodious voice echoed through the cabin.

He was going to miss that voice. Nate closed his eyes and took a deep breath, silently saying goodbye to Anna, his first love. Even if he came back onboard, it would never be the same. Opening his eyes, he glanced at his new love and his life. "Let's go home, boy."

⅓

Planet Regelence: Townsend Castle.

Nate stared at the stunning painting of Muffin and the Regelence Roses with a smile on his face. Pride swelled inside him. Aiden's art was worth sharing with the galaxy. It was something worth preserving, just like the man himself. Something Nate would die defending, if need be.

"Nate." Raleigh came in wearing a sword strapped to his waist, making the smile melt from Nate's face. Raleigh hadn't worn a sword inside the castle since Nate had arrived. Sitting behind the desk, he steepled his hands. "Steven is on his— There he is now."

"Jeffers, close the door and give us privacy, please." Steven strode into the room, crossing to the desk. Dressed much the same as Raleigh in starched pristine white neckcloth, light-colored waistcoat, dark trousers and boots and a scabbard with sword, Steven looked every inch the gentleman except for the strained expression he wore. "Raleigh, Nate." He dipped his head and perched himself on the front of the desk. "Shall we get started?"

"Steven, you make a better door than a window." Raleigh didn't wait for a response. He got up, came around the desk and sat on it next to Steven.

"You've called me worse, Raleigh." Steven looked at Nate. "Now, the reason I called this meeting is to go over what we've discovered."

Nate nodded. "I've got some news for the both of you too." The sooner he got this out in the open the better he'd feel. As it stood, he felt edgy. Sadly, that wasn't likely to change. He needed to ensure his boy's and his son's safety and he had a long fight in front of him to obtain that.

"Oh, well then, you go first, Nate," Steven said.

Nate nodded. The best thing would be to just lay it out there and see how they responded. "The IN wants to make me Aries Fleet Admiral."

Steven's eyes widened, but that was the only change in his appearance.

Raleigh nodded like it didn't surprise him. "And?"

"I believe they are trying to manipulate me into moving the Aries Fleet headquarters here. And I'd like your input. I had actually planned on finishing out my last year as a captain and retiring here on Regelence. I'd thought about starting a family and trying to give Trouble a more stable home life. But it looks like the IN is deeply involved with Braxton and whatever is happening on Englor, and I want my family safe. Aiden and my son are my main concerns. Because of who Aiden is to the two of you and Regelence, he, myself and any children we have can always be used as pawns. And I refuse to let that happen."

Raleigh sat forward, challenging him. "And what do you plan on doing about it?"

Crossing to stand in front of Steven, Nate knelt and bowed his head, showing his respect. It was so quiet in the room that

Nate became ultra aware of his own breathing. He'd never done this, not even for his own king, but to protect and provide for his family... He hoped Steven and Raleigh both knew what a huge step this was for him. Offering his complete allegiance and unquestioned loyalty to someone was not an easy thing for him.

The metallic hiss of the blade leaving its protective sheath made Nate hold his breath. He didn't expect to be struck, but old habits died hard.

Steven's shiny black boots came into view. "You honor my house, Nate, and I will gladly accept your oath." The flat part of the sword touched Nate's right shoulder. "You, being chosen to be one of the honorable company of the most noble order of The Black Rose, shall promise and swear by the Sacred Band of Thebes, that wittingly or unwittingly you shall not break any statute of the said order, or any articles in them contained. The same being agreeable and not repugnant to the laws of the IN, and the laws of Regelence as far forth as you belong, so help you."

What? Nate raised his gaze. He'd offered fealty and Steven had chosen to honor him with knighthood. "I do."

Steven brought the sword up and tapped him on the other shoulder. "Now rise, Sir Nathaniel."

As soon as Nate got to his feet and Steven replaced his sword, Steven pulled Nate into a hug, pounding him on the back. "I know you well enough to know you are not a man to give his loyalty easily."

"I love your son and I won't see him or the things he holds dear destroyed."

Dipping his head, Steven stepped back.

Nate hadn't seen Raleigh move, but he stood slightly behind Steven ready to take his place.

Offering his hand, Nate bowed his head, showing his respect to the king-consort as well.

Raleigh clasped his hand and pulled him into a back-pounding hug just as Steven had done. "Thank you, Nate. I want you to know that he has only knighted someone once and I was that person."

Nate stared. This was truly an honor.

"My father always said knights were for times of trouble and war. I have a feeling, unfortunately, both are upon us."

The hair on the back of Nate's arms stood up, the words were so significant.

Moving back to the desk, Raleigh took a seat on the edge of it. "This situation is going to get very ugly when and if what we've uncovered gets out."

"Yes. Which is what this discussion is about. I know I'm not the only one here that is questioning the IN's commitment to our protection and best interest, but until we know exactly what *is* going on we need to keep it to ourselves."

Steven nodded his agreement and leaned back on the desk between Raleigh's legs. "We will be making some drastic changes. This is what I wanted to speak to you about. We can no longer afford to trust the IN. Not only are radical changes in security going to have to take place, but we need to figure out what is going on."

"If I become an admiral...it would be an excellent way for us to keep tabs on the IN."

"I do like the way you think, Nate." Raleigh rested his chin on Steven's shoulder and grinned.

"Of course you would." Steven snorted, bringing his hand up to rest on Raleigh's cheek. "It sounds exactly like something you would do."

Raleigh lifted his chin, turning to face Steven. "What does that mean?"

"I wonder." The corner of Steven's lip twitched as he turned his attention back to Nate. "It sounds like a wonderful idea, given the circumstances. You should give them what they want and make your headquarters on Regelence. I think this needs to be a case of keep your friends close but your enemies closer."

Nate agreed. He was glad to see Steven shared similar views. It would make protecting what was theirs a bit easier. He took his seat back on the couch feeling much better. It also meant that he could stay here with Aiden.

Steven cleared his throat, resting his hands on Raleigh's thighs bracketing his hips. "I got a report back from Wentworth, the head of the royal guards. Braxton's townhouse didn't turn up much. They did find a substantial amount of Rapture though. Apparently, Braxton was hooked on the stuff. His butler affirmed he was using the drug at least twice a day. He was hard up for cash due to his drug use and his gambling."

Which would explain the spacey look in Braxton's eyes the day he tried to take Aiden while they were all shopping. "I'm not surprised. It also means he'd be easier to manipulate. Which lends credence to Benson's claims that he was a pawn."

Raleigh nodded, running his hand idly over Steven's arm. "Have the messages Trouble took from Braxton's ship been translated? I want to know how Englor fits into this."

"Not yet. But right now I think there is something more immediate that needs attention. The castle needs better security. Caldwell never should have been allowed to take Aiden and Trouble out of my suite, much less the castle. Are you aware there is a default loop in the security cameras and the princes have learned to get past it? It's how Aiden managed to get into my room unnoticed." Nate raised a brow at Raleigh.

"You have got to stop treating them, your children, like they are too young to understand. They're all grown men and they need to be told what's going on. This is their fight too."

Steven sighed. "You're right. It's only natural to try and protect your children, but you are correct, they must be told about this." He stepped out from in front of his consort and sat on the desk next to him. "Nate, since you mention children, we need to discuss yours. I believe Raleigh told you his suspicions about Trouble?" Steven rested his hand on Raleigh's thigh.

"Yes, he did. He thinks Trouble is Regelen." Nate was impressed his voice came out as unemotional as it did. He wasn't going to deny Trouble the opportunity to learn where he came from, but if anyone tried to take him away... The kid still had nightmares sometimes about being abandoned and having to fend for himself.

"Trouble is Regelen and we got the tests back. We are positive who his parents were." Raleigh laid his hand over the one Steven had resting on his leg and intertwined their fingers. "The men I told you about? Marcus and Patrick Summers. They were the Marquis and Marquis-Consort of Winstol. When they were killed, they had their infant son, Jeremy, with them. We assumed Trouble died too."

It didn't explain how Trouble had ended up on a space station, but for some reason it made Nate feel better. Maybe the kid's parents did not abandon him as Trouble thought they had. Not that it mattered, Trouble was his...and Aiden's now. "He has me and Aiden. Jeremy *is* my adopted son."

"And as such, you will be in control of one of the most vast estates in Regelence until Trouble reaches his majority. You and Aiden also have seats in parliament until your ward turns twenty-five or marries."

"My son," Nate corrected. *A seat in parliament?* Nate felt like someone dumped cold water over him. He wasn't about to deny Trouble what was his, but... "His name was legally changed to Hawkins. Will that be a problem?"

Raleigh shook his head. "I will see to it that it won't be an issue. As long as you and Trouble both wish it, his name can remain Hawkins."

"Your son comes from two of the oldest and most respected families in Regelence. I'm sure there will be some in parliament who want his name changed back to Summers, but..."

"Steven, you're stalling. Tell him the rest."

Shit. Nate didn't like the sound of that. He raised a brow at Raleigh.

Steven caught Nate's gaze. "Trouble was betrothed at birth to Rexley. Your son is to be the next King-Consort of Regelence."

Chapter Eighteen

Nate walked up the stairs with a sinking feeling in his gut. What was the worse that could happen? He'd tell Trouble, Trouble would probably get pissed off and run to his room to sulk, then Nate would have to talk to him again tomorrow. Nate had witnessed the kid's temper tantrums for years, he knew how to deal with them. But this felt different. There was the slightest doubt in his mind how Trouble would react and that worried Nate.

He had a lump in his throat the size of the Lady Anna. Which was ridiculous, this was good news. At least part of it was. Whatever happened, he'd handle it. Reaching his and Aiden's room, Nate opened the door. It was empty so he crossed to the sitting room that adjoined his and Aiden's room to Trouble's.

Aiden and Trouble were both there, looking relaxed and in their own little worlds. Aiden sat on the chaise lounge, in a pair of pants and shirt, no cravat or socks and shoes—his shirt wasn't even tucked in—sketchscreen propped on his bent knees. Trouble lounged in his pajamas on the rug in front of the fireplace, on his stomach, with his bookreader. Neither of them noticed as Nate entered the room.

"Ahem." Nate closed the door behind him.

Aiden glanced up and smiled. Jeremy shushed him, waving a hand absently in the air. *The brat.*

Nate took a deep breath and stepped forward. By the time he made it to the chaise, Aiden had put his sketchscreen away and was standing to meet him.

His boy's head cocked. "Everything okay?" Aiden wrapped his arms around Nate's neck and kissed his cheek.

"Yeah, everything is fine." Nate kissed Aiden's forehead and patted his back before turning his attention to Trouble.

Trouble glanced up from his reader, meeting Nate's gaze. "Whatever it is, Hawk, I didn't do it. I've been in here since you left. Ask Aiden." He nodded and went right back to reading his book.

Aiden chuckled. "He's been right here the whole time you were talking to my parents."

"Trouble, we need to talk."

"I already said I'm not the guilty party," he grumbled, turning off his reader, and flopped onto his side.

Nate grinned. He wondered what the kid had done. Whenever Trouble professed his innocence before being accused, he'd usually done something. Sitting on the chaise Aiden had vacated, Nate looked down at Trouble.

Aiden sat next to him, catching Nate's hand in his. Nate loved him even more for the gesture.

"Jeremy—"

"Uh-oh." Trouble sat up, crossing his legs, and gave Nate his undivided attention. "This must be serious if you are calling me Jeremy."

Squeezing Aiden's hand, Nate closed his eyes and took another deep breath. Trouble had always responded best to directness. So why was Nate having such a hard time being direct? "I know who your parents were. They didn't abandon you, they were killed. You're Regelen, Son."

Aiden gasped.

Trouble blinked several times. "Excuse me?"

"You're a marquis and you are from Regelence."

"Oh." Trouble frowned, looking down at his lap. He sat quietly for several minutes.

Aiden touched Nate's arm. "How did you find this out? What family?"

"Your sire saw the Regelence birthmark under his arm and figured it out. I'd seen yours but I didn't make the connection. Raleigh got a DNA sample from the Lady Anna's medical team and had it tested. His family name is Summers."

Aiden's eyebrows pulled together.

Trouble lifted his shirt and arm, looking at the birthmark. He dropped the pajama top and raised his head. "I had two fathers?"

"Yes. Your parents were Marquis and Marquis-Consort of Winstol. I don't know the specifics."

Trouble nodded. "Thank you for telling me. Do you think maybe Raleigh would tell me more about them before we go back to the ship?"

Now for the part Nate was dreading. "He said that he would, whenever you're ready to talk about it, but—" Nate glanced over at Aiden, reminding himself why he'd made this decision.

Aiden smiled and squeezed his hand, offering his support.

"We aren't going back to the Lady Anna."

"What?" Trouble glared and jumped to his feet. He positioned himself in front of Nate, hands on his hips. "What do you mean we aren't going back?"

"You are heir to a title and I'm being promoted to admiral."

"What? Admiral?" Trouble smiled for a brief second, then the scowl returned. "I don't want to stay on this tight-assed, uptight, prissy planet." He started pacing back and forth, shaking his head and grumbling under his breath.

Nate had known Trouble wasn't going to make this easy on him. He looked up, gathering his thoughts, then back at his son.

Aiden reached over, patting and rubbing the back of Nate's hand that was held in his. "I'll go and let the two of you talk." He started to rise, but Nate caught him. "You're part of this too. Stay." Leaning over, Nate kissed Aiden's cheek and stood. He reached out toward Trouble, but Trouble stepped away. Staying on Regelence was best for Trouble, for Aiden, hell even for him, but he hated hurting Trouble even if it was for his own good. "We have responsibilities now. You have to learn to manage your estate and—" *Fuck.* How was he supposed to tell the kid about Rexley?

Stopping, Trouble turned and jabbed his finger at Nate. "Don't you tell me about responsibilities and managing estates. You skipped out on your own inheritance—"

Nate froze. It felt as if someone had punched him in the gut. Staring at Trouble, he tried not to let on how much that had stung. "That was completely different. I shot someone, I had to leave to protect father's honor."

Throwing his hands in the air, Trouble let them fall to his side with a slap. "Well, if that is the only problem, where'd I leave my gun?" He glanced around the room like he was searching for something.

Trouble's accusation was said in desperation, but it still irritated Nate. He was older and wiser and he'd learned from his bad decisions. His job was to do the best by his son and consort, and that's what he was going to do. "Are you quite done being a smart ass?"

"Are you quite done with this idiotic idea that we are staying here?"

Nate growled, counting to ten under his breath.

Grimacing, Aiden pointed nervously at the door. "I'm just going to go and—"

"Stay!" Nate sighed. Damn it, he hadn't meant to snap at Aiden.

"Fuck this. As soon as I'm old enough, I'm outta here," Trouble said.

"Watch your mouth." Nate still had several years to change the brat's mind. "You can do whatever you like, when you reach your majority." And he damned well meant by Regelence standards—age twenty-five, not eighteen—but he wasn't going to share that information with Trouble just yet.

Trouble raised his chin a notch. "Majority? Sounds more like a jail sentence to me." He headed toward his bedroom door with his hands balled into fists.

"There is one other thing." Nate pinched the bridge of his nose, his head pounding. "When you were born, you were betrothed to Rexley."

Aiden gasped and stuttered, grabbing Nate's arm. "What? You can't let them do that. We have to stop it. It isn't fair. Trouble and Rexley are from two different worlds, it would be a disaster. It will ruin both their lives. Nate, this has—"

Trouble spun around. His mouth dropped open then slammed shut. He glared at Nate and Aiden. "Stay out of this, Aiden. I'm not going to be here long enough to marry the ice prince."

Nate was not going to stoop to Trouble's level. He was the adult and he was going to continue to act like one. "I'll get the betrothal annulled later."

"Is anyone listening to me? I'm not going to be here to marry anyone!" Trouble made an exasperated growling sound and stalked toward his door again. The ears on his bunny slippers flapped furiously, dampening his dramatic exit somewhat.

Nate watched him go. "I'm doing this for your own good."

Trouble stopped at the door, snarling back over his shoulder. "Are you? Or is it for your own good?"

Nate clenched his teeth together. He wasn't going to get pissed. "Trouble..."

"Nate, I am telling you I am leaving as soon as I am old enough and I am not asking for your permission on this matter." He slammed the door to his room.

Aiden reached up, running a hand over Nate's beard. "Do you think he'll be all right?"

Nate caught Aiden's hand and kissed it. "If we don't kill each other first."

⅓

Sitting quietly behind the desk, Raleigh watched and listened. He felt guilty about Rexley being affianced to Trouble. It was his fault. The contract had been signed before Rexley was born. Steven had broken his betrothal with Marcus to marry Raleigh. To atone for his and Steven's sins, they had to sign a contract promising their heir's hand in marriage to Winstol's first born.

Steven didn't hide his guilt nearly as well as Raleigh though. Having given Rexley the entire story, Steven paced back and forth in front of the desk. Every so often he'd look up at Raleigh then shake his head before going back to pacing.

Rexley's reaction should have lessened their guilt, but it didn't. It did just the opposite. Rexley was...well Rexley. He sat through the explanation perfectly still and expressionless, his amber eyes locked on to Steven, going back and forth as Steven paced. It wasn't at all surprising. Whenever Rexley was given what he thought of as a duty or responsibility, he seemed to go into what Raleigh thought of as control mode. He would calmly assess the issue and deal with it. No temper tantrums or accusations, it wasn't Rexley's style.

Raleigh felt tears welling up and his chest hurt. He desperately wanted for Rexley to be a child and have a carefree existence. A rebellion from him would almost be welcoming. He wasn't like his brothers—he never let himself be a kid. Out of all his children Rexley worried Raleigh the most. From birth, Rexley had been raised to be king, and he'd taken that responsibility easily but he'd built up walls to keep from getting hurt. It didn't work though, Rexley could be hurt, he just covered it well.

Finally, Steven stopped pacing and turned to face their son. "Say something, Rexley." Steven's voice was gruff, like he too was close to tears.

Rexley arched an ebony brow, looking so much like Steven. "What would you have me to say, Father? It doesn't sound like I have any choice." Rexley's composure made Raleigh's heart ache. He was such a good kid. Even as a baby he'd given Steven and Raleigh few problems.

Leaning against the edge of the desk, Steven ran his hands down his face and groaned. "Yell at us or something." When he set his hands back on the desk they were shaky.

"Why?" Rexley's brows drew together. "Ranting and raving wouldn't change the situation, Father." He got up from the chair and walked up to Steven, touching him on the shoulder, trying to console him. "It's honestly not your fault, not really. You had no choice after what happened and no control over whom you would love."

Which was the crux of the problem. Rexley should have someone who loved him, someone he loved too. He deserved that. Raleigh blinked back tears. All of his sons deserved to have what he had with Steven, but Rexley...needed it. He wasn't laid-back like Steven. Rexley needed someone to help him deal with the stress.

Steven sighed, his shoulders slumping. "We'll get you out of this, Son."

Rexley stepped forward and hugged Steven. He was as tall as Steven now, and looking at them together they could have been twins but for the gray at Steven's temples and the slightly wider shoulders. He patted Steven's back and stepped away. "Father, just let it alone for now and we'll see what happens. I can't say that I've really met him, but Muffin has and she likes him."

His behavior was so typical of Rexley, Raleigh smiled. Rexley would make a wonderful king. He always put others in front of himself. But it was that which bothered Raleigh the most. Rexley needed to enjoy life. He needed to do something for himself for once instead of always sacrificing for others.

03

I'm not going to kill him. Aiden unclenched his fists and opened his eyes. Nate wanted him to teach Trouble how to be a marquis. That included dancing. "Trouble. Leave the cravat alone and get back over here. You are not finished." That even sounded almost civilized for being ground out through his teeth.

Trouble looked up at him from his place on the floor and glared. "This is stupid. I'm not dancing tomorrow night."

"Yes, you are. Tomorrow's ball is to celebrate not just mine and Nate's marriage but also Nate being promoted to Admiral. You are Nate's son and Rexley's betrothed. You *have* to make an appearance. Now, get up." Having to shout over the music was giving Aiden a headache. Or maybe it was the situation, it was hard to tell.

Arching a golden brow, Trouble stood. "I thought I couldn't dance the waltz until I had some sort of come out party and bowed before the king?"

Aiden's jaw hurt from grinding his teeth together and he was developing the same tick Cony got in his cheek when he got mad. *Oh Galaxy,* he was turning into his sire. Aiden took a deep breath and reminded himself for the tenth time in the last thirty minutes that Trouble had not had it easy the past few days. He'd gained a title and a fiancé in one big swoop, not to mention having his freedom curtailed. For Aiden, finding out that Nate was taking the promotion and staying on Regelence was a blessing, but for Trouble, it seriously imploded planets. "You live under the king's roof. Everyone will assume the king has recognized your admission into society. Therefore, you're expected to attend such functions." Aiden held up his arms, ready to give it another shot.

"Just because I go to a ball, doesn't mean I have to dance."

"Why are you being so difficult?" Aiden's voice raised until the last word was practically a shout.

"Why are you? Shouldn't you be drawing or painting or something?"

The twitch in Aiden's jaw started again. "I would love to be painting or something, but instead I'm teaching you to dance."

"For the last time, I don't want t—"

Aiden grabbed Trouble's hand and his waist, jerking him closer. He was done talking about it. Trouble was going to dance and that was that. Listening to the music, Aiden counted. *One, two, three.* He stepped forward but Trouble didn't budge. They bumped heads. If he hadn't been so aggravated, it probably would have hurt.

Trouble staggered back. "Ow."

Grrr... Aiden threw his hands in the air and paced around his stepson. "Galaxy dammit! Can't you behave for five bloody minutes? Every day for the past week I've taken time out of my day to try and help you fit in and this is how you repay me. I'm sick of the whining about edict classes. I don't want to hear it anymore." He stopped several feet in front of Trouble and let his hands fall to his sides in exasperation. "Yes, I feel sorry for you, but—"

"I'm not cinder-fucking-rella. You can dress me up in this getup"—Trouble tugged at his cravat and waved a hand down his body—"teach me how to bow and say milord. You can even teach me to read Shakespeare sonnets but I'll be damned if I let some old letch cart my ass around the dance floor." Trouble fisted his hands, his teeth clenched. "What's next, Mommy?"

Aiden got right back in Trouble's face, pointing his finger. "I'm not your fucking mother!" *Oh yeah,* he was losing it. He'd never shouted obscenities at another person before. His blood was boiling, and he was so mad he was beginning to sweat. Most people probably would have backed down, but Aiden had been putting up with this kind of behavior all week. Trouble's constant criticism of Regelence culture was beginning to feel like a personal attack.

Trouble stepped toward him, raising his fist.

Aiden did the same. No way was he going to let Trouble cower him. He told Nate he'd make sure Trouble behaved and he would, even if it meant the kid showed up at the ball with a black eye.

"Ahem."

Turning to blast whoever was at the door, Aiden stopped dead in his tracks. *Rexley?*

"Problems, little brother?" Rexley looked at Trouble and held out a hand. "Jeremy, would you like me to teach you?"

Aiden rolled his eyes, like that was going to work. Who did Rexley think he was? "Rexl—"

Trouble blinked, and his lips turned up very slowly. It wasn't a smile, but it was close. He took Rexley's hand, staring into his eyes. "I'd love you to."

Holding his gaze, Rexley counted the music aloud and as one they moved together and began waltzing around the room, completely ignoring Aiden. Trouble even let Rexley lead.

Unbelievable. Aiden stared with his mouth ajar. He wanted to be mad at Rexley for interfering, but at the same time...

Trouble tripped and Rexley steadied him before he fell. Instead of yelling at Rexley and telling him he had big feet, Trouble caught his balance and let Rexley guide him in the proper form. Listening intently, Trouble nodded and leaned into Rexley, letting him count and get them moving again.

Who would have thought? Last Aiden heard Trouble was referring to Rexley as the "perky-assed Ice Prince". They actually looked and worked very well together.

Faltering again, Trouble frowned but quickly regained his composure. There was no yelling, just a few nods of his head when Rexley told him something. *Amazing.*

Rexley stepped on Trouble's foot while trying to turn them, and they stumbled. "I'm sorry, Jeremy."

Trouble beamed at him, then shrugged. "'S all right. It was my fault."

After that Rexley bent forward and quietly spoke directions in Trouble's ear. The whispering looked very intimate, but Aiden decided to ignore it. This was working and that's all Aiden cared about at the moment.

He glanced around the empty ballroom, set up for tomorrow's ball. It was done in red, black and white, Regelence colors. The red and black roses would be brought in tomorrow while everyone was at the ceremony, but the ribbons already decorated the railing of the balcony overlooking the ballroom and the marble columns along the perimeter of the dance floor. If Trouble could just learn to dance, tomorrow would be perfect.

Trouble got nearer every time Rexley gave him an instruction, but Aiden disregarded that too. This could be a good thing. Nate and Father had both been determined to get Rexley and Trouble out of this betrothal, but if this was any indication of what was to come, Aiden would make sure they thought twice about it. Rexley was actually smiling. He looked...happy. It was something that had occurred less and less over the years. It made Aiden smile to see it.

Trouble said something, making Rexley laugh.

Aiden found himself chuckling. Rexley hadn't laughed like that, over anything but Muffin, in a long, long time. Apparently, the perky-assed Ice Prince and the Hellion himself weren't such a bad match after all.

"What are you smiling at?" Nate came into the room, kissing Aiden's forehead, before focusing on the dancing couple. "What the—?"

"Shh... They look good together, don't you think?"

"Yes, but they are a little too close together, don't *you* think? If your sire comes in here and sees them so close, he's going— I don't think I've ever seen Rexley smile. And I know damned well I haven't seen Trouble without a scowl on his face all week. What did you do to them?" Nate stepped behind Aiden, wrapping him in his arms and staring over his shoulder.

Trouble was slightly shorter than Rexley, so he had his chin tilted up, but he wore a pleasant grin on his face. It had been there since they started dancing and he hadn't broken eye contact for more than a second or two at a time. The entire time Trouble and Aiden had danced—or rather tried to dance together—Trouble had watched their feet.

Aiden shrugged, leaning back and reaching up to caress Nate's face. The whiskers tickled his fingertips. "I didn't do anything. Rexley came in and asked Trouble if he wanted him to teach him and Trouble said yes. I'm as shocked as you. Before about twenty minutes ago, I was convinced Trouble was either tone deaf or couldn't count to three. Now he looks like he's floating."

Nate squeezed him around the waist, hugging him tighter. "Look at the way he's looking at Rexley."

"That's the way I look at you."

Chapter Nineteen

Aiden sat in the front center row of the large semicircular room of the House of Lords uncomfortably aware of how many eyes were on him. Being in the public should have gotten more comfortable with age but it hadn't. It made his skin crawl and his hands sweat. Having his paintings shown was much easier than being openly examined himself. And being in the House of Lord's meeting chamber had always been one of the worst public displays in his opinion. The room was a little on the daunting side, with its massive dome ceiling and high black, gold-veined marble walls.

Glancing to his left, he noticed Trouble looking around, seemingly oblivious to the scrutiny of the entire House of Lords. Maybe if Aiden had a sketchscreen he wouldn't be aware of being studied. Not to mention he could capture Nate's promotion as it happened. He leaned close to Trouble. "Do you remember what to do?"

"Yes. After Nate's promotion, I'm going to go up there and stand by him."

Well, that wasn't it exactly, but Aiden decided to trust that Trouble knew what to do since the basic idea was correct. "They'll call you forward. Don't worry."

"I'm not the one who's worried." Trouble gave him a pointed look. "Stop it. I'm not going to make a fool out of myself or Nate...or you. I'm not a complete heathen."

"I never thought that. My guess was only three-quarters of one."

Trouble smirked before facing the front again.

IN Admiral Carl Jenkins of Aries Fleet stepped up to the podium in his dress whites. "Lords of Regelence, I am honored to stand before your presence today to perform a military function that for most happens once in our lifetime. The promotion of an IN Captain to the rank of Fleet Admiral."

An anxious feeling came over Aiden. He was proud, but a little nervous too. Which was silly, this wasn't his promotion, but he couldn't help it. Nate was his. He smiled, remembering how Nate had looked in his uniform before leaving the castle. He'd completely lost count of how many times he'd had his hands pushed away and heard the warning, "Boy, behave." Which hadn't helped in the least. That good-natured chiding tone made him want to get his hands on Nate even more.

Trouble dipped his head forward, looking past Aiden across the aisle where Aiden's family sat.

Apparently, Aiden wasn't the only one letting his focus drift. He discreetly pushed Trouble back and turned his attention to Admiral Jenkins.

"It is my honor to have served you for all these long years but it is time for me to step down. I would like all of you present to recognize your new IN Fleet Admiral of Aries Fleet, Admiral Nathaniel Hawkins." Jenkins raised his hand and looked toward the rear of the assembly room.

The entire audience turned, following his gaze.

Nate stood right inside the double oak doors on the black carpet, in full dress uniform complete with his sword. He looked like a vision dressed in white. There wasn't a man in all the galaxy as handsome. The upper part of his face was shaded by a hat. It had a shiny black brim and huge gold brocade signaling his change in rank. It made the red and gold highlights in his dark beard and mustache stand out. Aiden's brain conjured Nate's chestnut eyes. Unfortunately, Aiden's memory took the image a step further and saw the twinkle there when Nate rubbed his whiskered chin across Aiden's nude body. His cock began to harden. Aiden closed his eyes and took a deep breath. A room full of stuffy uptight politicians was no place to get an erection.

He opened his eyes in time to see Nate salute the flag and drop his white-gloved hand back to his side. He'd already changed out his insignia to that of Admiral. His captain's black with gold shoulder boards had been replaced with the nearly completely gold ones of his new rank. Head held high, he followed Father toward the Admiral. Nate was so powerful and commanding Father was almost invisible, even in his crown and sharp formal wear. As they walked by, Nate turned his head, searching. When his gaze rested on Aiden, he winked, before looking back at the admiral.

Aiden let an appreciative noise slip out as Nate passed him. The man was as spectacular from the back as he was the front. The wide shoulders, lean waist, nice round arse. *Good Galaxy*, Aiden couldn't wait to get his hands on him. Maybe he'd see if Nate would leave the uniform on awhile. He liked how the starched uniform felt against his bare skin.

"You look like you are about to start drooling." Trouble elbowed him.

Snapping his mouth closed, Aiden frowned at Trouble. He had been lecturing Trouble on proper behavior all week and here he was ogling his spouse like he was a piece of meat, in public no less. Leave it to the brat to notice. It would probably come up the next time Aiden corrected him.

Admiral Jenkins bowed. "King Steven."

Father dipped his head. "Admiral." He took a seat next to Cony as Nate and Admiral Jenkins saluted one another.

Nate shook the Admiral's hand then handed over his captain's insignia.

After saluting Nate, Jenkins stepped aside, making room for Nate on the black-carpeted platform. "Now for a well-deserved retirement."

There was a chuckle amongst the crowd, before Jenkins joined a group of officers on the front row to the far left.

Standing in the middle of the platform in front of the large black marble podium with the Regelence rose etched into it, Nate addressed the group of IN officers. "Attention." His voice, so clear and deep, echoed in the vast room. It gave Aiden goose bumps. The urge to throw himself at Nate's feet and beg Nate to take him was strong, but he refrained...for now.

The entire group, including Jenkins, stood and saluted.

Nate saluted in return. "My first order is for you to move Aries Fleet Headquarters to Regelence by leave of the King of Regelence. Please carry out this command immediately."

The old Admiral stepped forward, "Aye, aye, Admiral Hawkins."

"Dismissed," Nate said.

Pride swelled in Aiden's chest as the IN officers turned and marched out in formation. His eyes got a little watery staring at his consort. What had he done to deserve such a man? For as long as he lived he'd remember this moment, watching Nate stand proud and tall before the entire Regelence House of Lords. And just as soon as he got the chance he was going to sketch it. Aiden could let himself forget that there was something going on with the IN for now, because this was an honor Nate deserved, for however long it lasted.

Nate caught his gaze, his mouth turning up on one side, and Aiden swore the temperature in the room ratcheted up a notch. Aiden smiled back, his heart speeding up.

Stepping off the platform, Nate slid into the seat next to him. Nate grabbed his hand and squeezed, holding it on top of his thigh.

It took every ounce of control Aiden had not to scoot on over into his lap. "Congratulations, sir," Aiden whispered.

"Thank you," Nate returned. His gaze lowered to Aiden's lips and he licked his own.

Aiden tilted his head, moving closer.

Nate leaned forward too but at the last minute he shook his head as if to clear it and turned his attention to the front of the room.

Dust. Aiden groaned and did the same.

Chuckling, Nate jostled their entwined hands. "Behave, boy."

Oh, that didn't help at all, his cock responded to that word like it was a command. He shifted a little and did his best to think of something unlustworthy. Like the man in front of them.

The Speaker of the House of Lords took Nate's place. The Speaker was a short, thin man with graying brown hair, dressed in black parliamentary robes. When he spoke it was nasally and clipped. "Lords of Regelence, your King wishes to address you."

Father stood and everyone—including himself and Nate—rose, showing their respect. When the king got to the podium the Speaker bowed and stepped away.

"Please be seated. I've some wonderful news." Father looked toward Trouble. "Most of you are aware Admiral Hawkins is my new son-in-law, but what you probably do not know is that he has an adopted son. Please come forward, Jeremy."

Trouble looked at Aiden and Nate, his color waning a tad.

Aiden nodded his encouragement and Nate stood, waiting for Trouble.

Getting up, Trouble walked forward with Nate and dipped his head, "Your Majesty." Regardless what Trouble thought, he was quite handsome in his beige waistcoat and navy knee britches.

Father returned the gesture. "Lord Winstol."

A resounding murmur echoed through the room before it fell completely silent.

"Jeremy Hawkins is the lost Winstol heir. I've taken the liberty of having his DNA tested against that on record of both his parents, the Marquis and Marquis-Consort of Winstol. I would like to have him recognized and his properties be relinquished to his guardian, his adopted father, Admiral Hawkins."

The room buzzed with excitement and conversation.

Trouble fidgeted and Aiden couldn't blame him. He felt like squirming too and he wasn't the one standing before a couple of thousand sets of eyes.

The Speaker went to the podium with Father. They talked softly for several minutes, then Father took his seat next to Cony.

"Myself and several noble persons confirmed the DNA results indicate that Jeremy Hawkins is Jeremy Summers, the Winstol heir." The Speaker spoke to the house. "All in favor of recognizing Jeremy Hawkins as the new Marquis of Winstol say aye."

There was a loud chorus of "Ayes".

"Do you recognize the Marquis of Winstol as your son?"

Nate dipped his head. "I do, milord."

"Your Majesty, Prince Rexley, please come forward."

Father and Rexley moved to stand next to Nate and Trouble. When Rexley got next to Trouble, he whispered something and the tension melted from Trouble's shoulders.

Aiden grinned.

"Your Majesty, Admiral Hawkins, are you prepared today to reinstate your commitment to the betrothal of Rexley Townsend, heir to the throne of Regelence and Jeremy Hawkins, the Marquis of Winstol?"

Nate and Father both said, "I do."

The entire House of Lords stood and cheered, Aiden included.

After a round of congratulations, Father and Cony led the way out of the chamber, leaving Rexley to take Trouble's arm and escort him. Nate and Aiden followed while Aiden's brothers and Lord Wentworth, the captain of the royal guards, brought up the rear.

Outside of the Parliament building, a large, noisy crowd gathered. Some appeared to be lords, but others were middle and lower classmen. The royal guards had cleared them a walkway to their lift and stood stiffly facing the throng of citizens. From here the royal family would go to the castle for a ball celebrating Nate's promotion, Jeremy's return and Aiden and Nate's nuptials.

In Aiden's peripheral vision, he glimpsed a man waving his arms. There were a lot of people and several were waving, but something about this man was different. He turned his head to see the man better. Aiden stopped and stared. Where had he seen the man before? He was tall, dark-headed and very handsome. His dress clearly proclaimed him a lord of the realm. An older man stood beside him, gazing intently at Nate.

Nate continued to walk, tugging Aiden toward the lift. "Aiden?"

Aiden stumbled, trying to keep the man in sight. Suddenly it hit him why the man looked so familiar. It was a slightly younger version of a face he knew and loved, only without the beard.

Nate's hand closed over Aiden's where it rested on Nate's arm. "Aiden what's— Jared? Father?"

CB

Nate leaned against the private balcony's railing overlooking Townsend castle's ballroom with a scotch in hand and his father by his side. There was so much he wanted to talk about but he couldn't find the words. It was a new phenomenon for Nate. He always spoke his mind, but his father made him feel like a child again. Where did he stand with the man? How had his father and brother come to be here?

Outside the parliament building his father had hugged him and told him how proud he was and how much he'd missed Nate, but with the hustle and bustle of the day, they hadn't had time to speak until now.

Swirling the amber liquid, he stared down on the dance floor. It was packed full of people but he found Aiden easily.

Aiden danced by with Jared, giving Nate that warm feeling inside he always got when he looked at Aiden. His boy looked happy, smiling and chatting. It made him even more handsome, if that was possible.

And Jared? Nate could barely believe his baby brother was here, much less dancing with Aiden. Jared looked even more like Nate now than when they were younger. If it weren't for the beard and mustache, they could be twins rather than having four years separating them.

Nate took in the splendor of the enormous room. It was nice, decorated in red, black and white. A very formal décor for a very formal occasion, yet here he was watching his own celebration from the sidelines, feeling unsure of himself. He didn't like the feeling. It wasn't one he'd dealt with in a long time and it made him irritable. Seeing his family again was something he'd yearned for, but never thought would happen.

Nate turned, studying his father. "Why?" It came out much harsher than he'd intended, but he didn't take it back.

"It took me awhile to find you. But, I've known where you were for the past ten years. After what I did I didn't think you'd want to see me."

Nate swallowed the lump in his throat, his anger dissolving somewhat. All these years he'd never thought...

His father turned to face him, giving him his full attention. "I regretted my actions as soon as you'd left. I never thought you'd actually run away from home. The next morning I went to your room to find you and you were gone." Squeezing his eyes tight, he exhaled a ragged breath. When he opened his eyes again there were tears in them.

"You told me to get out of your sight. You disowned me." Nate remembered it like it was yesterday. His stomach tied in knots, just like it did eighteen years ago. The hurt was as strong as it was then, the feeling of abandonment. A lump formed in his throat. Nate swigged the rest of his scotch, enjoying the way it burned as it went down.

"I was mad. Deep down I knew you hadn't done it on purpose, but I wasn't thinking straight. Daniel was a hotheaded arse, but he was still Kit's son. I was afraid Kit wouldn't— I'm sorry, Nathaniel. You're my son and I love you, please forgive me?" He tossed the rest of his drink back, his hands shaking.

Nate took the time to study his father. He'd aged in the last eighteen years. He was still the noble, handsome Duke of Hawthorne, but a few more strands of gray had joined the dark hair and wrinkles creased the corner of his eyes. Leland Hawkins had been known for his friendly inviting smile, but he wasn't smiling now. His lips were pressed tightly together. As a father he'd always been affectionate rather than stern. It was probably why Nate had such a hard time being strict with Trouble.

Trouble. How would Nate feel if this were he and Trouble? The rest of Nate's anger vanished. "I love you too, Dad. And yes I forgive you." Nate blinked, his own eyes blurry. *Damn it.*

Tears ran down his father's face, but the smile and the sudden ease of tension was even more telling. "Thank you." He grabbed Nate, hugging him hard. Nate hugged back before letting go.

His dad brushed the tears from his eyes and turned back to the scene below them. After a few moments he smiled over at Nate. "He looks like he's in his element. I like him. He's the reason I found you. King Steven contacted me. But Aiden is the one who asked him to."

Nate joined him, leaning over the railing again. "He told me." He'd have to remember to deal with Aiden later. His boy deserved a spanking for going behind Nate's back...*and* a good, long, hard kiss for it.

"Aiden is a good match for you. He looks like he can handle the social events that come with being a spouse of an earl and admiral."

Aiden did look happy, smiling and talking. Yeah, a spanking was definitely in order. Nate grinned. "He's a good actor. He hates these things. I forgot to pat him down before we left so I suspect there is a sketchscreen hidden in his waistcoat burning a hole in his pocket. This very minute he's probably looking for an escape route."

His father chuckled. "Ah, an even better match than I first thought. He'll keep you on your toes."

Nate took a deep breath, feeling much better. He searched the room for Aiden. "He certainly does. Between he and Trouble there is never a dull moment."

"I bet. Your son seems like a handful."

Nate glanced around the perimeter of the ballroom. Where was Trou— Rexley and Trouble waltzed around the floor, looking like they'd been dancing together for years. Even if it did appear that Rexley was counting aloud for Trouble. Nate's mood lightened even more. They complemented each other well. It was a nice surprise. He'd agonized over the betrothal when Steven had told him about it. He still wouldn't force Trouble to marry, but it appeared that he wouldn't have to if things kept up as they were. There was bound to be some friction eventually, but for now...

"You are going to have more children, aren't you?" His father raised a brow, practically beaming at him.

What? Nate blinked and then started laughing. He truly had his father back and apparently it was time to start thinking up excuses to the endless badgering about grandchildren.

○ℨ

"Don't look so grim. He has table manners; he's been to formal dinners with me before." Nate squeezed Aiden's hand that rested on his forearm as Trouble walked into the dining room in front of them.

Aiden grimaced. "There is that, I suppose." Pausing, Aiden jostled his arm. "You talked to your father?"

"Umm…" He wondered how long he'd get away with that non-answer. *One, two, thr—*

"Umm? What does that mean? What did he say?" Aiden's eyes narrowed, his nose scrunching.

Nate arched a brow, trying not to smile. "That you deserve a spanking for not asking me first."

Scoffing, Aiden resumed walking. "I seriously doubt he sa—" He stopped, his eyes widened and he smiled, showing off even white teeth. "Do I?"

Laughing, Nate started them moving again. When they rounded the corner leading to the dining room, they noticed someone—it looked like Colton but it was hard to tell since his head was around the corner—at the other end of the hall.

Stopping in front of the dining room, Nate pointed and looked at Aiden.

Aiden shrugged and disengaged his arm from Nate's, heading toward his sibling. He reached the end of the hall and peeked around the corner. Groaning, he grabbed Colton's arm. "Come on."

"But— You have become a stick in the mud, big brother," Colton grumbled, jerking his arm away from Aiden. He nodded at Nate and went into the dining room.

"What was that about?" Nate offered Aiden his arm again.

Aiden smiled and took it. "Lord Wentworth was inspecting the guards."

"The captain of the royal guards?"

"That's the one."

Oh damn. Nate chuckled, wondering if Raleigh knew his son had a hard-on for the head of castle security. Probably not, the man was still employed.

In the dining room, everyone was just sitting down. A huge twenty-foot rectangular table dominated the middle of the room and several smaller round tables flanked it. Nate escorted Aiden to the large table that had been reserved for family and close acquaintances. Near Steven's end of the table, there were empty chairs for them. Nate pulled out Aiden's chair then his own and took a seat. Across from them and to Steven's left sat Rexley and Trouble. Nate had a sneaking suspicion Aiden had a hand in that. It was a smart move. Between, Nate, Aiden, Steven and Rexley, one of them was bound to be able to control Trouble.

Steven nodded to them and motioned to the footmen to start pouring the soup. They started at Raleigh's end of the table, so it gave them a little time to talk. Unfortunately, with everyone present, they couldn't talk about what really needed to be discussed.

Taking a drink of his wine, Steven set his glass down. "Nate, with all that has happened I don't believe I told you congratulations on making Admiral."

From the corner of his eye, Nate noticed Trouble cocking his head back and forth at the empty soup bowl in front of him.

He tried to ignore it and carry on his conversation with Steven. "Thank you, Your Majesty."

Aiden put his hand on Nate's knee under the table. "I have a gift for you."

Nate turned to his boy, surprised. "You do?"

Smiling, Aiden nodded. "I do. It's upst—" Aiden's head jerked around, facing Trouble. "Oh Galaxy."

Trouble held up the blue and white bowl from in front of him, looking at it. "I did not know you could do that. Nate, have you ever done that?"

A feeling of dread hit Nate before he even glanced down at the plate in front of him, trying to figure out what Trouble was talking about.

Rexley started coughing.

Steven covered his mouth with his napkin, snickering, and Aiden kept up a steady refrain of "Oh Galaxy" under his breath.

He was going to kill the kid this time. The plate depicted nude Greek wrestlers, at least that's what Nate thought it was. It certainly was open for interpretation. It could have been an image from the Regelence Kama Sutra... No, not in the castle, he was pretty sure it was wrestlers. He gave Trouble the look, and noticed Rexley turning red next to him. Was the kid choking or laughing? He was slumped so far down that he was nearly on the floor.

Apparently, Aiden's friend Rupert wasn't sure either. He started pounding on Rexley's back.

Trouble looked up at Nate, his eyes twinkling. *Oh, the little shit.*

"Trouble..."

Trouble turned the bowl, showing it to Nate. "Whaaat? I'm just saying..."

Rexley righted himself, took a deep breath and wiped a tear from the corner of his eye. "Jeremy," he whispered as he reached for his drink.

Just like that, Trouble set the bowl down and took a drink as well. Rexley looked up at them over his glass, arching a brow. That was when Nate noticed only one of his hands was visible. *Hmm...*

Aiden, at some point, had stopped his song of "Oh Galaxy," and patted Nate's thigh. "Close your mouth."

CB

After the ball, Nate retired to the study with the royal couple, his father, brother and Aiden. Aiden had only lasted thirty minutes before he started yawning and said good night. Jared stayed about an hour. Nate had thoroughly enjoyed his family's company and Steven and Raleigh's as well, but he was getting anxious to get upstairs to his boy.

"Nate, I don't believe in arranged marriages, and I won't make Rexley and Trouble marry if they don't want to, but I have to say I think this might be a very good match. I don't think I've ever seen Rexley laugh so hard." Steven's lips twitched again, just as they did every time the dinner was brought up.

Taking a drink of his scotch, Nate leaned back in the leather love seat, trying not to smile. He and Steven had gotten along well from the beginning, but now the man was becoming a good friend. Nate wasn't sure if it was due to his marrying Aiden or swearing fealty, but even Raleigh had lightened up around him. "I'm glad you thought that was funny, Steven." All right, it *was* funny, but the brat had poor timing. And Steven had a very valid point. Trouble and Rexley did appear to be suited to each other.

Nate's dad chuckled and took a drink of his own scotch. "I don't know why you're complaining, Nathaniel. It sounds exactly like something you would have done at his age."

Nate pushed his father's knee with the foot he had crossed over his own knee. Nate knew he could trust his father, but he hadn't told him everything about what was going on, not just yet. They were still trying to find their footing with one another. And there was a little resentment on Nate's part, even though he tried not to let it stand in the way of getting to know his father again.

They all laughed for a few more minutes, then Nate cleared his throat. "How's Englor, Father?"

"Not very good, I'm afraid. There are a lot of rumors flying around."

Steven swirled his drink, pretending only vague interest, but Nate wasn't fooled.

"Oh? What about?" Nate took a sip of his drink, making eye contact with Raleigh.

His father shook his head. "Vague mentions of the royal scandal, not good at all."

Raleigh set his drink on the coffee table in front of them and leaned back. "Prince Simon is an Englor Marine officer, isn't he, your grace?"

"He is. He's a colonel and a very highly respected one." Turning toward Nate, his father frowned. "Nathaniel, I really think you should make a point to visit Englor now that you are Aries Fleet admiral."

Nate nodded, looking at Steven and Raleigh before turning his attention back to his dad. "I think you are right, Father. A trip to Englor is definitely in order." Tossing back the rest of his scotch, Nate stared at his feet. He needed to plan a trip to Englor, but it could wait until the morning.

His father stood, clapping him on the back. "Gentlemen, I hope you will forgive my rudeness, but I believe I'm ready to call it a night." He stood, dipping his head. "Your Majesties, it's been a pleasure. King Steven, I thank you again for contacting me."

Steven stood, offering his hand. "You're most welcome, your grace."

Getting to his feet, Raleigh shook hands, and then Nate's father turned to Nate. After giving Nate a hug and extracting a promise to go riding tomorrow from him, the Duke of Hawthorne left.

Nate stretched, covering a yawn. "Steven, Raleigh. Shall we meet back here tomorrow morning to discuss business?"

"Indeed we shall, Admiral." Steven slapped him on the back.

"Father! Cony! Nate!" Payton came running into the study, his face red. He was breathing hard.

Raleigh started forward immediately and Payton waved him away.

"I'm fine, Cony." He looked at Nate. "You know those messages Trouble downloaded?"

Nate nodded.

"Well, Trouble couldn't crack them so he asked me to take a look at them. I haven't cracked them either, but I've figured out that the encryption is definitely Englorian."

Epilogue

The first thing Nate saw when he opened his bedroom door was Aiden standing bareassed in the middle of the bed. Then his gaze landed on the silver chain collar and lock he'd given Aiden before the ball when they'd snuck back here for a quickie. Not a bad thing to open the door to. His cock was rock hard in seconds flat, but what the hell was Aiden doing?

Grinning, Nate closed the door quietly and walked closer. Aiden was fiddling with the painting above their bed. Funny, Nate didn't even recall what the subject matter in the painting was. It certainly wasn't one of Aiden's pieces. And Nate didn't pay attention to the artwork now either. How could he when that delectable little ass was eye level? "Boy, you are going to fall on your head."

Aiden turned toward him, smiling ear to ear as Nate's thighs bumped the edge of the bed. "What do you think?" He lifted his hand toward the picture but Nate's gaze stayed on the view in front of him. Aiden was a work of art all by himself.

Nate wrapped his hands around Aiden's waist and pulled him closer, burying his nose in the dark hair above Aiden's prick. Inhaling deeply, he savored the warm musky smell. He knew the scent would be stronger further down, but it was still nice, still Aiden.

"Mmm... You're not looking." Aiden's fingers tangled in his hair, petting. His cock hardened, nudging Nate's neck.

Oh, fuck yeah. Grabbing the hot hard cock, Nate covered the head with his mouth and slid slowly down. His other hand cupped his boy's tight little ass, dragging him forward.

Aiden's fingers gripped his hair, his thighs stiffening. "Sir..." His voice was like a purr. His legs wobbled, threatening to give out.

Nate groaned and pulled back, letting the glistening tip of Aiden's prick bob free. He didn't want to do this with Aiden standing on the bed. He smacked Aiden on the hip. "Down from there, boy."

Grumbling, Aiden sat on the edge of the bed, his hand going to the button of Nate's uniform pants, a huge grin tugging at those full lips.

Oh, it was so tempting, but he wanted Aiden begging for him. "Lay down." Nate batted his hands away and undressed himself.

After putting his clothes away he started to get into bed, but froze, sitting on the edge when his gaze landed on the painting he'd forgotten all about.

"Do you like it?" Aiden crawled across the bed on his knees, looping his arms over Nate's shoulders and pressing himself up against Nate's side.

At any other time it probably would have distracted him to have the firm little body rubbing on him. But this time all he could do was stare in awe.

Aiden had painted a picture of the Lady Anna. It was an incredible likeness of her sailing through space. The Regelence Space Station was on the port side and slightly behind the vessel, like she was coming to Regelence.

Nate was speechless. He sat there with Aiden on his knees next to him, still looking at the painting. It was beautiful, just as Aiden's other pieces were, but this was even more so. It was painted out of love. A gift painted especially for Nate, something Aiden had known would be treasured.

Aiden looked at the artwork, resting his cheek against Nate's face. "Her last trip under your command. She's sailing to Regelence..." Smiling softly, he turned back to Nate, his hands going to Nate's beard. "Bringing you home, sir."

Home indeed. Nate blinked away tears. The sterling silver around the pale throat caught his attention. His boy was worth way more than any IN destroyer. Fusing their lips together, Nate pushed Aiden flat on the bed, coming down on top of him. Aiden felt so right, fit perfectly against him.

Wrapping his legs around Nate's calves, Aiden squirmed, already pushing himself up against Nate. His hot cock nestled against Nate's hip, his hands clutching at Nate's back. "Please, sir..."

Nate moaned, his own prick filling. Pulling back, he braced himself on his hands above his boy. "Thank you." *For everything.*

Still trying to rub against Nate, Aiden nodded. "I wanted to give you something special."

"Be still, boy." Balancing on one hand, Nate pressed Aiden to the mattress, halting his moving hips. He smiled down into the handsome face just below his. "I already have something special. I realized that the day you snuck into my room."

"You knew." It wasn't a question. "That's why you said the things you did."

"Of course, I knew. I was trying to save you and scare you off." And instead he'd found the perfect partner.

Aiden grinned and shook his head. "It didn't work, sir."

Thank Galaxy. Nate chuckled. "So I've noticed, boy." Dipping his head, Nate rubbed his beard against Aiden's chin and cheek. Just knowing how excited it made Aiden when Nate did that, made Nate's heart race and his breath hitch. He couldn't wait to feel the tight heat wrapped around his dick and watch Aiden flush with pleasure, begging for Nate to fuck him harder.

Aiden moaned and rubbed back, his hips pushing up again, frantically trying to get friction on his cock.

Damn. Nipping Aiden's jaw, Nate reached for the headboard, getting lube on his fingers, and brought it down between them, pressing into Aiden's crease, looking for the snug little hole.

Aiden bucked toward Nate's fingers, impaling himself. He groaned and writhed, closing his eyes for just a second before he opened them again. His gray eyes widened and focused on Nate's as Nate added a second finger.

Nate moved in and out, opening his boy for him. His cock ached and his balls drew closer to his body. He wanted inside his boy so badly.

Adding a third finger, he angled them upward, finding Aiden's prostate. Nate loved watching Aiden squirm, trying to fuck himself on Nate's fingers. As always, Aiden's need matched his own.

"Oh, yes. Oh, please, sir..." Precome seeped from Aiden's hot prick, smearing on Nate's abs.

Sitting up, Nate pushed a fourth finger inside. Using his other hand to get more lube, he caught Aiden's gaze and spread the slippery gel around the outside of Aiden's hole.

The whole time, they held each other's gaze. Saying everything without opening their mouths. Nothing outside the room existed at the moment. There was no IN, no corruption, just the two of them.

Aiden drew his legs up, bending his knees and planting his feet on each side of Nate. He thrust up, making his prick slap against his lower belly.

Fuck, that was a pretty sight. Nate licked his dry lips, remembering the feel of Aiden in his mouth. After, he promised himself. He'd taste after.

"Sir?"

He loved hearing the love and respect in Aiden's voice when he said that, so easily and naturally. Without removing his fingers, Nate braced himself on his hand and knees above Aiden before slanting his mouth over Aiden's, kissing him deeply. His tongue stabbed in, staking his claim.

Aiden returned his kiss with equal fervor, all the while bearing down on Nate's fingers, trying to get them deeper.

Pulling away, Nate nipped Aiden's lip. "What, boy?"

"Remember what you said that day? About my heart?" His voice was low, a whisper.

Oh fuck, yes. Nate's cock throbbed, jerking at the thought of his entire hand in his boy's ass, feeling his heartbeat— His cock was so hard it hurt, but for Aiden, for this, he'd wait. Moaning, Nate stared down into his boy's eyes again. *Mine. My boy.*

Nate glanced down at the collar he'd bought Aiden. He'd never expected to find someone to share his life with, much less a lover who shared his desires. Pulling his fingers out a little, Nate fitted his thumb in and pressed slowly into Aiden's hole. "You're mine now, boy, all mine."

About the Author

JL has been talking since she was about seven months old. To those who know her it comes as no surprise, in fact, most will tell you she hasn't shut up since. At eighteen months, she was speaking in full sentences. Imagine if you will the surprise of her admirers when they complimented her mother on "what a cute little boy" she had and received a fierce glare from said little boy and a very loud correction of "I'm a girl!" Oddly enough, JL still finds herself saying that exact phrase thirty-some-odd years later.

Today JL is a full-time writer, with over ten novels to her credit. Among her hobbies she includes reading, practicing her marksmanship (she happens to be a great shot), gardening, working out (although she despises cardio), searching for the perfect chocolate dessert (so far as she can tell ALL chocolate is perfect, but it requires more research) and arguing with her husband over who the air compressor and nail gun really belongs to (they belong to JL, although she might be willing to trade him for his new chainsaw).

To learn more about J.L. Langley, please visit www.jllangley.com. Send an email to J.L. at 10star@jllangley.com or join her Yahoo! group to join in the fun with other readers as well as J.L.! http://groups.yahoo.com/group/the_yellow_rose/

Look for these titles by
J. L. Langley

Now Available:

Without Reservations
With Love

Coming Soon:

With Caution

Can a straight-laced business student and an indie boy with a thing for extremely personal electronics turn one night's wild ride into a trip to last forever?

Catching a Buzz
© 2007 Ally Blue

Adam Holderman isn't your typical twenty-something college boy. He prefers jazz to Goth, shuns body piercings and street-waif clothing, and despises the lack of vocabulary among his peers. Some call him uptight, but Adam doesn't see it that way. Just because he prefers his men articulate and well-groomed doesn't make him a stick-in-the-mud. He simply has standards, unlike most guys his age.

The new employee at Wild Waters Park, where Adam works, single-handedly throws a monkey wrench into Adam's orderly world view. Buzz Stiles wears eyeliner and black clothes, listens to emo bands, and talks like a teenage skate punk. He's the polar opposite of Adam's avowed "type". So why can't Adam get him out of his head?

When Adam finally agrees to go out with Buzz, he finds there's much more to Buzz than a hot body, a sharp wit, and a Goth fashion sense. Buzz is someone Adam can see himself being with for the long haul. But you need more than mind-melting sex to make a relationship last. Can they keep their hands off each other long enough to find out if they have what it takes?

Warning, this title contains the following: graphic language, explicit male/male sex, inappropriate use of personal electronic devices, and gratuitous disco dancing.

Available now in ebook from Samhain Publishing.

GET IT NOW

Printed in the United Kingdom
by Lightning Source UK Ltd.
129252UK00001B/226-231/P